READING YOU

READING YOU

LUBOV LEONOVA

First Printing, 2024

ISBN
978-1-7782003-9-7 (Hardcover)
978-1-7782003-7-3 (Paperback)
978-1-7782003-8-0 (eBook)

Fantasy Romance, Mystery, New Adult

Contents

*"If women truly want to make a positive change,
we must heal our hearts first.
The only way for light to triumph over darkness
is to become the light."*

- Lubov Leonova

1

Unwanted Date

Lana twirled in front of her tall mirror, admiring her reflection. Her favorite dress, as always, looked stunning on her petite frame. The light-beige fabric almost perfectly matched her flaxen locks, accentuating her big brown eyes. The leather corsage hugged her waist. With the hem grazing her knees and in her heeled boots, she resembled a porcelain doll.

Becca will be jealous, Lana thought with a smile. Tonight, she was thrilled to see her best friend. It was such a relief to have this freedom – to dress up and spend time with someone she genuinely liked without the pressure of finding a suitable fiancé. *How long until Dad brings up that topic again?* Pushing aside the anxious thought, Lana grabbed her coat and hurried down the stairs.

In the living room, Lana found her father, Bernard Morris, in the company of an unfamiliar man. They were seated in chairs, engaged in conversation, with the fireplace casting a warm glow on their brandy glasses. Lana tried to tiptoe past them, but her heels gave her away with a loud click on the wooden floor, capturing their attention.

"Lana, there you are!" her father exclaimed.

Lana greeted him with a polite smile. "Good evening."

Her father approached her, his face now illuminated by the fire, revealing wrinkles on his forehead and around his tired brown eyes – the telltale signs of his stressful work. His gray mustache stretched as he smiled at her. "Will you join us for dinner tonight? My old friend Maynard just arrived from the capital."

Lana's gaze shifted to Maynard. He lounged in a guest chair with his long legs stretched towards the fireplace. He was slender, with a short beard and strands of gray mingling with his once-black hair. His round glasses accentuated his dark eyes, giving them an air of intelligence, though lacking in kindness. They gleamed with arrogance as he ogled Lana, focusing primarily on her decolletage.

Lana tightened her coat around her, warding off his lecherous stares. "I wish I could stay," she muttered, eager to make her exit. "But Becca is expecting me. There's a circus performance tonight."

"Ah, the circus," her father said, his tone tinged with sadness. "I completely forgot about it."

"So, may I be excused now?"

"Hold on." Her father turned to Maynard to make introductions. "This is my daughter, Lana. I was just telling you about her."

Lana offered a slight bow. "Nice to meet you, sir."

Maynard remained seated, his thin lips stretching into a grin. "Beautiful! How is it that such a lovely woman is still unmarried?"

Why do you care? Lana gritted her teeth, resisting the urge to respond sharply. She reminded herself that this man was not here for an arranged meeting. *Or was he?* With a silent plea in her eyes, Lana shot a glare at her father.

"She is a bit shy," her father offered apologetically.

Lana shook her head. It seemed that most men found shyness appealing in women. Perhaps it was because it made them more compliant – obedient wives never questioned their husbands, no matter how cruel or deceitful they may be. She suspected that Maynard was no different.

"Fortunately, I admire modest women," Maynard confirmed her guess, swirling his brandy glass. The amber liquid shimmered like a blade of copper. "I am a widower, by the way, and we were just discussing the possibility of remarriage."

Lana's throat tightened as she sensed the direction of the conversation. She was trapped, with her father blocking her path to the exit. She had two options to extricate herself from this uncomfortable situation. The first was to feign assistance with the dishes and slip out through the kitchen door. However, it would only be a temporary escape. Given Maynard's connection to her father, Lana suspected he would find another opportunity to approach her. His predatory gaze confirmed it.

The second option was to act swiftly and utilize her Gift of mind-reading to uncover any unsavory secrets about this man. Lana was sure that Maynard had skeletons in his closet, and if she played her cards right, she could use this information to disrupt the awkward dinner. The only drawback was that delving into Maynard's mind would take time, potentially causing Lana to be late for her meeting with Becca. However, Becca was her best friend, so she would understand the delay.

With a resigned sigh, Lana removed her coat. "Fine, I'll stay for dinner then."

"How delightful!" her father beamed, pleased by her compliance. "Dinner will be ready in five minutes! I'll ask Molly to put an extra plate."

"Sounds good," Lana replied with a nod. "I'll take the opportunity to get acquainted with our esteemed guest."

As her father departed for the kitchen, Lana approached Maynard. As a mind-reader, she could tap into the memories of others. It required physical touch, though. Since Maynard remained seated, Lana moved closer to him from behind.

"You appear to be a fine specimen of a husband," she murmured. "How do you maintain such a good physique? Are you a guardian?" *Flattery.* This tactic often worked to distract men like him and divert their attention. It was precisely Lana's intention.

He relaxed and rested his hands on the armrests, one hand tightly gripping his glass. "No. I teach architecture at the university."

Awesome! Unlike most guardians, Maynard wasn't employing mental blocks to shield crucial memories. He was an easy target for her mind-reading abilities. Leaning in closer, she whispered into his ear, "I have a fondness for old buildings. They hold so much history."

"They certainly do," he responded, sinking further into his chair. The trembling of his glass indicated conflicting emotions.

It's now or never. Gently placing her hand on his shoulder, Lana closed her eyes and focused on connecting her energy with his, delving into the shadows of his troubled past. Over the past year, she had honed her skill to access the most poignant memories with precision.

In Maynard's mind, Lana witnessed the scene from his perspective. A young girl accepted a glass of orange juice from him and took a sip as they sat together on the sofa, engaged in quiet conversation. From Maynard's memory, Lana discovered that they were in the living room of his new lake house, where he had recently painted the walls white. The scent of fresh paint lingered in the air, adding to the vividness of the recollection.

Unexpectedly, Maynard leaned in closer to the girl and touched her neckline. It sent shivers down his stomach as his desire consumed him. Lana, trapped in his mind, felt a wave of revulsion and guilt washing over her. Despite her discomfort, Lana resisted the urge to break the connection immediately. She had to stay connected to uncover what Maynard was about to do.

Lana erected a mental barrier to shield herself from Maynard's intense emotions. It allowed her to observe the scene as a detached spectator. It was like watching a theatrical performance, albeit a disturbing one.

Maynard continued to touch the girl, whispering in her ear as his hands ventured under her blouse. He persisted despite her attempts to resist, his actions becoming increasingly aggressive. Lana felt a surge of relief when the girl fought back, struggling to break free from his grasp. The moment the girl struck Maynard's head with a table lamp, Lana was overwhelmed by a wave of pain and dizziness, mirroring his physical sensations. She barely maintained the mental barrier between them.

Damn it, Lana muttered under her breath as she scrolled forward, desperate to avoid being ejected from Maynard's mind. She needed to witness the outcome.

As the scene unfolded, it was nighttime, and Maynard pursued the girl along the lake shore. Despite her efforts to flee, she stumbled and was unable to escape his grasp. In a display of dominance fueled by anger and lust, Maynard forcefully pulled her to the ground and began tearing off her clothes.

Suppressing a scream, Lana fast-forwarded through the harrowing events, landing on a scene a week after the disturbing night.

Maynard sat in his small office, sipping whiskey and seemingly lost in thoughts of repeating his predatory behavior.

"Dinner is ready!" her father's voice broke through, causing Lana to snap back to reality. She found herself still in the living room behind Maynard. Her vision was blurred from the intense use of her Gift, her head throbbing. Overwhelmed by the shocking revelation she had uncovered, Lana gripped the chair tightly, fighting the urge to faint.

Maynard rose from his seat and turned towards her, his dark eyes boring into hers. "Are you alright?"

Lana's heart raced, yearning to break free from her ribcage. Among all the unsettling potential suitors she had encountered through her Gift, Maynard stood out as a true monster. "Uh-huh," she managed to mumble, her voice barely above a whisper.

Her father interjected, dismissing her reaction. "I told you she's shy."

"I see," Maynard remarked with a mocking glint in his eyes as he killed his brandy glass. "I'm certain she's full of surprises."

You have no idea. Lana clenched her fists, steeling herself as she gathered her composure. "This evening is full of surprises. And it's only just begun."

2

A Skeleton

The thick candles blazed with fury, casting a warm glow over the dinner table and the men's faces as they chewed their food and enjoyed each other's company. *What a farce!* Lana sat in silence, staring at her plate with no appetite. She hadn't spoken since they had started eating, her mind consumed with thoughts of how to expose Maynard.

As her father told one of his famous jokes, Maynard burst into squeaky laughter. Lana remained indifferent.

"What's wrong?" her father asked in a soothing voice, momentarily making Lana feel safe. *If I only had someone as reliable as him!* Unfortunately, luck had never been on her side.

"Nothing," Lana replied, flashing him a sarcastic grin. "Just pondering how to overcome my shyness."

Their maid, a young woman named Molly, brought more wine and refilled her father's glass. Lana took a sip of her lemon water, relishing its refreshing taste. She always avoided alcohol because it had a negative impact on her. As a mind-reader, Lana was more emotional and sensitive than most mages. Her brain was constantly active, allowing her to solve complex problems. However, it also made her more susceptible to stress.

As Lana sipped her citrus water, she kept her emotions in check. Despite having seen troubling memories in Maynard's mind, it wasn't the right time to expose him. Lana needed to bide her time and wait for the perfect moment when Maynard wouldn't be able to brush off her accusations with a joke.

It may have been unsettling to share a meal with a rapist, but Lana couldn't pass up this rare opportunity to prove her worth. Perhaps then, her father would finally take her aspirations of becoming a detective seriously.

Maynard wiped his lips clean of grease. "So, Bernard, I've heard you have a vacant position at a Guardian House."

Her father's expression turned somber. "Yes, it's been a concern of mine. Triville is expanding, and we need more guardians to ensure the town's safety."

"Oh, really? I didn't realize it would be so challenging to find capable people."

"It's not a matter of quantity. We've already hired several new guardians this year. The issue lies in finding experienced mentors to guide them. It's been more difficult than I anticipated. I ended up hiring a younger man, hoping for the best."

Maynard gave him a knowing look. "Why didn't you consider me for the role? I have twenty years of experience as a head teacher."

"You teach architects."

"So what? I understand the importance of discipline in building a strong team. Trust me, I can provide that."

"But... you reside in the capital."

Maynard shrugged, a mischievous grin on his face. "Life in Middle Lake has become too chaotic. I've been considering a move to a quieter place... like Triville."

What a hypocrite! Lana winced at his words. How could he be seeking to be a part of the guardian team after committing such a heinous crime?

Her father smiled. "In that case, your assistance would be greatly appreciated. These cadets are proving to be quite a handful. They lack experience but are overflowing with ambition."

Maynard glanced at Lana. "All young people are like that. They're dreamers who struggle to rein themselves in."

Lana took a deep breath to steady her racing heart. That was true – her father viewed her as nothing more than a naive dreamer who occasionally offered to help with his work. He had dismissed her, claiming her presence would only serve as a distraction to the other guardians. Now, she had a chance to prove her true capabilities. It was the perfect moment for Lana to reveal her cards and show that she could be a valuable addition to their team.

"What's wrong with having dreams, father?" Lana inquired, fluttering her eyelashes. "I've read that good people dream because they envision a better future and strive to make it a reality."

Her father leaned back in his chair, intrigued. "That's an interesting perspective, Lana. So, does that mean, according to the books, that bad people don't have dreams?"

Maynard chuckled, finding the conversation amusing. "It does make sense. Unlike villains, dreamers aren't driven by selfish motives. They are the ones who bring about positive change because they care about others."

Lana sneered. "So, are you claiming to be a good person?"

"Well, I've made mistakes in the past that I'm not proud of. But I've changed, and I'm striving to lead a better life."

Lana set her glass of water down on the table, restraining herself from splashing it in his deceitful face. "And how exactly do you plan to make that change?"

Her father observed them with interest, taking a sip of his wine but refraining from intervening in their conversation.

Maynard shrugged. "I want simple things – to find fulfillment in my work, start a family, and raise children."

Lana frowned. "I couldn't help but notice how you spoke about your teaching experience. I think it's creepy."

"What do you mean?"

Lana gave him a piercing look. "It's inappropriate for you to be working with guardians. Because you raped one of your students."

Her father choked on his wine, clearly taken aback. Maynard regarded Lana with a somber expression, likely guessing where she had obtained this information.

Lana handed her father a napkin and paused, allowing him a moment to process the unfolding situation. Then, she resumed her confrontation. "Crime is a serious matter, Maynard, even though you managed to conceal it effectively. You may have silenced her, but I know the truth. You won't escape justice."

Maynard coughed into his fist, casting a suspicious glance at her father. "What's happening, Bernard? Is this some kind of joke? Because if it is, it's not amusing."

Her father's expression darkened. He slammed his fist on the table, causing the dishes to rattle.

Lana's heart raced with anxiety. Her father would likely choose to believe his friend over his own daughter. *Would he?*

"Is this true?" her father demanded in a stern tone, his gaze unwavering as he focused on his 'old friend.'

Maynard shot Lana a disdainful look before averting his eyes. "Bernard, I swear on my honor, I would never commit such an act. I have no idea what this young lady is trying to achieve."

Her father turned his gaze towards Lana, a silent question hanging heavily in the air.

Lana steadied her voice and locked eyes with Maynard. "You called it an 'extracurricular activity' that you orchestrated last summer at your lake house. It was deceptively innocent. You staged it as a voluntary tutoring session for students struggling in your subject. However, your true motive was driven by your infatuation with one particular student – the one who rejected your advances.

"Despite her refusal, your obsession persisted. You meticulously planned for that night, concocting a drink laced with a sleeping potion. To mask any suspicions, you had prepped the walls with fresh paint to confuse her senses. Your intention was to violate her while she slept. However, your scheme was thwarted when she declined the alcohol and opted for juice instead. You had a limited supply of the potion, so your plan unraveled. When she realized that you started touching her inappropriately, she hit your head with the table lamp. That's why you have this little scar on your forehead."

As Lana recounted the events, Maynard's hand went to his forehead, tracing the scar as if hoping it would vanish.

She continued. "That girl... she fought back and attempted to flee, but you pursued. And then you raped her. Violently. If anyone in the university knows, your career is over. You are a criminal, Maynard. Just admit it."

Her father observed in silence, his gaze fixed on Maynard, awaiting a response.

In a sudden outburst, Maynard rose from his seat, tossing the napkin onto the table. "Everything your daughter is spouting –"

"... is the truth," her father said. "Because she's a mind reader, and she accidentally delved into your darkest memory."

"Accidentally?!" Maynard exclaimed, aghast. "This is an invasion of my privacy! You should teach her some manners."

"Enough, Maynard. Something transpired last year that you're trying to escape by relocating from the city – to evade the rumors until the storm settles," her father said.

Maynard's grin twisted into a sneer. "So, now you accuse me of crimes I never committed? Well, I won't stay in this house any longer!"

"Fine, leave! And kindly remember to shut the door behind you."

Maynard's face flushed with anger, his breaths coming in heavy gasps as he stormed towards the door and made his swift exit.

They sat at the table in a heavy silence, Lana's mind swirling with thoughts. She pondered whether her assertiveness had been too much. After all, her father had stood by her when she needed him most. *Does it mean I made an impression on him? Will he consider allowing me to work alongside him?*

Lana lifted her gaze to meet her father's eyes. "I'm sorry for disrupting dinner. Again."

"It's not your fault, Lana. Not this time. Perhaps I should reconsider these dinners. Look at the company I've brought into our home!"

Lana reached out and touched his hand, offering a sense of solace. "It's your Gift, Father. You always see the good in people, but you overlook their darker aspects. It saddens me that you fail to see anything in me."

He regarded her with a sorrowful expression. "I see you as a gifted mind reader, Lana. As your father, who has watched you grow, I'm deeply concerned for you."

"Why?"

"People fear your Gift. With your ability to read minds, you could uncover the truth about every criminal in town. If you were to pursue this path, no one would escape justice."

"Isn't it a great ability?"

Her father let out a heavy sigh. "Not for you. Once criminals perceive you as a threat, they may attempt to harm you. I can't bear the thought of losing you."

Lana shook her head, unwilling to accept his grim words. It seemed her father's concerns were clouding his judgment, envisioning worst-case scenarios to protect her. "I can still be of great assistance at the Guardian House. I don't have to directly engage with criminals. Working with witnesses alone would be beneficial. Please, just give me a chance."

He withdrew his hand and raised his voice firmly. "Lana, this discussion is concluded. I will not permit you to work alongside me. That's final."

"Can I at least continue visiting the library?"

He gazed at her in silence, his eyebrows furrowed in contemplation.

The maid, Molly, entered the room carrying a tray. Despite being relatively new to the household, Molly had quickly become a familiar presence. She was a nice young woman with a warm smile and a pleasant demeanor. Also, she was the same age as Lana, so they shared a mutual fondness for each other.

Molly seemed taken aback by the absence of the guest, indicating that she had missed the recent drama. Her gaze met Lana's, silently acknowledging the tension that had unfolded.

"Would anyone like more wine?" Molly offered.

"Why not?" Lana's father stood up and retrieved the entire bottle of wine from the tray. He glanced at Molly before departing. "I'll be in my office. Please, don't disturb me."

Molly nodded, her hands clutching the now-empty tray.

Once her father's footsteps had faded, Lana buried her head in her hands. "Why is my life such a disappointment?"

Molly approached, gathering up the dishes. "Oh, come on. Your father may be upset now, but he is a kind man. He will come around. Just give it some time."

At the mention of time, Lana sprang to her feet, glancing at the mirror adorned with time crystals that emitted a lilac glow. "Oh, crap! It's nearly nine! I'll be late for the show!"

Molly chimed in with a smile, "Also, refraining from swearing might improve his mood."

Lana chuckled. "That's one promise I can't make."

A Weirdo

Becca shuffled her feet, standing at the town plaza. Late November evenings were short, and now the cold was creeping under her coat. She rubbed her palms and exhaled a vapor into the frosty air. *Where the hell is Lana?* Despite her deep affection for their friendship, Becca couldn't help but feel a twinge of annoyance at Lana's tardiness. Lana, being the bookworm she was, might be lost in the pages of her favorite novel, completely forgetting about their plans.

Becca glanced at the circus entrance. The show was about to begin. The crowd with tickets was making their way inside the bright yellow tent, seeking refuge from the cold. Becca couldn't wait to join them and escape the chill. She retrieved two tickets from her pocket, featuring a vibrant image of a mage holding a flame circle. With a sigh, Becca returned them to her pocket. She still had a few minutes left, and she could wait for her best friend.

"Hey, weirdo!" The voices of her schoolmates broke the silence, startling Becca.

Oh no. She slowly turned to face two girls from her class. They were twins and dressed identically. Their raven-black pigtails were adorned with pure-white ribbons. They wore heeled boots, short skirts, and beige stockings that accentuated their slim hips. Their elegant upper bodies were clad in fancy jackets, with the top buttons left open to reveal their delicate decolletage lines.

Becca adjusted the collar of her gray coat, trying not to feel self-conscious about her more modest attire. With her strict mother's influence from serving in the church, she would never be allowed to wear something as fashionable as the twins. They often teased her for her reserved appearance and quiet demeanor, and Becca found the best way to deal with them was to ignore their taunts.

"Did your mom even let you come to the show?" the first twin inquired.

"You know, there will be men with bare torsos," the other one added.

They were not only similar in appearance but also in name – Mina and Mira. Having known them closely throughout her school life, Becca could easily distinguish between the two. Mira had a charming mole above her left eyebrow, and her eyes had a softer shade of gray. She was also a bit kinder, and Becca believed she might be a good person if not for Mina, whom Becca referred to as the 'evil twin.' At times, Becca suspected that Mina's goal was to make her sister as unpleasant as herself. They rarely interacted with Becca, except when the teacher assigned them to the same group for school projects.

Becca let out a heavy sigh, contemplating the best way to respond in order to divert their attention away from her. "I think I'll manage just fine. Thank you for your concern, though."

The twins chuckled in unison. "Of course."

"Actually," Mina's cold gray eyes narrowed, "I don't believe you're allowed to be here alone. There should be a chaperone."

Becca felt a lump form in her throat. It was true – she was only permitted to attend with Lana, who was currently absent. If her mother found out, there would be consequences.

"So, where is your friend?" Mina continued to probe. "That awkward mind-reader?"

Becca folded her hands. "I don't think that's any of your business."

"It is our business. Because if I inform your mother that you came here alone –"

"Please, don't," Becca interjected. Perhaps it came out too fast because the girls giggled in response. "What do you want?" Becca asked, her tone firm as she refused to let them see her discomfort.

The girl with the mole, Mira, gave Becca a curious look. "We were just wondering about your friend. How much older is she?"

Becca swallowed. Lana was four years older, and their friendship was not solely based on their fathers' connection as family friends. Lana was the most understanding person Becca had ever known, the one she could always rely on.

"It's impolite not to answer when people talk to you," Mina said, her gaze unwavering.

"Four years. So what?"

The twins giggled once more, causing Becca to roll her eyes in annoyance.

"It's so pathetic that she's your only friend," Mina remarked, clearly enjoying herself. "Who else would even want to talk to you? You're just too weird."

"You're talking to me right now," Becca retorted.

"Yeah, but it's not because I like it."

"Then why?"

The girls exchanged glances before Mira, the kinder twin, spoke up. "Because you'll ask your friend to buy us some booze."

Becca furrowed her brow. "And why on earth would I do that?"

Her sister, Mina, flashed a cold smile. "Well, I see at least two good reasons. Firstly, your friend clearly doesn't care about you. Just look around – she ditched you. And here you are, standing in the cold."

Becca bit her lip. She was indeed left waiting in the cold, hoping for Lana's arrival. *What if the girls tell the truth?*

Sensing Becca's uncertainty, Mina continued, "And the second reason is that in exchange, we'll keep today's events a secret. We won't breathe a word to your mother, even if you go in alone. How does that sound?"

Like nonsense. Becca glanced at the warm light emanating from the entrance, beckoning her inside. The idea of making a deal now and dealing with the consequences later seemed almost reasonable. However, Becca hated the thought of being manipulated. Despite appearing a meek church mouse, she was not one to be underestimated. It was time to show them that this mouse could bite.

Stepping closer, Becca caught Mina off guard, causing her eyes to widen in surprise. "You know what? If you two dare to breathe a word about me visiting the circus alone, you'll be going down with me. I can easily expose your ridiculous proposition to your parents. How does *that* sound?"

Mina's eyes narrowed in anger, and before Becca could react, she felt a forceful push that sent her stumbling backward, struggling to maintain her balance.

Are these two really going to fight right now? Becca thought, her heart racing as the girls advanced towards her with menacing smiles. Desperately seeking help, she scanned the deserted plaza. Even the ticket controller had vanished from sight. The cold had driven everyone inside the circus, leaving Becca alone with these bullies.

Threatening them was a foolish move, she realized. *It's two of them, so I won't stand a chance.* Panic began to grip her throat. Becca glanced once more at the circus entrance. It was just fifty steps away. If she could reach it quickly, she might be able to escape the twins' grasp. Once inside the crowd, they wouldn't dare to bother her, and hopefully, they would abandon their foolish proposition. With the leverage she held, it wasn't in their best interest to complain to her mother.

Taking a deep breath, Becca sprinted towards the safety of the circus tent. She managed to take ten strides before she heard the clicking of heels behind her. Suddenly, a forceful hand pushed her, causing Becca to stumble and fall to the ground.

She landed on all fours, feeling the sting in her palms as she pulled herself up from the rough ground and settled into a sitting position. "Crap," Becca muttered under her breath, her heart pounding.

The two pairs of polished boots approached Becca, surrounding her as they stopped by her sides. A skinny hand grabbed her braid, forcing her to look up at their grinning faces. *Gee, why did I think these two were beautiful?* At that moment, the twins appeared to be menacing monsters, with their crooked smiles and dark shadows around their eyes. Becca couldn't help but smirk with disgust.

"We didn't finish discussing our deal," the girl holding her hair stated.

"There won't be any deal," Becca retorted, trying to maintain her composure. "Now, let me go. The show is about to start."

"Maybe we should let her go," Mira, the second twin, interjected, glancing at her sister. "Please, release her."

"But she can rat us out," Mina countered.

"She won't!" Mira gave Becca a playful look, her eyebrow mole moving up and down. "Right?"

"I won't say a word about our conversation," Becca assured.

Mina tightened her grip on Becca's hair. "I can believe that. But the issue of your friend remains unresolved. Promise that you'll make her do what we want, and then you can go free."

Becca shivered. *Will I really have to involve Lana?* Still on her knees, she raised her eyes to the cold, indifferent sky, silently sending prayers for some form of rescue. Perhaps a passerby, not indifferent to the peace of the town, would intervene.

"Hey, what's going on here?" A young man's voice cut through the tension like a ray of hope.

The grip on Becca's hair loosened, and she smiled gratefully at her savior – a tall young man with dark hair and gleaming brown eyes. He stood a few steps away, his expression puzzled. Becca recognized him from school. Unfortunately, she had never learned his name. Boys and girls studied in separate wings, and their paths rarely crossed. It seemed that fate had brought them together in this unexpected moment.

"What's up, Stan?" One of her tormentors now stood beside her, attempting to charm him with batting eyelashes. Becca couldn't help but feel a sense of satisfaction at the shift in power dynamics. Perhaps this unexpected intervention would help rectify the situation.

Stan glanced at Becca, causing her to question her appearance. She stood up and examined her coat, now dirtied from her fall. Frowning, she began to shake off the dirt marks from her clothes.

"Are you always like that?" Stan directed his question towards the twins.

"Pretty and gorgeous?" Mina replied with a wide grin. "Yes, we are."

Stan smiled, clearly amused by their response. Becca stole a glance at the entrance once more, yearning to escape from this situation.

"Hold on!" Stan's voice made her freeze in place.

Will I ever make it to that entrance?

"Right, wait here, weirdo!" Mina said.

"It's not funny," Stan's tone held a hint of disappointment. "You were about to harm this girl. Gee, I thought you were better than that."

"It's not what you think, Stanley," Mina attempted to maintain an innocent facade. "Becca fell, and we were just helping her up."

Stan folded his arms, unconvinced. "I saw you push her."

The twins exchanged uneasy glances, realizing they were caught in their lie. Becca couldn't help but smile inwardly. *Yes, you're cornered now!* It seemed that Stan was a decent guy, and any chance one of the twins had with him was likely ruined by their behavior. This was the consequence of revealing their true colors.

Stan's question made Becca's heart race. "What did this girl do to you that made you act like that?"

"We had our reasons," Mina replied confidently. "And we were in the middle of a discussion, so there was no need for you to interfere."

Keep up the hostility, Becca thought with a smirk. *It will only push him further away.*

Turning to Becca, Stan's curious gaze met hers. "Maybe you can tell me. What did you do?"

Unable to find the words to explain herself, Becca lowered her gaze. Despite her current disdain for the twins, she knew that complaining to the boy one of them clearly liked would only invite trouble. Becca was certain the twins would find a way to make her life miserable if she spoke out. Instead, she decided to try and defuse the situation, hoping it would ease their anger towards her.

"So?" Stan prompted, waiting for an explanation.

Taking a deep breath, Becca spoke, "Mina is telling the truth. I was in a hurry to get to the circus performance and ended up falling. They helped me up, and we started talking."

"What about the pushing?"

"It was just a harmless joke that didn't go as planned," Becca replied with a small smile. "But everything is fine now. Thank you for intervening, though."

Stan shook his head, still not entirely convinced by her explanation. He then turned his attention to the twins. "Alright then. But if I ever catch you behaving like this again, you won't get off so easily."

"What do you mean?" Mina asked, clearly irritated by Stan's words. "Is that a threat?"

Stan calmly tucked his hands into his pockets, his voice steady and reassuring. "No, not at all. I consider you two my friends, but you make it hard for me. If you're willing to harm this nice girl, who knows what else you're capable of?!"

Becca blushed. *Does he really think I'm nice?* She might have overreacted, but she couldn't help it. She had never received a compliment from a boy, especially one as good-looking as Stan. So, consequences be damned, she embraced this moment of victory.

Watching her, Mira shook her head, her eyes filled with disdain.

Unlike her sister, Mina remained composed. "We've all explained it was a misunderstanding. I have nothing more to say." With that, she grabbed her sister's elbow, and they began to walk away from the plaza.

As the clicking of the twins' heels faded away, Stan turned his attention to Becca. She felt her head spin at the warmth in his gaze. She had never imagined that a boy would take notice of her, let alone come to her defense. Overwhelmed by gratitude, she struggled to find the right words.

"Thank you, Stan," Becca managed to say, her voice trembling slightly. It felt strange to say his name, but she found herself liking the sound of it.

"No problem, Rebecca," Stan replied, easing the tension with his casual demeanor.

Wait, he knows my name?

"I believe people should help each other in times of trouble," Stan continued. "I just hope those two learned their lesson and won't bother you again."

Becca smiled in agreement. "I hope so, too."

The distant sounds of music signaled that the circus show had begun. Becca glanced around, searching for Lana. If her best friend couldn't make it, she didn't want to miss the performance entirely. Besides, she saw an opportunity to show her gratitude to Stan by inviting him to watch the show with her. The question remained: *would he agree?*

Before doubts could dampen the moment, Becca reached into her pocket and pulled out two tickets, flashing them at Stan. "If you have some time, you can join me. My friend couldn't make it tonight, and I... I don't really want to go alone."

"I would love to," Stan replied, taking one of the tickets and offering her a cheerful smile.

4

A Beautiful Stranger

Lana ran through the town streets, paying no mind to the rare pedestrians who gawked at her. Perhaps she did look strange, with her coat flapping open and her hair tousled from her fast pace. She didn't care.

As she neared the town plaza, she collided with two twin girls. They stood in the middle of the road, their faces clouded with gloom. Lana's heart raced with concern as she recognized the girls from Becca's school. She forgot their names, but she could still check on them.

"Hey... Are you okay?" Lana asked.

"Not really," one of the twins replied.

A sense of unease crept over Lana. "What do you mean? What happened?"

"It's about your friend, Becca," the other twin said with a hint of disdain. "She didn't wait long for you. I saw she gave a ticket to the boy. Looks like she betrayed you."

A boy? Lana furrowed her brow in confusion. Becca had never mentioned liking anyone enough to leave her behind. There had to be a logical explanation. "Are you certain it was Becca? Rebecca Turner?"

"Yes," they replied in unison. Then they turned and resembled their walk.

As Lana reached the yellow circus tent, she came to a halt. The music blared from within, indicating that the show had already begun without her. Entering through the main entrance now would likely disrupt the audience and distract the performers. Rubbing her throbbing temples, Lana pondered if there was another way to sneak in.

She considered crawling under the tent's side. Even if the ticket controller caught her, she could attempt to explain the situation and pay for a ticket. Then, she could locate Becca and unravel the mystery. With determination, Lana lifted the edge of the yellow curtain and slipped inside.

The space buzzed with activity as visitors filled the area. The stage, adorned with tall candle holders, illuminated the eager faces of the spectators. The host stood at the center, announcing the first performer. Every bench appeared occupied. The task of locating Becca in the crowd seemed daunting.

"Excuse me. Do you have a ticket?" a man beside Lana inquired.

Startled, Lana turned to face him. Lost in her own thoughts, she hadn't noticed his presence before. Furthermore, she didn't recognize him as a local resident. He was handsome – a young man dressed in a black coat, his cheeks dimpling as he smiled at her. *If he works here, I'm in trouble!* Apparently, sneaking in without a ticket wasn't a good idea.

Returning his smile, Lana attempted to sound convincing. "Hey. I don't have it on me. My friend –"

The sound of drums interrupted her awkward excuse. Lana helplessly turned her gaze to the stage, where the performer was engaging with the audience.

"Okay, I happened to have two tickets today," the man said. "But it seems like everyone is here in pairs, so... it would be a shame to waste one."

"It would," Lana agreed, slipping her hands into her purse. "How much?"

"Don't worry about that. It was a gift from my new employer, so I'm happy to share it. I noticed a couple of empty seats at the back." Without waiting for her response, the man gestured for Lana to follow him.

They reached the far end, where benches lined the stairs. He found an empty spot and patted the seat, inviting her.

"Thanks," Lana said as she took a seat.

His bright blue eyes sparkled with curiosity as he gazed at her. Then, the room plunged into darkness, and a hush fell over the audience. Lana turned her head towards the stage, anticipation building in the air.

The voice from the stage resonated with a tragic tone. "Silence allows us to hear our own voice clearer. And darkness lets us see the light." The orange sparkles danced in the air, revealing the performer who gestured his hands. With a snap of his fingers, all the candles surrounding the stage burst into flames.

It was the Gift of Fire, one of the highest in the magic hierarchy. Those bestowed with this Gift possessed resistance to flames and other destructive physical spells.

"Hey, what happened? Did you lose your ticket?" the handsome stranger whispered to Lana.

It took her a moment to register that he was addressing her. "No... It was just a coincidence. I was running late, and my friend, who had both our tickets, had already entered."

"It happens," the stranger replied, offering Lana a sympathetic look before returning his attention to the stage.

Who is he? Lana took a moment to study him closely. The flickering flames cast a glow on his clean-shaven face, revealing that he was in his late twenties. Lana bet there was much to uncover if she delved into his thoughts, but she needed to refrain from using her Gift further. She had already exhausted her abilities. Pushing herself beyond her limits could result in fainting, a risk she wasn't willing to take.

Turning towards her, the man remarked, "If I knew people were watching me instead of the show, I'd charge for it."

Lana blushed. "Sorry, I've just never seen you before."

"And...?"

Lana gestured with her hand, explaining, "It's a small town. Everyone is familiar with each other's faces. But maybe it's for the best that you don't know me."

"I'd like to know your name. If that's okay."

"Lana. And you?"

"Charles," he introduced himself, extending his hand.

She shook Charles's hand, feeling a pleasant warmth but refraining from delving into his mind. "So, what brings you to Triville, Charles?"

"I'm here for work."

"What kind of work?"

"I'm a Gift reader," Charles revealed.

Lana's eyes widened in surprise. "I've never heard of that ability before."

"I can sense others' powers, and my role is to help them unlock their full potential," Charles explained.

Lana's heart raced. If his Gift worked the same way as hers, Charles might have discovered her ability to read minds once he touched her hand. *Did he take this advantage?*

"I believe that power should be used for positive change," Charles continued. "Perhaps you'll share yours with me when you're ready."

She breathed out. *Good, he doesn't know what I'm capable of. Not yet.* It meant she had some time before her abilities might frighten him away, as they had with other men she had encountered. "Maybe I will," she replied mysteriously.

The people in front of them turned back, shushing Lana and Charles.

"Sorry," Lana whispered apologetically.

They exchanged smiles, silently agreeing to continue their conversation later. Lana redirected her focus to the stage, where the performer with the Gift of Fire had just concluded his act.

Next, an illusionist emerged and declared that he could conjure anything from thin air. He invited the audience to suggest material objects they desired to see materialized.

"A hat!" a woman from the front row called out.

The illusionist elegantly waved his hand, enveloping it in a cloud of mist. As the mist dissipated, a lovely purple hat with a delicate veil appeared in his palm. He presented it to the woman, who placed it on her head.

Within minutes, the hat vanished as if it had never existed. Lana blinked in astonishment. It was a remarkable Gift she had read about before. *What else can he fake?*

Charles raised his hand and requested a rose from the illusionist. With a smile, the illusionist performed his trick once more, conjuring a beautiful red rose on a long stem. He handed the rose to someone in the front row, and the flower was passed back through the audience until it reached Charles. He then gave it to Lana, a smile lighting up his face.

Her heart skipped a beat as she accepted the rose. Though it was merely an illusion, the thorns felt sharp and real. Lana caught a whiff of a faint, sweet scent and savored the moment. Maybe the flower's beauty would soon fade, but holding it in her hand was so exciting!

Charles gave her a playful look. "You're welcome."

"Thanks," Lana whispered, touched by the gesture.

For the first time since reaching 'the bridal age,' Lana found herself appreciating the attention of a man. Charles was unlike any of the typical suitors she had encountered – he was a young, handsome stranger. He represented a new mystery for her, a puzzle waiting to be unraveled.

It was midnight as Lana and Charles strolled along the dimly lit street. The tree barks emitted a faint purple glow, casting a subdued light on their path. It was the darkest time of the year, signaling the completion of the magical cycle – all the leaves had fallen, and the colors had faded. Despite the somber atmosphere, Lana found the night to be bright with new experiences.

As Charles accompanied her home, they shared laughter and discussed the magic tricks they had witnessed. His soothing, velvety voice put Lana at ease, and before she knew it, they had arrived at her doorstep.

Not ready to part ways just yet, Lana locked eyes with Charles. "I appreciate that you didn't press me about my Gift. Why didn't you read me to discover who I am?"

"Why would I?"

"Weren't you curious?"

"I find it much more intriguing to discover people slowly," Charles explained. "Also, even if I knew your abilities, it wouldn't change a thing. Through my experiences, I've learned that our magic doesn't define us; it's how we choose to use it that matters. All I wanted was to get to know you better, Lana. And so far, I really like you."

His words quickened her heartbeat. She needed to confess her truth before it was too late, and she liked him too. It was time to reveal her secret. "I'm afraid you won't like this part of me."

"Why not?"

"People avoid me because of my Gift. I've tried to use it for good, but it's only caused me trouble so far."

"You wouldn't believe how many people express the same concerns at the start of our training," Charles reassured her.

"How many people dislike their powers?"

"I'd say almost everyone," Charles replied, taking both of Lana's hands. "But I can help you if you let me. What's your biggest concern about your Gift?"

Lana cast her gaze downward. "I despise uncovering the dark secrets hidden deep within people's souls, all their ugly truths... Sometimes, I wish I had never become a mind reader."

Despite Lana's admission about her Gift, Charles did not withdraw his hands. This reaction was unusual; most people were guarded upon learning that she could potentially uncover their secrets by touch.

"I could read you if I wanted to," Lana cautioned.

"If you intended to read me, you would have done so already," Charles responded calmly. "Why haven't you?"

Because I've had my fill of secrets for today. Lana mustered a smile. "I try to respect personal boundaries."

"I appreciate that," Charles acknowledged with an encouraging smile. "Listen, every Gift can be both a curse and a blessing. It's not about the magic itself, but rather the intentions behind its use."

"Peeking into others' secrets... what purpose does it serve?"

"If you put it like this, it could be seen as... intriguing to some perverts." Charles chuckled, easing Lana's concerns. "But seriously, Lana, your Gift is remarkable. You have the ability to perceive others' fears and provide them with comfort and security. You have the potential to do so much good."

Lana's heart swelled at his words. Charles was undoubtedly a professional, and his perspective resonated with her. She had primarily used her power to uncover truths and jeopardize her potential suitors. Tonight, she had pushed herself to impress her father. But she had never utilized her Gift to aid those in need. Perhaps, this was her true calling all along. What if it was the key to changing her father's mindset?

Damn, this man sounds convincing. Does it mean I can trust him? To resist the temptation of delving into his mind, Lana released his hands. She was still in the process of recovering her powers and couldn't risk falling ill at that moment. However, she could test Charles's intentions by posing a provocative question. Stepping back, she asked, "If I have the ability to read someone, shouldn't I use it?"

"Why do you feel the need to do so?"

Lana shrugged. "It's better to be safe than sorry. For instance, what if you're just pretending to be normal? What if you're a maniac who preys on young, naive women?"

Charles chuckled. "If I were a criminal, I wouldn't be escorting you safely home." He gestured towards the entrance door, emphasizing his point. "Don't you think so?"

Lana crossed her arms. "That's exactly what a criminal would do – gain trust first and then discover where I live –"

"So, you're starting to trust me," Charles said, a smile playing on his lips.

She exhaled. "A little."

Charles scrutinized her with narrowed eyes. "Do you happen to read a lot of mysteries?"

Damn, he reads me like an open book! "Maybe."

"It explains a lot," Charles remarked with a soft chuckle. "Well, then. I'll see you again later, I suppose."

A smile graced Lana's lips. Perhaps her concerns had been unfounded, and she could simply savor the moment of this newfound acquaintance. "I would love to see you again."

"Then let's meet tomorrow," Charles suggested.

Lana's heart raced. She had never truly dated anyone before. While she had briefly encountered the men her father introduced to their home, those encounters didn't count. In Triville, dating was strongly discouraged for young women like her. Once she had reached sixteen, a 'bridal age,' she was no longer free to have male friends. Being seen in the company of a man could lead to malicious rumors. Lana detested this restrictive rule, but she had never met anyone worth breaking it for. Now, she was willing to take the risk.

Lana licked her dry lips, feeling as though she was on the verge of committing a transgression. Strangely, the idea of this forbidden date exhilarated her. "Okay. What time?"

"Well, it will be my first day at work, but I hope to see you afterward."

"Sure. Where shall we go?"

"Would you mind showing me around the town?"

"I would love to," Lana replied, her heart glowing with joy.

"Then I'll meet you here at six in the evening," Charles said, leaning in to kiss her hand. His touch left a pleasant sensation on her skin.

5

Girlish Secrets

The next day was foggy, so it was perfect for reading. With her eyes wide open, Lana lay in her bed, fully immersed in her favorite fantasy romance wrapped in mystery. She had read it many times, and each time, the story awoke something deep within her heart. But today felt different. The rustle of its crispy pages pulled her into a welcoming embrace, each scene with the male lead reminding her of Charles. *Oh, I can't wait to see him again!*

A loud knock on the door interrupted her reverie. Lana blinked and shifted her gaze to the bedroom door. *Locked.* She exhaled a sigh of relief, hoping the unwelcome visitor would walk away and leave her alone with her romantic journey.

The knock repeated, followed by her best friend's voice. "Open up! It's Becca! I know you're in there!"

Lana closed her book with a sense of regret. The main character, a girl with flapping red hair, gazed at her from the cover, her smile teasing.

"It's alright," Lana whispered to her, "we'll continue later."

On the other side of the door, Becca continued to pound on it. "Can you open the door already?!"

Lana placed the book on her nightstand and walked over to un-lock the door.

Today, Becca was clad in a high-school uniform, her long choco-late-brown hair cascading down her chest. *Perhaps she came here straight after her classes,* Lana observed.

"What's the matter?" Lana asked, frowning at her.

Becca stared at her with anxious blue eyes. "Seriously?! You missed the show last night!"

"Oh...right," Lana said, mustering her best apologetic look. Af-ter meeting Charles, she completely forgot about her friend and her original plan to find Becca in the circus to resolve the ticket misunderstanding. Admitting this out loud would be the worst ex-cuse ever, so Lana chose to remain silent.

"I can't believe you missed it!" Becca shook her head and en-tered the room without waiting for an invitation. She climbed onto the bed and glanced disapprovingly at Lana's book. "Maybe the problem is that you are more interested in fictional stories than in real life."

"Maybe it's because my real life has been taken care of," Lana retorted. "Thanks to my father."

"Yes, he is trying to arrange your marriage. He does it because he loves you and wants the best for you. Isn't that sweet?"

Lana rolled her eyes. "Unfortunately, my dad's idea of a suitable husband is strange. Ever since I turned eighteen, he has been ar-ranging these ridiculous dinners, trying to find a perfect match for me. You know how much I hate it."

"I know, but –"

"And yesterday was a complete mess," Lana interjected, relieved to have a perfect excuse for missing the show without revealing her encounter with Charles. "Listen, Becca, I'm really sorry we didn't meet last night. But I couldn't. Just before I was about to leave the house, my father introduced me to his 'good old friend' from the capital. I tried to find a way to dismiss him, but the things he was hiding... Long story short, I managed to make him confess to his crime. Even my father supported me when I exposed him!"

"A crime?" Becca asked, her eyes widening.

"Yes. He raped his student," Lana revealed.

Becca stared at her blankly, as if Lana had just said something extremely inappropriate. *Right, Becca is a regular schoolgirl, and such dark secrets are shocking to her.* Lana made a mental note to be more careful with her word choice in the future.

"Yes, here's the thing... He committed a crime months ago, and he thought he had gotten away with it," Lana explained in a softer voice. "He used his high position in the university to ensure that no one would believe the victim."

"What about the girl who..." Becca hesitated, unsure how to phrase her question. "Who was assaulted? Is she okay now?"

Lana shrugged. "I hope so." The saddest part of the story was that no one seemed to care about the fate of the victim, except for Lana, who had learned the truth the previous night, and now Becca. Unfortunately, they couldn't do anything about it. The crime had happened months ago, which was too late to get involved.

Becca glanced at the book resting on the nightstand. "Everything seems easier in a fictional world. There, everyone gets their justice."

Lana furrowed her brow. Becca loved the story, but unlike Lana, she was skeptical about its ideas and resistant to change. Nevertheless, Lana felt it was worth trying to open Becca's mind. "Maybe that world is thriving because women are allowed to do a man's job?" Lana proposed. "What if we could protect people from the injustices and cruelties of life? I believe it could make things much easier for everyone."

"Women will never be allowed to do such things," Becca countered.

"You sound just like my father," Lana teased. "But grumpiness doesn't suit you. Unlike him, you are young and have a creative mind. Can you use your imagination?"

Becca rolled her eyes. "Sometimes, I think your imagination is too much."

"Come on." Lana touched her shoulder in an attempt to break through Becca's resistance. "What harm could come from giving yourself a break and embracing the possibility of change? What if you could do the things that men take for granted?"

"Because it's false hope," Becca replied, brushing Lana's hand away. "And it only breaks your heart in the end."

"Maybe. But what is life without hope?"

"This hope it built on a lie that you choose to believe in for some unknown reason. As my mom says, *'the truth may be bitter, but accepting it is a way to navigate through life.'*"

Lana let out a sigh of disappointment. Perhaps she sounded like a foolish dreamer, but she wasn't ready to give up.

"I'm sorry, Lana," Becca said, giving her a remorseful look. "It's just... It's difficult to see you trying to escape your fate."

"My fate?"

Becca nodded. "Women are gifted with the ability to create new life. Isn't it wonderful to have a family?"

Not when you can be raped and silenced, Lana thought, but she held back the harsh words. She shook her head, gazing out the window. Outside, the bare trees stood still, vulnerable yet defenseless against the impending winter. Perhaps her desire to change the status quo was delusional. But Becca was also delusional, influenced by her mother's beliefs. Maybe that was a card Lana could play. "Alright, then. But as your mom also says, *'Divine's ways are mysterious.'* What if the time comes when we are called upon to help someone seek justice?"

Becca nodded in agreement. "Then, I'll do whatever is necessary."

"Good." Lana smiled, content with their resolution. "Now, tell me about last night. Did you manage to watch the performance?"

Becca placed her hands on her lap, her black school uniform skirt covering her knees and revealing her long, plain boots. "Yes, about yesterday... I was waiting for you, and it was getting late..."

Lana smiled at her friend. Becca's reluctance to talk about her mysterious boyfriend was endearing. "Is it true that you met a boy?"

Becca furrowed her brow, likely suspecting where Lana had heard about it. "Yes... But I'm not really into Stan. He's just a friend who helped me out once."

Lana got intrigued. It seemed Becca needed more time to get to know this Stan guy better. Who knew, maybe she would develop feelings for him? "What did he do?"

"Last night, I ran into twins from my class. Those girls started mocking me, and Stan intervened," Becca explained.

"I actually encountered those two girls on my way to the circus," Lana said. Now, it was clear why they had been so hostile towards her. "They seemed really upset with you!"

"Yes, we had a little misunderstanding," Becca admitted, glancing at the time crystal on the wall. It emitted a yellow glow, indicating it was around two in the afternoon. Time crystals like this were scattered throughout Lana's house, changing color to show the time of day.

"Actually, they are the reason why I came to see you today," Becca said.

"Huh?"

"Today, when I got back from school, my mom mentioned that something had happened to one of those girls."

Lana frowned. "I'm not surprised they got themselves into trouble. They are so mean!"

"I know, right?!" Becca rolled her eyes. "They didn't show up at school today, and my mom asked me to go check on them. As I've been told, their mother went to church to pray for their health."

Lana placed her hand on her chest. "Oh... I had no idea it was something serious. I'm sorry for what I just said!"

"I'm pretty sure they're pretending to be sick just to avoid seeing Stan," Becca said, visibly irritated by the situation. "Last night, their pride was wounded, so I'm sure they won't return to school without a plan for revenge. But my mom thinks I'm friends with them, so she asked me to visit and see if they need anything. Can you believe it?"

Lana gave her a supportive look. "If you want me to come with you, I'm in."

"Thank you!" Becca's eyes sparkled with gratitude. "I just can't face them alone. Not after what they tried to do last night."

"Okay, tell me everything. Then, I promise, we'll go together and give them the treatment they deserve!"

6

A Tactic

Becca and Lana strolled along the street where the twin girls lived. Their family occupied a large household – a three-story building made of red bricks that stood out among the smaller, paler houses. Becca stopped at the crossroad as her stomach churned. It was fortunate that Lana was nearby, as she needed her courage to approach.

Lana touched her elbow with her free hand. "Are you okay?"

"Yes," Becca lied. She glanced at her friend – in her other hand, Lana carried a wicker basket filled with muffins that their maid had baked that morning. The muffins had been recently reheated in the oven and smelled of cranberries, making Becca's mouth water. "I'm still unsure if the bullies deserve all this amazing food you are bringing."

"That's the tactic that works all the time," Lana explained as they resumed their stroll to the twins' house. "Here is the thing – when someone mistreats you, they expect aggression in return. This is how the bully is confident that you are no better than them. It fits their worldview, so they keep being aggressive and get the same reaction in response."

"So you decided to kill them with kindness," Becca suggested with a smirk. After she had told Lana about last night's events in detail, her friend came up with a strange plan.

"Exactly," Lana confirmed, her eyes sparkling with excitement. "You see, when you help the person in trouble, despite how they had previously treated you, you change their perspective. Now, instead of seeing you as a scavenger who shamelessly feasts on their problems, they see you as a strong, reliable person who is wiser than they first thought." She pointed at the red-brick house. "And this, my friend, is the best moment ever to deal with your enemies."

"Oh, I got it now," Becca remembered the old saying. "Keep your friends close and your enemies closer."

"That's right."

At the wide porch with five stairs, they stopped. One of the twins, the girl with long raven hair, sat on it. She didn't even notice their arrival. With her face buried in her hands, she was too busy crying. Her sobs made Becca cringe.

Lana poked her shoulder, her lips barely moving as she whispered, "Go check on her!"

Becca took a deep breath and approached.

At the sound of her steps, the girl raised her blurry eyes to her. They were dark-gray, but the whites were now red from crying. The mole above her left eyebrow indicated that it was Mira. *At least I get to face the less evil twin.*

Becca handed her a clean napkin. "Here. Take it."

Mira winced but didn't object. She wiped her puffy nose and crumpled the napkin between her palms. "What are you doing here?"

"My mom told me that something bad happened last night," Becca said. Now, she could clearly see that it wasn't one of their games. This girl, Mira, might have been mean to her last night, but right now, her state of upset made Becca frustrated, too. "I came to see if I can help somehow."

Mira sighed and gave her a look full of doubt. Then she shifted her eyes to Lana. "And you brought your friend? So you would sniff around and laugh at us? How silly!"

Becca blinked. "No, that's not why we're here –"

"Oh, go away already!" Mira stood up, intending to go back home. "We don't need anyone's pity!"

Becca gave Lana a perplexed look. She had no idea how to handle the situation. Maybe they were supposed to leave her alone and go home? *Oh, well... At least, we tried.*

"Hold on!" Lana raised her hand, causing Mira to freeze at the threshold.

"What now?"

Lana stepped closer and handed her a wicker basket. The enticing smells reached Mira, and she eyed the baked goods with interest.

"I made it for you," Lana said in a syrupy voice. "Please, take it as a gesture of my support. I know that you were mean to Becca and me last night, but right now, it doesn't matter. Whatever happened to you, you don't need to explain anything to me or anyone else. I just hope your sister will recover soon."

"Thank you," Mira replied in a trembling voice. Then her shoulders started shaking again, and tears rolled down her cheeks.

Lana gave her a hug, patting her shoulders. "Hush... It will be okay."

Becca stared at them in disbelief. Not that she was heartless, but damn, this strategy worked! Just a small gesture of kindness turned this lioness into a meowing kitten.

Lana gave Becca a meaningful glance as if to say, *"What are you waiting for?"*

Becca stepped closer and hugged her former enemy. It was awkward at first, but comforting this vulnerable girl felt good.

7

A Crime

In the spacious living room, Becca occupied a corner of a leather sofa with a screaming-red shade that matched the curtains on the tall windows. Among all the houses she had ever been invited to, this one was the furthest from being cozy.

Mira, the girl they had met on the porch, walked from the kitchen with two steaming cups of tea. She placed them on a coffee table and sat nearby. Becca hesitated for a moment, afraid that Mira might add some potion to it. *No, it would be too inappropriate considering the situation*, she decided as she took her cup.

"You are brave, weirdo," Mira teased her.

"My name is Rebecca," she replied, trying to be patient. The last thing she wanted was to argue now.

"Rebecca sounds too long," Mira whined. "What if I call you just Becca?"

She rolled her eyes. "Sure. Why not?"

Mira gave her a curious look. "So, how long have you been friends with Lana?"

She shrugged, still not used to questions that weren't meant to be mocking. "All my life. Our fathers are –"

"Working together, right?" Mira smiled at the recollection. "I think you talked about it in school. They both are guardians."

"Good memory." Becca smiled back, trying not to sound too sarcastic. Everyone in this town knew Bernard Morris, a Guardian Captain, and both twins were aware of who Lana was. In school, Becca often mentioned that her father was a guardian, mostly to feel safe from all the bullies surrounding her. Now, Mira had just put two and two together. *What an achievement for her small mind!*

"Listen, I'm sorry about yesterday," Mira said. "And all the trouble we caused you."

Becca exhaled a sigh. *'Forgiveness is the way to greatness,'* as her mother liked to repeat. Becca found it too difficult to let go of her anger, however, she had to focus on the tactic. *Keep your friends close... right.* "Don't bother about it. I just hope Lana will help Mina as much as she can."

Mira nodded. "Me too."

They sat in silence, immersed in their thoughts. After their truce-making on the porch, Mira explained that her sister had fallen into a long somber state, and even their family doctor couldn't awaken her. Mira simply couldn't talk about it without crying, so Lana suggested checking Mina using her Gift. As Mina rested upstairs in her bedroom, Becca was left face-to-face with the other twin, Mira. The tension between them grew stronger with each minute of silence.

Becca gave her a suspicious look. This one wasn't that tricky or cruel, but still, it was hard to believe that Mira would change her attitude so easily. It must have been something terrible happening to her sister because she had agreed to accept Lana's help. *What really happened?* Becca was afraid to ask.

"You know, we were both so mad at you last night," Mira said. "Just pissed!"

"I can imagine," Becca said, trying to appear polite.

"Really?!" She narrowed her eyes. "I bet you were glad when Stan treated us like shit."

She shrugged. "I'm not responsible for his reaction. He saw you pushing me, so he got upset."

"Nevertheless, you used the opportunity and invited him to the show," Mira said, fixing Becca with her gaze, which sent shivers down her spine. "Why did you do that?"

Because I thought you'd never learn about it. Becca swallowed. It was better for Lana to hurry up; otherwise, it would be another fight. "Listen, I only shared the ticket out of gratitude. But I'll never see Stan more than a friend, especially knowing how much you like him –"

"I don't!"

Becca blinked, taken aback by Mira's reaction. They were in high school, not in kindergarten, so being so shy about her feelings was awkward. "Well, whatever the status of your relationship is..."

"I mean, Mina likes him, not me."

That explains a lot. Becca nodded in understanding. "Whatever. I said I'm not interested in him, and it's true. I'm pretty sure your sister can restore their connection once she wakes up."

"*If* she ever wakes up," Mira said gloomily, ending their uncomfortable small talk.

Fortunately, Lana walked down the stairs. She lowered herself on the sofa and exhaled an exhausted sigh.

"What happened?" Becca asked, impatient to find out how Mina had ended up being so sick.

Lana gave her a weary look. "I need a moment to pull myself together." Becca handed her a cup of tea, and Lana took it. "Thanks."

"You're welcome," Becca said in a rushed voice. "Did you manage to read her?"

"Uh-huh." Lana took a sip of tea, making both Becca and Mira fidget in their seats.

Mira glared at her like Lana was her only hope. "Will she ever wake up?"

Lana waved her hand in reassurance. "She'll be alright."

"How do you know?"

Lana placed her empty cup on the coffee table before replying. "The last memory that I managed to find in her mind was before she went to bed. And it was the day before yesterday. It explains her deep slumber – her memories of the whole day were erased!"

"Erased?!" The girls said together.

Lana nodded. "Damn, it must be a very strong potion. I'm still dizzy after reading her!"

Mira brought her palms to her burning cheeks. "Are you sure Mina will be okay?"

"Yes. I read about this potion. It's forbidden because it has a severe side effect – it can cause mental health maladies. However, Mina's other memories look in order, so I'm sure nothing like that happened. Her mind needs to recharge after such stress. I think she'll be awake by midnight."

Mira exhaled a sigh of relief. "Thank you, Lana."

"No problem." Lana smiled. "From now on, this case will be in the hands of the guardians."

"What? Why?"

Lana gave her a compassionate look. "You said your family doctor checked her, right?"

Mira nodded.

"It means he must have taken a blood sample for analysis. After he found the presence of the forbidden potion in her system, he must have reported it to the guardians. It's a crime, Mira, so it must be investigated thoroughly."

Mira kept staring at her in silence.

"Was it you who talked to the doctor?" Lana asked.

"No. But I heard his talk with my parents. He never mentioned it was a potion. All he said was that it was the impact of alcohol that we both tried last night..." Her lower lip trembled as she got back to the painful memory. "He said she might never wake up and advised us to pray for her health!"

"Well, prayer would never hurt," Becca implied.

Lana frowned. "Maybe. But the doctor never checked her properly, and it's completely wrong. I bet he just ran an alcohol test and was satisfied by what he found – a young woman who misbehaved. It was enough to confirm his stigma. He didn't even bother to dig deeper." She sighed. "It's just cruel that he chose to keep you in the dark instead of trying to find the real cause of her slumber. Why would he do that?"

"It's something else," Mira lowered her eyes, her cheeks blushing. "He checked her innocence and found... he found that it was... gone."

Lana shifted on the sofa, leaning closer and lowering her voice. "You mean... She was assaulted?"

Mira nodded, not raising her eyes. "I was so scared when I learned it! But thanks Divine, I didn't suffer, so I guess I'll just be by her side when she wakes up."

Lana placed her hand on her shoulder. "Mira, if someone erased her memories, it was done with only one purpose – to make her forget about this assault. And he did it by giving her an alcohol with an illegal potion in it. Now, we must find this person. Don't you think so?"

Becca shifted her eyes between them. Again, Lana attempted to play detective. And as she knew, it never ended well.

"Please, tell me what happened last night," Lana insisted.

Mira shook her head. "Nothing. I hope I'll forget it, too. As if it was a nightmare."

"Okay," Lana said, her gleaming eyes, however, indicating she was not going to give up on this case so easily. "Keep silent. Then, the person who did it to your sister will get away with it. With time, he'll grow bolder. Then, he will repeat his crime with another young girl who was foolish enough to try some booze."

Mira and Becca swallowed synchronically. It was creepy – to know that somewhere in their town, there was a rapist who gave the schoolgirls free alcoholic drinks with Forgetting potion.

"I'm not sure I can help you with that," Mira said gloomily. "I have no idea what happened!"

"All you need is to tell me all the details you can recall about last night," Lana said. "Then, I can start an investigation."

"Are you capable of finding the criminal?"

"I can handle this," Lana assured her. "I read a lot of books on law and have access to the Guardian House library. I'm pretty sure we can figure something out."

"But you aren't a guardian."

"My father is. So, all I need is to find the truth, and then I'll pass this case on to him. Trust me, with the evidence, he will arrest the man who had assaulted your sister."

"Fine." Mira exhaled a heavy sigh, finally convinced. Then she started her story, "It happened last night. After that accident with Becca, Mina and I were too pissed to go home. So, we decided to check the West End."

Becca frowned. The West End was the most troublesome part of the town, occupied mainly by poor people who loved to get drunk and fight with everyone who dared to argue with them. It also had multiple taverns and underground stores where people sold illegal potions and herbs meant to make the mind blurry. Drugs, as people called them. *What two schoolgirls forgot there?*

Mira caught her look. "Hey, don't judge. Our dad works there. He owns the dance club."

Becca nodded, doing her best to look like an understanding person.

"So, we were going to check on our dad and watch a couple of dances. You know, they have a nice stage."

"What happened next?" Lana rushed her. "After you left the club?"

"On our way back, we met our chemistry teacher, Mr. Burke. He was a bit drunk, and we decided to make fun of him." She paused, her cheeks beet-red. "We asked him to spare us a drink, and he invited us to his house."

Lana gave her a worried look. "And you accepted his invite?"

Mira's voice quietened. "We just were curious, okay? And we asked him rather as a joke, but he agreed to give us a drink. We decided to try 'a special tea,' as he called it. Then I had my drink and fell asleep."

"Did you wake up at his home?"

"No. At sunrise, I woke up close to *my* home. I was on our lawn, to be precise, and Mina lay nearby. I assumed we got too drunk and knocked off close to our house..." She rubbed her puffy eyes. "I tried to wake Mina, but I couldn't. I got terrified. I screamed, and our parents ran outside. It was such a shame! I smelled of alcohol, and my clothes were all wrinkled. I first thought it was my fault. I was afraid Mina had an overdose or something. And I slept through the whole thing..." She covered her mouth with her hand, unable to continue this confession.

"It wasn't like that," Lana said in a soft voice. "Trust me, alcohol is bad, but it's another kind of potion. If you get too drunk, the worst thing that can happen is a morning headache. It's not just a sip of drink that you took, Mina. Your teacher, Mr. Burke, knocked you off on purpose, using a sleeping potion. But as for Mina... He raped her and erased her memory. He just used your inexperience with alcohol to cover his crime. Burke probably was confident that you wouldn't tell anyone about him, assuming that it was all your fault."

"But it *was* our fault."

"Only partially. It was your teacher who took advantage of you, and he will pay for that."

"Will he?!" Mira's voice was full of doubt. "I have no idea what fantasy world you live in, but in reality, it never happens like this. Bad people get away with their crimes, and the innocent ones die!"

Becca swallowed. It was precisely what she had told Lana earlier that day – they could do nothing against the cruelty of this world. However, if it was so, she had no desire to live in such a world. She had to do something. Otherwise, her heart would just bleed out.

Maybe Lana's hope to become a detective was foolish, but she had good intentions, and these girls needed her. Becca only needed to support her best friend. She turned to Mira. "I know it won't be easy. But you aren't alone in this, Mira. You have me and Lana. To-gether, we'll bring him to justice."

Mira stared at her, stunned by her words. "How exactly?!"

"We'll investigate this mystery," Becca said, glancing at Lana. "Right?"

Lana nodded. "Of course. We can start by finding the witnesses. If Burke carried you here, someone must have seen him. We only need to ask around."

Becca nodded in support. "I'll help you with that."

"Thank you, girls," Mira said as her eyes darted to the stairs. "I just want her to be alright."

Lana placed her hand on her shoulder. "Mina will recover. I promise."

8

A Thin Knit

In the evening, Lana was busy working in her room. Surprisingly, she was quite skilled with yarn when she was moved by her detective passion. She had a new purpose – to help Mina find justice, and this time, she wasn't going to stop until she found the criminal.

She started by attaching a white sheet to one of her bedroom walls. The pins helped secure the ends of the sheet to the wallpaper. Lana then cut the pictures from her magazines that resembled the key people in this crime. She used the pins to attach a portrait of the suspect, chemistry teacher Mr. Burke, to the center of the sheet. Once her visual aid was ready, she took a wicker basket filled with colorful yarn that her father had given her as a present. Red knits connected the suspect with his victims – two young women with black hair, Mira and Mina. Lana then connected the blue knits with possible leads that she needed to investigate – such as the street names where the suspect could be seen walking with the two girls.

Lana bit her lip, deep in thought. *How exactly did he deliver the girls to their home?* Lana grabbed a clear sheet from her notebook and attached it near the suspect's portrait. With her pencil, she wrote a possible clue: *A cart.*

Despite being a strong man, Burke probably wouldn't carry two girls all the way to their home using just his hands. It was too risky – someone could bump into him and start asking questions. It would be much more convenient for him to place the girls in a cart and cover them with a blanket. This theory was easy to verify – Lana believed that people might have seen the man pulling the cart or at least heard some noise. The nights in Triville were typically quiet, especially in the neighborhood where the twin girls lived. If her hunch was correct, they would find the cart in Burke's stable and have solid evidence of his crime!

Lana chewed on her pencil, contemplating more potential scenarios. What other information did they have on Mr. Burke? She knew for sure that he possessed a Telekinesis Gift. This type of magic was a perfect fit for his profession – in his laboratory, Burke could manipulate any ingredients, even toxic ones, without physical contact. This ability allowed him to create various mixtures that were contained within a glass cube, eliminating the risk of inhaling harmful fumes. Perhaps this was how he concocted the potions to sedate his victims. It might be worthwhile to investigate his workstation to uncover any forbidden potions.

Where did he conduct his potion-making activities? If Burke had prepared the potions himself, it would have been too suspicious to keep all the equipment at home. It was more likely that he utilized the school laboratory. Lana raised her hand and jotted down another note in pencil: *Check the lab.*

She took a step back, admiring the creation she had just completed. Her heart swelled with pride as she realized it resembled the investigation boards she had seen at the Guardian House. There, detectives typically used a whiteboard to establish connections between the evidence they had gathered, piecing together a clearer picture of the crime. Through this method, they slowly unraveled the motives behind the crimes and ultimately apprehended the culprits. Although such occurrences were rare in Triville due to its safe and tranquil nature, when a crime did occur, it was a significant event.

Oh, if only I could become like them! Lana pressed her hands to her chest, lost in a daydream of joining the guardian team. Despite her father's lack of belief in her detective abilities, Lana pondered the possibility of solving this case. If she succeeded, she could prove her worth to her father and perhaps even earn a place at the Guardian House.

A sudden knock on her door jolted her back to reality. Lana swiftly removed the pins securing the sheet to the wallpaper, causing it to fall to the floor.

"Yes?" Lana asked, smoothing the sheet and ensuring that her 'investigation board' remained intact. To her relief, it appeared undamaged. She quickly slid it under her bed to conceal her activities.

The door creaked open, and her father entered. He looked impeccably dressed in his pressed black uniform, adorned with a golden dragon embroidery on his left shoulder and two golden stripes denoting his rank as a Guardian Captain.

"Good evening!" Lana greeted him with a hug.

"Evening," he replied, his expression turning surprised as he noticed the basket of used yarn. "Have you taken up knitting at last?"

Lana stifled a laugh. "Let's just say I've started working on a project."

"Very well." He nodded in approval. "You know, there are many other interesting pursuits besides solving mysteries."

Lana smiled mischievously. "I'm pleased to see you in good spirits. I trust you haven't forgotten your promise to cease arranging dinners for my potential suitors."

He gave her a somber look and settled into Lana's chair. She perched on the edge of her bed, bracing herself for the conversation.

"Lana, I'm an old man," he began, his voice tinged with melancholy. "I may be here now, but I'll be gone in ten or fifteen years."

Her heart sank. "Please don't say that!"

He raised his hand, halting her futile attempt to comfort him. "It's the natural order of things, my daughter. We are born, and one day, we'll pass on. In the time in between, we must embrace a multitude of experiences. Life can be a source of great joy if you open your heart to new possibilities."

She smoothed the hem of her dress nervously. "Well, the term 'new' doesn't quite capture the essence of all the men you bring into our home."

"They are seasoned and independent, though," he countered.

She rolled her eyes. "Oh, please! I have no desire to be with a man of your generation. It just feels... too strange."

"Perhaps you're right."

"Am I?" Lana blinked, taken aback by her father's unexpected response.

"I'm just weary of these trials and disappointments," he elaborated. "Perhaps you should consider going to the capital, where life is markedly different. There, you could pursue studies and potentially find a job that aligns with your aspirations. It may lead you to true happiness, even if it means being far from me."

The notion of leaving Triville and starting anew in the capital held a certain allure. However, the idea of leaving her father alone in their home weighed heavily on her heart. "How can I leave you, father?"

He offered her a reassuring smile. "It's alright. I only want you to find happiness. Who knows, you might even encounter a suitable young man there! Besides, the capital is just a three-day journey away. You can always visit me whenever you wish."

Lana let out a heavy sigh. Her life had been rooted in Triville thus far, but she also felt the pull of new beginnings. She yearned to explore the Kingdom, yet bidding farewell to her home and the people she held dear was a daunting prospect. "I need some time to consider it."

"Of course. There's no rush to make a decision," her father reassured her, his kind brown eyes easing her apprehension. "Let's revisit this discussion in the spring."

"I wouldn't mind assisting you at a Guardian House," she suggested.

His expression turned weary. "Lana, please. If you bring up that topic again, I'll have no choice but to enroll you in Maynard's study program!"

"Sure, because being an architect is all I've ever dreamed of!" Lana retorted sarcastically.

"Why not?" he mused. "Architects are constantly in demand as cities expand. Perhaps you could specialize in interior design and create beautifully decorated spaces."

Lana shot him a bewildered look. "Seriously?! After what he did to his student, you're considering sending me there?"

"His guilt hasn't been proven. You may have read Maynard, but what if it was merely a figment of his imagination? A twisted fantasy that crosses the minds of all men at times?"

"I can differentiate between imagination and a genuine memory!" Lana gasped. "Why won't you believe me?"

"I stood by you last night and intervened when he was disrespectful to you. Isn't that enough?"

I wish it were. Lana shook her head. "It's disheartening that people like him can evade accountability."

"Well, if he truly is a criminal, as you suspect, then I hope our actions have deterred him from committing further assaults."

"And if not?"

"Then he'll face the consequences sooner or later. That's how justice operates. When you violate the law, it's a matter of luck to avoid being apprehended. We're all fallible and prone to mistakes," he concluded.

"I understand," Lana replied, harboring doubts about whether Maynard would face justice anytime soon. However, viewing the situation from a different angle, attending an architecture university didn't seem like a bad idea. Given Maynard's criminal background as a teacher, she could potentially pose as a student to uncover his illicit activities. "Fine, I think I'll consider becoming an architect."

Her father nodded, content with their decision. "Then it's settled! I'll look into their study programs, and you can select one."

"Great," Lana responded wearily. She was too drained to argue further. If she wanted her father to consider her for a detective position, she needed to crack a real case. Gathering evidence and presenting it to him was the only way to prove her capabilities. She was prepared to put in the hard work to achieve her goal.

"Good." Her father clapped his hands together before rising from his seat. "By the way, I've invited my new colleague for dinner tonight –"

"Seriously?! Didn't we discuss calling off my potential engagements?"

"Relax," he reassured her with a smile. "It's the new coach I mentioned last night. He's not on my matchmaking list."

"Why not?"

"He's too young for my liking."

Lana chuckled. "In that case, I already love him."

9

A Fragrance of Love

The fire was blazing in the fireplace as they sat in the living room, waiting for dinner to be ready. Lana was curious to meet her father's new colleague. Also, she couldn't wait to get back to her work. The next day, she would start her investigation.

Lana glanced at the crystal of time on the wall, glowing light-blue. *Almost six in the evening*, she noted. Then, another memory hit her. *Charles!* She had been so preoccupied with her new investigation that she had completely forgotten about the handsome man who had promised to come to her porch tonight for a secret date. *What if he knocked on the door?!*

She glanced back at the entrance doors, her breath ragged. "I must go outside. Now."

"Is everything alright?" her father asked.

"Certainly," Lana replied, her shaking voice betraying her. Her life had never been so full of secrets before. Living in a quiet, conservative Triville, she could only dream of catching criminals, let alone having an admirer. Now, she didn't know how to handle so many contradictory feelings and cover all her lies. "I mean... I'm just a bit excited about my future studies. I might need some fresh air before dinner. Or better yet, skip the meal."

He narrowed his eyes. "Knowing you, you must be up to something. Is it a chronic avoidance of men?"

"Quite the opposite," she shrugged, trying to look innocent. "I'd better go."

The bell over the entrance door chimed, and Lana jumped to her feet. While the servant was opening the door, her father stood to greet the visitor. Lana squinted her eyes, hoping it was someone other than him...

"Sergeant Braun," her father said in a cheerful tone. "Welcome to our house."

It's his colleague, then. At least Lana could meet him properly before leaving. She put on her nicest smile and turned to the guest. Once her eyes locked with his, she lost her breath.

It was the man she had met last night, Charles. And now he stood by the entrance, smiling. The dimples on his cheeks made his face magnificent. In his hands, he held a bouquet of white lilies. *No freaking way!*

Her father came closer and patted her shoulder. "You can unfreeze now."

She blinked, realizing that she had been staring at Charles, numb. *Wait... How does my father know him?*

The answer didn't make her wait for too long. Charles took off his coat, revealing his black uniform. It was the same as her father's but with a dragon embroidery and one golden wave. Her brain quickly connected the dots – Charles was a Guardian Sergeant. He had obviously prepared for this visit, and it meant one thing – when he promised to see her again last night, he knew he would come to their house as a visitor. *Why didn't he tell me anything?*

"Hi, Lana," Charles said, giving her the bouquet. "It's nice to meet you finally."

Lana accepted the bouquet and inhaled its rich aroma, which made her head spin. Strangely, this sweet gesture helped eliminate her shock. Charles apparently decided to pretend that it was their first meeting. Well, she could only follow his lead. Anyways, she couldn't tell her father that she had already met this man last night and agreed to see him again.

"I was told lilies are your favorite flowers," Charles said.

Her heart melted. "They are. Thank you so much."

He smiled again, chasing away all her worries. *Damn, this man has power over me.* "Who told you about my flower preference?"

"The seller in a flower shop nearby. I'm not used to small towns like this, but I know about its benefits. Almost everyone knows people living around."

"That's true," she agreed.

Her father coughed, attracting their attention. "Sorry to interrupt. But dinner is ready."

They exchanged glances and followed him to the dining room.

In the evening, Lana walked through the central park with Charles, holding onto his elbow. Despite the chilly temperature, it felt cozy near him. The naked trees with dark-purple barks glowed around them, illuminating their path. Now, she didn't have to hide Charles from her father anymore, and it made things less tense. They had a nice dinner, and her father didn't mind when Charles asked Lana to show him the beauty of nighttime Triville.

"Last night, you knew that I was your boss's daughter," Lana raised the question that she couldn't ask during dinner. "Why didn't you tell me anything?"

"Well, I didn't know that until I followed you home last night," he explained. "Only then did I realize it was the house of the Guardian Captain that I saw when I first came to town. I was told he had a capricious daughter who rejects all her admirers, but honestly, I had no idea it was you!"

"Trust me, I had a solid reason to reject all of them," she explained. "Anyhow... When you figured out who I was, you decided to schedule the same meeting time with me and my father. Didn't you think you would put me into a confusing situation?"

"Oh, it was hilarious!" He laughed.

"Was it?!" She poked his shoulder. "I almost had a heart attack when you showed up at my doorstep."

He mustered an apologetic look. "Sorry. I didn't know you decided to keep me a secret."

"I didn't," she mumbled. Well, now she had one less secret. "And I have more important things to hide."

"That's intriguing." His blue eyes shone with interest. "Maybe I can help with resolving some of these things?"

Lana looked into his face. He sounded quite sincere. Also, he had training in the Guardian Academy, which meant he certainly knew how to catch criminals like chemistry teacher Burke.

"Or keep it to yourself," he said.

"I think I will."

"Okay. But if you ever change your mind, let me know."

His mindfulness was touching. Lana wanted to tell him everything immediately, but she stopped herself from this silly move. No, she had a good investigation plan, and she must carry it out without anyone's help. After all, she barely knew Charles, and she couldn't trust him. Not yet. What if he complained to her father about her plan? It would put her in a bad light and wouldn't leave a chance for this investigation to succeed. This meant Mina would never find justice. No, she couldn't risk it. Not before she had read Charles properly and made sure she could rely on him.

Meanwhile, they neared the bridge of wishes. It was an old stone bridge with metal railings stretched above the running river. It was around nine in the evening because the time crystals mounted in the railings shone lilac. Under their glow, the river seemed to be made from liquid amethysts.

They walked on the bridge, and Lana touched the wood that covered the top of the railings. "This is our special sightseeing."

Charles looked around. "Time crystals look amazing everywhere; that's why people use them in public places. I saw many of them on the fountains in city squares and sometimes on the bridges."

"It's not the time crystals that make this bridge so unique." Lana spread her hands, introducing him to one of the World's wonders that happened to be here, in Triville. "This is a bridge of wishes. It can make one of your biggest dreams come true."

"Any dream?"

She snickered. "Of course, it should be a realistic one. You cannot wish for the sky to turn green or to be able to fly. Also, the bridge will make your dream come true only if you sincerely want it."

Charles moved his hand along the railing. "What's the catch?"

She gently touched his hand. "Be careful when you make a wish because it's only one you can make per your lifetime."

His face became intrigued. "Did you make yours?"

Lana paused. What could she say? *Yes, I made my wish two years ago when I realized that no one in his right mind would ever let a woman become a guardian. It never came true, even though I still have hope.* No, Charles didn't have to know about it. He would laugh at her then. All she wanted was to tell him about the bridge without looking silly.

He smiled. "I see. It's a big secret, and you can't tell anyone; otherwise, it won't come true."

Lana lowered her eyes. "No, I just... never told anyone that I wasted my wish on that."

He touched her chin, and she looked into his eyes. "It's so important for you that you spent your once-per-lifetime wish. It proves it wasn't a waste. Don't you think so?"

Her heart beat somewhere in her belly, and goosebumps spread all over her skin. Luckily, she wore a coat, so he didn't notice her bodily response. "Maybe. But why would I reveal my biggest secret to you?" she asked. "I don't even know you."

"So get to know me, then."

Lana might have pondered on the question she could ask him, but her mind was clouded by the sensation of his touch. Then he leaned closer and kissed her.

She closed her eyes, tasting his warm lips. Like candle wax, her body melted in his hands that held her waist with care. He was a good kisser, and the flames of his passion captivated her body. For a moment, she lost herself in his arms, but still, her mind-reading instinct was working.

Lana let her consciousness open to him, and she glanced under the curtain of his mind. It was not easy to do because emotions blinded her, smashing the images, but for a second, she saw two men in guardian uniforms in the same room with Charles. They were arguing with Charles, but Lana couldn't distinguish their words. Then, Charles left and slammed the door after him. After this scene, everything became blurred, like she was immersed in a thick, milky fog. Her heart beat calmly, overfilled with joy.

Lana opened her eyes and took a step back. Speechless, she looked at Charles. She knew that her mind-reading Gift might become weaker under strong emotions, but she had never experienced anything like that. *What was it? Attraction? Love? How foolish was it to fall for him?* Lana never thought it was possible. Not for her.

Charles gave her a puzzled look. "Did I do something wrong?"

She inhaled a sharp breath. "No. I liked kissing you. A lot. But –"

"You read me," he guessed.

She nodded. "Sorry."

He moved closer. "Listen, Lana, I'm not really hiding anything, but I'm not allowed to talk about my work. You know, I'm a guardian, and I don't want to compromise anyone. If you saw something classified –"

"No, I didn't see much. Maybe how you left your previous work. That's it."

He was visibly relaxed by her answer. "They just didn't want me to leave. But I had to. I had nothing there to hold on to."

"You slammed the door."

He smiled. "It just got too emotional. I hate long goodbyes."

"I see. Just give me a minute." Lana turned away and walked down to the nearest tree, trying to pull herself together.

The dull-purple pine tree bark shimmered in front of her blurred eyes. More than anything, she wanted to be sure that Charles was a good, reliable man who could also become her ally when the time comes. But she couldn't even read him due to her overly emotional state. And how was she supposed to check on him now, when her heart chose to melt and block her Gift?

Was it worth it to give him a chance for a relationship? During dinner, Charles confessed that he wasn't even sure if he would stay here permanently. He might be gone soon, leaving her behind. The idea of secretly dating him seemed so childish now. It would only ruin her life and all her future plans. She had to sober up.

Charles came closer. "Well, I guess it's too late. I can escort you home."

She shook her head. "There is no need. Don't you know that Triville is one of the safest places in our Kingdom?"

"Crimes can happen anywhere."

She nodded. The case she was secretly working on was proof that criminals remained active, even in quiet Triville. Some of them were just hiding their crimes well. "Anyways, I'm a captain's daughter, so who will dare to mess with me?!"

"Well, as you wish." His eyes became sad.

She sighed. Maybe she didn't know him well and couldn't check on him. But she still could be sincere because he deserved it. "Charles, I really like you, but... we can't be together as a couple."

"Did you decide it after you read me?"

"Maybe."

"Lana, you seem to be a smart woman, but still, I can't understand you."

"Well, here is the thing. My father is your boss."

His eyebrows twitched. "So what? I want to date *you*. Not *him*."

She gave him a sad smile. "I'm touched by your proposal to date. Unfortunately, dating is impossible in this town. I'd hit a 'bridal age' a while ago. So, there is only an engagement option now. You might get used to life in a big city, but here, as soon as everyone knows about us, they will spread dirty rumors. And engagement will make things way too complicated – if something goes wrong, it might affect your work relationship and even your career."

He took her hand. "I'm not afraid of taking this risk. And if something goes wrong, it won't be your worry."

"Still, it might affect our lives badly."

"I see. I think you aren't ready for a serious relationship. But we can still see each other as friends." He gave her a small smile. "And whatever your dream is, I can help you."

"It's not about my dream."

"Really?!"

No. Lana sighed. She hated the thought of being stuck in a senseless marriage and burying her desire to help people. The thought of her sitting in the comfort of a big house, hoping that her five kids would fill the void in her soul, made her heart bleed. She knew that in the future, the kids would grow up and start living their own lives, but what would her life be about? She didn't see any sense in such a pathetic existence – without any chance to do what she was passionate about. No, she wasn't ready to abandon her hopes. Not so easily.

"I'm sorry, Charles," she finally said. "You won't be able to help me with it."

He nodded. "Fine. I won't try to reassure you now. Instead, I'll do my best to earn your trust."

"Okay. But we won't be dating," she reminded him.

He kissed her hand. "Of course."

"I can sense sarcasm."

He gave her a sly look. "Put it as you wish."

10

Rumors

"Are you sure you didn't hear anything unusual that night?" Becca mustered her best pleading look.

The woman on the other side of the threshold frowned. "Yes. It was as calm as always."

Becca sighed. It had been three days since they started questioning people in the neighborhood where the twin sisters lived and where the tragic incident had occurred. So far, they had found nothing.

"And you know what?" The woman continued to glare at her in disdain. "You should stop disturbing people around."

Her words made Becca's heart sink. "What do you mean? I just want to help –"

"Isn't your father a guardian?" she interrupted. "Leave it to him."

"He does nothing to investigate this case."

"A case?!" She frowned. "Girl, please. I know you're trying to do a good thing, but your friends lied to you. The girls just got drunk, and one of them suffered badly. All the narratives they spin just show how shameless they are!"

Becca widened her eyes. "Who told you that?"

Her thin lips stretched into a grin. "It's Triville. Here, rumors fly faster than the wind."

Indeed, she was confident in her knowledge of the 'truth,' even proud. Hopeless, Becca was about to burst into tears. Instead, she took a deep breath and thanked the woman for her help.

The door closed shut, and Becca walked down the stairs, her head spinning. Well, this woman was right about one thing for sure – they lived in a small town, and if rumors started flying around this neighborhood, it meant that their chances of finding a witness were close to zero. No one would even want to talk to them now. She had to find Lana and Mira to discuss it.

Her friends were in a small park at the end of the street. The sky above them was as gray as her mood. Lana stood under the crooked birch tree, her face stern as she thought deeply. Mira, the twin helping with the investigation, sat on the bench, swaying her feet.

Her sister, Mina, had awoken exactly as Lana had predicted. However, she still suffered from the side effects of the Forgetting potion – headaches and intense nightmares. The other doctor, invited by her parents from the capital, explained that Mina's mind had forgotten what happened to her, but her body still retained the memory of that night. Therefore, Mina was assigned to visit a therapist to help her recover from the traumatic event. The sessions lasted around two hours, so Becca and Lana spent this time with the other twin, Mira.

It allowed them to continue working on their part of the plan without divulging too many details about their investigation to Mina. They did it for her own sake, being careful not to worsen Mina's condition by giving her false hope.

Becca approached them. "You won't believe what just happened!"

Mira raised her dull gray eyes at her. "Let me guess. Someone just advised you to fuck off."

Her cheeks flushed at such a blunt and surprisingly accurate remark. "How do you know?"

"We just received the same response," Lana explained.

Mira's eyes were glossy from tears. "This is so messed up! I can't believe someone is spreading these rumors!"

"They're not exactly rumors," Becca reminded her. "If you hadn't put yourself in that situation, it wouldn't have happened.!"

Her comment caused Mira to lose her temper. She jumped from her bench and raised her voice. "So it's all my fault now? You know what?! If it wasn't my sister, then he would have raped someone else!"

Breathless, Becca stared at her, trying to recall why she had started helping her in the first place. Mira was still the same bully as before, and nothing would ever change that.

Mira crossed her arms. "I must find the one who is spreading this rumor. By the way, isn't it you?"

"Me?" Becca touched her chest, her heart pounding. "Why would I say such things to anyone?"

"Because you are just like them!" Mira pointed to the houses that stood along the street in silence. "Judgmental, cold-hearted bit–"

"Enough!" Lana stepped between them, waving her hands. "Don't you see?! This is what he wants – to divide us."

Becca blinked, utterly puzzled. "Who wants it?"

"Burke." The sound of his name made both Becca and Mira fall silent.

Lana looked around them. "Just think about it. Besides the three of us, it's only him who knows the whole truth. I bet he learned that we were trying to find witnesses, so he had to make his victims look untrustworthy. He started talking to other teachers in school, and this rumor spread like a plague. Now, no one will help us find any evidence against him."

"It makes sense," Mira said before turning to Becca. "I'm sorry for being on edge. It's just unbearable to live through this. I feel so helpless."

"It's okay. I'm sorry, too." Becca mustered a small smile. Dealing with this girl was unpleasant, and she couldn't wait for the end of the investigation. It had become too emotional for her. Perhaps it was one of the obstacles that Divine had sent her, and she must handle it with grace. She shifted her eyes to Lana. "What should we do now?"

"What if you just read him?" Mira suggested.

Lana gave her a sad look. "I would, but... my Gift has been acting unusual lately."

Mira knitted her eyebrows. "What does that mean?"

"It's all because of the new guardian," Becca explained. "Since he arrived, nothing has been the same."

Lana knitted her brow. "Don't make me regret telling you about him."

Becca smiled at her. "You know that you can tell me anything. After all, we're best friends, and I'll always support you no matter what."

"Aww..." Mira's eyes sparkled with interest. "I think I saw that man. Is it love?"

"No!" Lana exclaimed, but her reply didn't convince anyone.

Mira gave Becca a sly look. "See? Her cheeks are blushing, and her eyes are gleaming at the mention of him. If she isn't in love, then she is about to fall ill with fever."

Becca smiled at Lana. "I knew it! This is why you have been so pensive these days. You can't forget him."

"Yeah, when you love someone, they are always on your mind," Mira confirmed. "Do you think of him all the time?"

"I think we can't be together," Lana said, crossing her arms protectively. "Let's focus on our problem, okay?"

Becca and Mira exchanged looks and snickered.

"So," Lana continued, "My Gift wouldn't be useful here. Even if I could read Burke, no one would believe me anyway."

"Why not?" Mira asked.

"Because in court, the advocate could easily prove that I have a personal interest in this case. After all, I started helping you right after I learned about what happened. So, I can't be considered a reliable witness."

"You mean... They would assume you lied to protect me?"

"Exactly." Lana nodded. "We need to come up with another plan. Let's brainstorm on it."

Becca rolled her eyes. "Another plan?! Maybe we should just let it go and trust in Divine justice to do the job?"

Mira shook her head. "You read too many fairy tales. In reality, people commit crimes and get away with it all the time. They don't even feel guilty about it. I have no doubt Mr. Burke is already looking for his next victim."

Becca didn't give up. "If he continues to commit crimes, he'll be caught sooner or later."

"And how many other girls must suffer before he is caught?"

Becca gave Lana an inquisitive look. "What do *you* think?"

"I think you're both right," Lana said, touching her lower lip as she thought deeply. She did this every time she was building a plan, and Becca could only hope it was a good one.

"Both?" Mira's face became puzzled. "So what should we do? Give up or keep trying to find a witness?"

"Neither," Lana said with a mysterious smile. "Instead, we'll let Burke target his next victim. But this time, we'll watch him closely, aware of every step he takes. And when he tries to harm the next girl... boom!" She raised her hand suddenly, making the girls flinch. "We'll catch him red-handed!"

"Sounds like a plan," Mira agreed. "But who will agree to become bait?"

Lana shrugged. "Not you, obviously. He's already messed with your family, so I doubt he would take such a risk."

"And you are the captain's daughter," Mira pointed out. "And a mind-reader who can easily expose him."

They looked at Becca, causing her to shrink under their gaze. The way their eyes glittered didn't bode well. She swallowed hard. "You want *me* to be the bait?!"

Lana nodded. "I promise – it will be a piece of cake. You'll be supervised all the time, and we'll catch him before the year ends."

"Are you sure there is nothing else we can do?"

"Well, we have asked all the potential witnesses around and found none," Lana explained, counting their failures on her fingers. "Also, as Mira confirmed, he has no lab in his home, which means the only place he can prepare his potions is the school lab. If we can prove he is making these potions there to commit crimes, he will be imprisoned for years!"

"Come on, Becca," Mira pleaded. "You can help prevent so many disasters!"

Becca raised her eyes to the cloudy sky, seeking a sign. It felt improper for her to involve herself in such a plan by seducing an adult man. There was a risk to her reputation if things went awry. At the same time, it was for a noble cause. *Should I really do it?*

A pure, fluffy snowflake twirled around her head and landed on her forehead, leaving a cold but pleasant sensation on her skin as if she had just been blessed. Becca smiled. "Fine. I'll do it."

Unexpectedly, Mira rushed to her and embraced her tightly.

Lana chuckled. "See? We must never let our doubts divide us. Only together can we bring about change."

"This is true," Mira agreed, clapping her hands. "You know what?! I can help Becca with makeup and clothes."

"What's wrong with my clothes?" Becca asked.

"Well, let's just say they aren't too appealing," Mira replied.

Becca gave her a dirty look.

"She's right," Lana confirmed. "You need to dress provocatively to attract Burke's attention."

"What's your job then?" Becca asked in response.

Lana sighed and looked at the street. The first snowfall of the year started covering the houses like a thin white veil. "I have to pay a visit to the Guardian House."

Mira snickered. "Oh, I see. You decided to get help from that attractive guardian?!"

Lana's cheeks blushed. "No! I mean I'll check the library. There should be information about the potions he is possibly making. We can use it as proof later."

Mira gave her a teasing look. "Got it."

11

A Game

The Guardian House, a stunning three-story building constructed of black stone, stood proudly on the central street of Triville. A metal dragon perched atop the golden roof, now dusted with a thin layer of snow.

Interesting, is Charles there? Lana shook her head. It had been a few days since their last conversation, but she still found pushing him out of her mind challenging. Stubbornly, her thoughts returned to the handsome guardian with bright blue eyes and a charming smile. Lana had to admit – when she thought of visiting this place, she hoped to catch a glimpse of him. *I need to stop it*, she decided as she took a deep breath. She had a mission to focus on, so there was no time for a foolish, impossible romance.

She ascended the stairs and halted at the massive doors. A young guardian dressed in a black uniform gave her a surprised look. He was nineteen years old, just like Lana, and she knew he had started working there last year after graduating from the Academy.

Lana couldn't recall his name, but she knew his Gift was Paralyzing. He had the ability to make people freeze by touching them.

Not that she was afraid he would use his magic on her, but she stopped five steps away from him just in case. "Hey there!"

"Hi, Lana," he replied with a polite smile. "Has anything happened?"

She returned the smile. "Everything is alright. I just need to see my father... I mean, Captain Morris. Is he here?"

He shook his head. "No, he left to check the West End."

"Again?"

"Yeah. You know, it's busy there on the weekends. So, he is instructing the new guardians about that place."

She nodded in understanding. It was almost the end of the week, the days when all regular people usually visited each other to share food and have a pleasant conversation. The people of the West End often did the same, but their gatherings involved heavy drinking and frequently ended in arguments and fights. That's why Lana's father always placed more guardians to patrol those streets on Friday and Saturday nights – in case the conflicts escalated, they could prevent the next homicide. Her father had a challenging job, and now Lana was relieved that her visit wouldn't distract him. It was the perfect time to visit the library.

Lana rubbed her frozen palms. "Gee, it's so cold today. He asked me to come to discuss an important matter. Would you mind if I wait for him inside?"

"Of course," he replied, beaming as he opened the door for her.

This part was easy, she thought, smiling as she walked inside.

Squeaky, old stairs led her to the upper floor. The library was in the corner room with expansive windows on two walls, making it a perfect vantage point for the guardian on duty – from here, most of the town was clearly visible, so it was easier to monitor safety in Triville.

Usually, Lana entered this room after visiting her father, and a couple of times, she even caught moments when someone sent a Light signal, indicating that town dwellers needed help. Today, she didn't think about the signals or any other crimes, except for the one happening at school.

Lana walked inside. Surprisingly, the room was empty. *Perhaps the guardian on duty walked away.* Lana could use this time wisely. She reached the shelves with books on applied magic and found one titled *Forbidden Spells and Potions.* She took it, blew the dust off the cover, and sat on the floor to read. Her index finger slid down the table of contents and stopped at the letter *F.*

She turned to the page and read:

Forgetting Potion

The Forgetting Potion has a sour taste and a rich green color, with ingredients including nettle root and rhubarb leaves. Its usage results in permanent memory loss of all events occurring 24-48 hours prior to intake. The potion may cause severe side effects such as headaches, permanent amnesia, disorientation, full or partial paralysis, and speech loss. The potion is strictly prohibited for public use, sale, or resale.

It can only be taken if the memories acquired pose a real threat to health and safety, and only when the risk after taking the potion is not greater than the risk of retaining the memories. It is strongly recommended to undergo a complete medical check-up by a licensed doctor before administering the potion to the patient.

Lana skimmed through the next couple of paragraphs to find the information she was searching for.

Punishment for using the spell without permission:

If the potion is used with the intent to commit a crime, the punishment is 3-5 years of imprisonment, in addition to the term for the crime itself.

If the potion is used by regular mages without special permission but without the intent to commit a crime, the punishment is 2-6 months of imprisonment, depending on the harm caused.

Lana slammed the book shut and placed her palms on the cover. Chemistry was a tricky science, but Burke could easily concoct the potion in his school lab using his knowledge and skills. This was how he took advantage of his female students. Did he realize the harm it could cause to Mina? To anyone else he assaulted? Lana doubted he ever cared.

These thoughts brought tears to her eyes. *How dare he prioritize his own dirty interests over the health of the girls?* Several years ago, Lana had been a student herself, and Mr. Burke had been her teacher. At that time, her Gift had not yet manifested. And if it had, could she have foreseen such a sinister outcome? Could she have read him to prevent this crime?

She didn't know. Back then, she had been young and oblivious to the dark truths that people hide in their minds. Now, Lana was an adult, and the secrets she had uncovered terrified her. At the same time, they were the driving force behind her dream of becoming a detective. Now, she was determined to do her best to stop the criminals who caused so much pain.

The door squeaked, and heavy steps approached her from behind. Lana froze, clutching the book in her hands, trying to compose herself.

"Do you come here often?" a male voice asked with a chuckle.

Charles. She would recognize his voice among all the men working there. It immediately eased her worries, and she looked up at him. He was smiling, his dimples warming her heart.

His smile faded as he noticed her tears. "Is everything alright?"

She wiped her eyes and stood up. "Yes. I come here sometimes to read."

"I see." He glanced at the book in her hands and furrowed his brow. "I'm not much of a bookworm, but I never thought such reads could be sentimental."

She laughed. *Damn, I missed him so much!* Now, with him standing before her, everything seemed so much simpler. She could talk to him about her problem. Even though they hadn't become a couple, Charles had kept his word and hadn't told anyone about their kiss. If he had spoken to anyone in Triville, the rumors would have already reached her father. And her father would never take it lightly. It meant that Charles was a trustworthy man. Lana could seek his advice without revealing the whole truth.

She returned the book to its place and turned to him. "Sometimes my father and I play a game where he gives me details from a case file, and I have to guess who the criminal is. Today, I came here to check some facts about a potion."

He leaned against the bookcase, seemingly convinced by her small deception. "What an intriguing game. Can I join in?"

"Of course. But on one condition."

"What's that?"

"My father must never find out that you're helping me."

"Deal."

"Okay, then." Lana smiled, grateful to have such an experienced advisor. "Right now, all I know is that the suspect recently used a Forgetting potion to make his victim forget about the assault he had committed."

"How interesting." Charles scratched his chin, deep in thought. "Why do you think it was a potion? Did anyone run a blood test?"

The question took her aback. According to Mira's words, the doctor had run the test on alcohol and never looked deeper. "I'm afraid the victim wasn't checked properly. However, the witness claims that one man gave the victim a drink prior to the accident, so..."

"You think he added something to the drink? "

"Yes. Also, all the side effects match – memory loss, headaches, mood shifts, and so on. I'm sure it was a Forgetting potion."

Charles nodded. "I understand this theory, and it might be correct. However, as a person who specializes in Gifts, I can tell you that Hypnotic magic might have the same side effects. To confirm the suspect, you must consider it, too."

Lana pondered on his theory. Was it possible that someone else had assaulted Mina? Burke was the primary suspect because he was the one who gave the drinks to the girls. What if there was someone else? Charles was right – she had to exclude the other suspects. This crime happened on the same night when she had met Maynard, and Lana had no idea what his Gift was. Even though she had read him, she never checked what his magic was. Fortunately, she could inquire about his information from her father. After all, Maynard was his friend.

"In case you didn't know," Charles continued, "Hypnotic power and all the other Gifts of mental influence must be officially registered. Since the Gift manifests in adolescence, all the high school students have mandatory check-ups. The school doctors must report all the information to the local Guardian House. This is how we have the information on locals with all the possibly harmful Gifts that could be used in committing a crime."

"It makes it easy to verify the names and find the ones who might do it," Lana said, making a mental note to check the *Gift Registration Book*.

"Exactly. Now, back to your potion theory."

"Right. There is another detail I didn't tell you about."

"Which one?"

"After I talked to the witness, I found out that the person she points to is a teacher. So, my theory was that he likely brews a Forgetting Potion in the school lab."

"Why do you suspect he makes it in the school lab? Is there any evidence to support that?"

"Well, he is a chemistry teacher," Lana replied.

Charles narrowed his eyes, studying her face intently. "It's a plausible theory, then. If you catch him mixing ingredients and prove he is making a forbidden potion, he will undoubtedly be arrested."

"You think so?" His encouraging words lifted her spirits.

"Yes," he affirmed. "But I wouldn't bank on that theory."

"Why not?"

"Well, for one, it's too risky and time-consuming. It's difficult to spy on someone working in a closed room without alerting them. Secondly, just because he knows chemistry doesn't necessarily mean he is the one making the potions. The most potent potions of mental influence are typically crafted by a herbalist with the Gift of Persuasion. My guess is he purchased it."

"But selling it is illegal!"

He chuckled, clearly amused by her innocence. "Lana, all crimes are illegal. Yet, people still commit them."

His point made perfect sense, and it gave Lana another theory to consider. "Where could he buy such a potion?"

"That's a good question!" Charles raised his index finger. "To answer that, I need to know where these crimes are occurring."

"What do you mean? In Triville, of course."

He gave her an intrigued look. "So this game is quite real, huh?"

She blinked, momentarily confused about what game he was referring to. Then she remembered her white lie. "Right, the game that I play with my father. Of course, we try to make it realistic so it's easier for me to investigate."

"Sure. Let's see." He walked over to the wall where the map of Lake Kingdom hung.

The capital, Middle Lake city, was in the lower right corner of the map, and the other major city, Santos, located on the seashore, was in the upper right corner. Triville, along with other smaller towns, was a tiny dot somewhere in between. There was a separate map of Triville itself pinned near the larger map.

Charles took a pencil from his chest pocket and pointed to the map area labeled '*West End,*' the impoverished area of their town. "Here. I recently discovered there is a drug store there run by a woman with the Gift of Persuasion. I've received two complaints from people alleging that she is selling illegal potions."

"Interesting... Who would file complaints against her?"

"The church community," he replied with a hint of displeasure. "They are quite strict around here, from what I gather."

"I know, right?! I feel the pressure from them constantly."

Charles locked his eyes with her. "I'm sorry about my dating proposal, by the way. I realize now how foolish it was."

Her heart raced. Lana had turned down his offer to date, fearing it could jeopardize her dream and her father's reputation. She never expected it would bother him as well.

"Let's get back to our case," he swiftly changed the subject, and Lana was grateful for the shift.

"Yes?" she prompted.

"The community alleges that she is selling potions designed to prevent conception."

"To prevent what?" Lana batted her eyes in confusion.

"Having a baby."

She blushed. "Oh."

"Exactly." He smiled at her. "These potions aren't officially restricted in the Kingdom as they cause no permanent damage to health, so the guardians usually turn a blind eye. So, the question is – if she is making potions that aren't approved in this community, could she potentially create ones that erase memories?"

"Even if she doesn't, she may know someone who does," Lana said. Damn, working with a skilled guardian was proving to be highly beneficial for her. She didn't doubt that everything she had learned from him was a promising lead to pursue.

He smiled and tucked his pencil away. "I'm glad I could be of help today."

Their eyes met, and her heart glowed in her chest. Staying close to him, Lana could detect his scent – a faint cologne mixed with the aroma of tree nuts. His lips looked inviting, igniting a desire for another electrifying kiss. It would have been highly inappropriate, yet strangely, it stirred something within her. Lana moved closer, seeking his embrace.

His hands encircled her lower back, his warm breath brushing against her lips.

"Charles?" Her father's voice echoed from the corridor, jolting her back to reality. "Are you here?"

Lana took a step back, her heart pounding. *Almost busted!*

Charles flashed her a mischievous smile as he responded to her father, "On duty! Come on in!"

The door swung open, and her father entered. Upon seeing Lana, his eyes widened in surprise. "Lana? What are you doing here?!"

She opened and closed her mouth, her breath caught in her throat, rendering her unable to speak. She had lied to the man at the entrance, then to Charles to continue her impromptu investigation. Lana was a terrible liar, and she had no idea how to explain herself to her father without embarrassing herself.

Thankfully, Charles stepped in on her behalf. "Lana helped me locate a book I needed for work. She's quite knowledgeable about your library, sir."

Lana shot him a grateful look. "Thank you... for the compliment, I mean."

Her father turned his attention to Charles. "Which book?"

"A book on potions," Charles smoothly transitioned into his explanation. "I received two complaints from the church community recently and wanted to verify if there are any regulations regarding a specific potion."

Her father waved his hand dismissively. "Don't concern yourself with that. They are always too meddlesome."

"Understood." Charles nodded. "How can I assist you, sir?"

"Well, I actually came to invite you for dinner that we are hosting at our house tomorrow," her father announced, his gaze shifting to Lana. "We hold it every last Friday of the month."

Lana looked at him in bewilderment. They always had dinners at the end of the month, with her father usually inviting his best friend, Lieutenant George Turner, and his family. It was an opportunity for her to reunite with Becca, and she was accustomed to it. However, she had never heard her father mention inviting another colleague, especially Charles. *Was he up to something?*

"Thank you so much!" Charles glanced at Lana. "Unless it would be too much trouble for you."

"Not at all," she replied as calmly as she could. "I would be happy to see you."

"I'll come," he promised.

"Then it's settled!" her father exclaimed, rubbing his hands together.

12

The Art of Seduction

Becca sat with her eyes closed, patiently waiting for Mira to apply a layer of powder on her face. The fumes tickled her nose, and Becca sneezed.

"Bless you!" Mira chuckled.

"Thanks." Becca opened her eyes. The large bedroom was filled with plush toys sitting on the beds, chairs, and wall shelves, but she never found a single book in there. Unlike her best friend Lana, these girls preferred to learn about life on the streets. It wasn't the safest way, but she had to admit – they knew how to look attractive.

Now, as she looked in the mirror, she was stunned by her long charcoal eyelashes framing her innocent blue eyes. Her cheeks had an attractive blush, and her lips were shining from the glossy gel that Mira had applied.

"So, how do you like your reflection?" Mira asked, her eyes sparkling with excitement.

"Good job!" Becca admitted. "I just fell in love with myself."

"It's easier than you might think."

Becca touched her lips – they were a bit sticky, but her smile looked charming.

"It's my sister's favorite lip gloss," Mira said, lowering her eyes and suppressing a sob.

Becca gently patted her shoulder. Mina, the twin who was assaulted, was assigned to the therapy, and she had her ups and downs. That's why Mira was often distraught, even though she did her best to mask her uneasiness. "I prayed for your sister's health. I hope she'll find her way to healing."

"Thank you. The therapy works, so we have hope." Mira smiled at her, her eyes glossy. "And you look like candy. A forbidden one that he would like to eat."

Her words sent a shiver down her spine. "I don't want to be eaten."

"Relax, our plan is good, and it's all under control," Mira cheered her up. "Just try to provoke him in some way."

Inwardly, Becca was disgusted by the whole idea, but her purpose propelled her forward, making all the inconveniences seem insignificant. "In what way?"

"Give him a couple of compliments. Men like it."

Becca rolled her eyes. "*I hate it.*"

"By the way, the winter ball is coming up," Mira reminded her, changing the subject.

Becca sighed. The winter ball was a big event that most school-girls looked forward to. It was meant to greet the coldest time of the year with grace. The young women who attended the ball could wear lovely dresses in all shades of blue, Becca's favorite color. But she was too shy to go alone. She had hoped Stan would invite her as a friend, but he still hadn't made any moves.

"Why are you so sad?" Mira asked.

"Nothing."

She pulled her hand. "Come on. Tell me. You know that I can help. Do you need a nice dress?"

Becca shook her head. "No, I have a proper dress. It's more about the dancing partner."

"And why does everyone care about a partner? If you go there alone, you can enjoy the dance with whoever you want."

"So you would dance with me if I go?" Becca asked hopefully.

"Of course I will," Mira assured her. "But what about Stan?"

"What about him?"

"Come on! I know you like this guy. And Mina is no longer talk-ing to him, so... You might use this moment to invite him."

"I don't know... Honestly, I thought men must make such a move."

"Come on, it's Stan. You need to be a bit bolder with him."

Bolder? Becca knitted her brow. "Why do you think so?"

"I just know him too well. He's been our neighbor for years, and both Mina and I used to play with him when we were kids."

"He lives nearby?" It was something new. Since that evening at the circus, Becca had only met Stan twice, and they had small talks after school. He wasn't very open about himself. Oh, she wished she could get to know him better! At least now, she could satisfy her curiosity using Mira.

"He lives next door," Mira continued explaining. "And he might be shy at times."

"And what if I push him away?"

Mira shrugged nonchalantly. "If I were you, I wouldn't worry about him too much. I mean... You can enjoy this freedom to have different male friends as long as you don't hit the 'bridal age.'" She waved her hand dreamily. "After sixteen, things can get awkward. As for me, I aim to get out of this town as soon as my school days are over."

"Why don't you stay here and create a loving family?"

"I doubt it's my thing." Mira sighed for no apparent reason. She glanced at the crystal timepiece on the wall. "Alright, it's almost three in the afternoon, so we need to hurry up."

Becca nodded. Burke held extracurricular activities every Friday. They both signed up for it yesterday after an unsuccessful trial to find the witness. She could only hope their plan would work.

"Potions, prepared properly, can heal," Mr. Burke explained as he walked along the row of desks. Today, the teacher wore a checked shirt and a purple mantle. His long chestnut hair rested on his shoulders. "But if you cook them in the wrong way, it may hurt you."

Becca stood at the end of the room, her cooking station tidy and organized. Her Calming potion, a yellowish liquid smelling of chamomile, was boiling in a glass vessel, almost ready.

"Look what we have here." Mr. Burke loomed over her, so Becca smelled the sour odor of his clothes. "Nicely done."

It took Becca a huge effort not to wrinkle her nose. She raised her eyes to him. "Thank you so much, sir!"

"It's an honest feedback," he smiled, eyeing her inappropriately unbuttoned shirt that revealed her décolletage line. "Everything looks yummy. Don't you mind if I taste this sweet potion of yours?"

Is he referring to my body or to my work? Now Becca was grateful for the solid layer of powder that covered her burning face. "Erm... sure."

She stepped aside and glanced at the opened door, wishing only one thing – to get out of this stiff room as soon as possible. Then she shifted her eyes to Mira. This girl was in the middle of the classroom, watching her every move.

Noticing Becca's hesitation, Mira gave her a strict glance, crushing her idea of running away. Becca not only had to handle the teacher's greedy glances but also flirt with him. *This is my role to play, and I assigned to it voluntarily*, Becca reminded herself. *Now, I must stick to my mission.*

Mr. Burke still stood at her desk, examining her potion vessel. He distinguished the fire and waved his hand, using his Telekinesis Gift to make a couple of drops of the potion separate from the rest of the liquid and form into a ball. The tiny ball flew to his mouth, and he swallowed it.

"Wouldn't it make you sleepy?" Becca asked.

He licked his lips. "Not in this amount. Plus, this isn't a Sleeping potion, just a Calming one. It's weak, so you have to take at least ten drops to fall asleep. And as for me... I might need 20 drops."

"Okay then... So how do you like it?"

"A lot," his tone was satisfying.

Becca batted her eyes. "I had a good teacher."

Mr. Burke smiled like a cat who just killed a jar of sour cream. *Disgusting.* He turned back to the class. "Good job to everyone who managed to prepare a quality potion. Remember – a good sample must be golden and transparent. You can take it with you and try it tonight. And for everyone who didn't get it right... I hope you learned something, too, and good luck next time." He clapped his hands, announcing the end of the lesson. "Let's call it a day!"

Students started packing their books, eager to rush outside to the snowy schoolyard. Becca had no doubt there would be a serious snow battle tonight, with both boys and girls finally able to relax and have some fun after a hard week of studies.

Becca was never fond of such fun, so she packed her things without rushing. First, a heavy chemistry book, then her notebook, and a box of colored pencils.

She took her glass vessel. It had a pretty white sticker on it with her handwritten name on it. *Rebecca.* Burke had prepared all the bottles and stickers in advance prior to giving them to the students. Now, she had to close it properly to carry it home.

Becca looked around in search of a bottle cork. The classroom was empty now, except for Mr. Burke. He sat at the teacher's table, filling his class journal. She could try to slip away without disturbing him. It was enough for her for today. Plus, her ally, Mira, was now away, probably forgetting about their mission and getting carried away with her other friends.

Becca was at the door when it closed shut just in front of her face. Her heart sank. Slowly, she turned to Mr. Burke. He was at his desk, still staring at the journal, with one of his hands raised. *Have he just used his magic to block my way out?* She coughed, attracting his attention.

Mr. Burke raised his eyes, his look apologetic. "Oh, sorry Rebecca. I didn't notice you. I just wanted to close the door as it might get cold in the classroom."

Liar. She nodded, mustering understanding. "It's okay. Just let me go."

He put his pencil down and folded his hands. "You know what? You have a real talent in chemistry. With the right guidance, you can even make a career in it!"

She blushed, buying his appraisal. For a moment, she believed he wasn't a criminal. He could be just a caring teacher who sincerely wished to help her. *Maybe the girls are wrong about him?* After all, when Mira upgraded her image, it was Becca who felt awkward all evening. What if Burke was only triggering her discomfort?

"If you stay longer next week, I can show you more complex recipes," he suggested.

"That would be nice."

He stood up and picked a cork from his desk. Then he came closer and gave it to Becca.

"Thanks." She plugged her potion bottle.

"You're welcome." He smiled and waved his hand, opening the door. "See you next time, then."

"See you," she promised before walking away.

In the corridor, there was another surprise for her. Stan stood by the window, his arms in his pockets. He smiled as his chocolate-brown eyes locked with hers.

"Hey!" Becca said as she neared him.

He embraced her and planted a kiss on her cheek. However, even this sweet gesture didn't eliminate her stress.

"It's so nice to see you again," he said. "And you look so gorgeous today!"

"Thanks." She touched one of her cheeks, grateful for Mira's assistance with her makeup. Somehow, it made her a bit more confident when she was talking to him. "What are you doing here?"

He pointed at the darkening yard where the students were throwing snowballs at everyone walking out of the main doors. "It's madness outside. I just thought I could escort you home safely."

"How considerate of you!" she said, pulling her coat on. "By the way, do you plan to attend the winter ball?"

"Only if you join me."

A smile graced her lips. Indeed, Mira had given her valuable advice – to be a bit bolder. Maybe this girl wasn't as hopeless as Becca had initially thought.

13

A Dinner Party

In the hallway, the night-blooming indoor plants unfurled their buds and illuminated the space. This was what Lana couldn't help but admire about her world – the beauty and wisdom of nature. Everything seemed to have a perfect balance when it wasn't created by humans. Unfortunately, people were often too consumed by their greed and self-interest to focus on making the world a better place.

Lana smiled at a delicate flower and made her way into the bustling dining area. Following their good neighborhood tradition, the women from the invited families arrived early to assist with cooking and setting the table. Since Lana's family had a maid, her responsibilities were limited to minor tasks. She circled the dinner table, draped in a pristine white cloth, and arranged the paper napkins beside each plate.

"One day, you'll make a fine housewife," the woman in the room remarked.

Lana raised her eyes at her. It was Mrs. Turner, Becca's mother. Just like Becca, she had a thick dark-brown braid and serene blue eyes. She stood by the opposite end of the table, holding a tray of empty glasses. Mrs. Turner was a highly involved member of their local church, at times perhaps overly so, which tended to irk Lana.

"Thanks," Lana replied with a grin. "Becoming a housewife is my ultimate dream."

Mrs. Turner let out a scoff. "You're still so young, Lana. You may believe you're more clever than the rest, but I can see right through your sarcasm."

Lana approached and took the tray from her hands. "Thank you for your assistance, but I'll manage the rest on my own."

With a sharp glance in Lana's direction, Mrs. Turner made her way to the kitchen.

As Lana began arranging the glasses beside each plate, the task helped her focus her thoughts on Charles. Despite her best efforts to avoid him, she found herself in his embrace yesterday. It was a moment that nearly led to an embarrassing encounter in front of her father.

Charles had been invited to their dinner, prompting Lana to devise a plan. After some contemplation, she decided that sitting at the far end of the table away from Charles and avoiding conversation with him would ensure a smooth evening.

"The table looks lovely," Becca remarked as she entered the room.

"You're here!" Lana rushed to embrace her friend. "How did everything go?"

"Quite well," Becca replied, glancing around to ensure privacy. "He invited me to the Winter ball! I pushed him a little, though... but it worked just fine."

Lana's eyes widened in disbelief. "Seriously? Since when can a teacher invite his students to events like this?"

"I meant Stan," Becca clarified. "Come on, Lana! Can we set aside this investigation for just one evening? I simply want to enjoy my social life."

Lana's heart swelled with joy at seeing her best friend so happy. Becca had always been somewhat solitary, but now she had genuine friends and was actively engaging socially. "Aww... I'm thrilled for you!"

"And I'm thrilled for you!" Becca continued to smile. "Please, tell me you saw your handsome guardian yesterday."

Lana sank into a chair, her head spinning. "I've never been this confused in my life! I don't know what to do, honestly. On one hand, I want to avoid him and focus on building my life. On the other hand, I can't get him out of my mind!"

"That's why you're dressed like this," Becca observed.

Lana glanced down at her attire. Today, when selecting her outfit, she opted for an elegant scarlet silk dress that complemented her complexion and made her stand out among the guests. "Yes, I dressed up a bit. So what?"

"You dressed for *him*."

"No, I didn't."

"Oh, come on! Can't you see it?" Becca fixed her with a knowing gaze. "Your heart has chosen him, so you need to trust it!"

"I wish I could trust Charles."

"Why can't you?"

Lana shot her a frustrated look. "Because I can't even read him now! My Gift... It has its limitations. I can't discern the thoughts of people I love or once loved."

Becca chuckled. "So what? Yes, you may not be able to know his every doubt or second thought about you. But isn't it wonderful to simply enjoy your time with him? Love hinders your ability to read him because nature is wise enough to impose such a limitation on your Gift. Why can't you trust in that?"

"Because it feels like I'm standing on the edge of a cliff."

"Then take the leap and see what happens," Becca encouraged.

Placing her hand over her heart, Lana hesitated. "But what about our mission? And my dream of becoming a guardian?"

"I believe a good man will support you in pursuing your wildest dreams. However, if you never share them with him, you'll never know if he is capable of supporting you. By the way, this is how most normal couples navigate such matters."

Lana nodded thoughtfully. "Alright, I'll consider it."

"Great," Becca said, glancing over her shoulder. "Because he's here."

She rose from her seat and turned to face the man who had consumed her thoughts. Lana's breath caught in her throat as Charles flashed a smile in her direction. Tonight, he was clad in a white shirt, holding a bouquet of red roses in his hands. He presented the flowers to Lana, who accepted them, speechless.

"I was informed that these are your second favorite flowers," he remarked with a smile.

Lana's head spun. She stood there like a silent, smiling statue, which might have drawn attention to her unease. *Come on, say something, Lana*, she pushed herself, but her tongue refused to obey.

Thankfully, Becca intervened. "Are you the new guardian?"

Charles smiled at her. "Yes, I'm Charles Braun, a Gift Reader."

"Really?" Becca's eyes widened. "Can you determine what Gift I possess?"

"Let's find out." Charles took her hand and closed his eyes, his expression becoming focused. After a few moments of silence, he opened his eyes. "I don't perceive any Gifts within you. Has it recently manifested?"

She shook her head. "Actually, no. It's about to manifest soon."

Lana exchanged a curious glance with Becca. Typically, all mages acquired their special powers during adolescence, and Becca seemed on the brink of discovering hers. The uncertainty of what Gift one would receive often led to surprises when the power first emerged.

"Becca, I'm confident it will happen for you soon," Lana reassured her friend.

"I just thought he could check what it might be like," Becca said, looking at Charles with hope.

"I'm afraid that's not possible," Charles explained. "There's no way to determine it before it manifests. Even Oracles cannot predict it. Every mage experiences this mystery. You'll be fine."

"I hope so."

After Charles departed, Becca gave Lana a mischievous look. "You know, when you gazed at him, you seemed a bit like..."

Lana fidgeted with the bouquet in her hands. "Like what?"

"Like a dummy."

She chuckled. "I wish I could appear more composed."

Becca reached out to touch one of the roses. "You know what? If things don't work out with Charles, I'll be there for you."

Her heart fluttered in her chest. "Oh, Becca, that's so sweet of you. Unfortunately, a romance between us is impossible. But I truly value your support."

"That's what friends are for – to help each other."

Lana smiled. "Indeed. If anything goes awry with the guy you fancy or with your Gift, I'll be there for you as well."

14

An Offer

As everyone took their seats at the tables, Lana's father extended an invitation for Charles to sit beside him on his right, as a new guest. Being the daughter of a captain, Lana was expected to sit next to Charles, which disrupted her initial plan. To divert her attention, she focused on engaging with the other guests.

Lieutenant George Turner, her father's close friend and Becca's father, occupied the seat on his left with his wife. He was a slender man with pale blue eyes and a short black beard. He appeared patient and wise in Lana's eyes, especially in how he managed his wife.

Becca was seated beside her parents, currently serving herself mashed potatoes. The Turners also had a ten-year-old son, Kyle, who was absent from the gathering due to illness.

As the dinner commenced, Lana's father expressed gratitude to all the guests and raised a glass of wine. "This year has been particularly special for me. We welcomed a successful addition to our guardians. As many of you are aware, Charles Braun is a Gift Reader with a remarkable talent for aiding individuals in mastering their powers. I am confident that he will elevate our team to new heights."

In response, Charles raised his glass. "Thank you, Captain Morris. I'll not disappoint you."

Lana observed Charles closely. It was evident that he was trying to win her father's favor, and her father was encouraging it. She understood her father well and knew that everything he did was deliberate. If only she could read his thoughts! Unfortunately, their familial bond imposed a limitation that prevented her from peering into his consciousness.

Her father then turned his attention to Becca, offering her a warm smile. "Have you already decided on your plans after completing school?"

Becca shrugged. "I'm not sure yet. I still have another year to figure it out. I believe that once I discover my Gift, I'll determine how I can contribute to society."

Mrs. Turner smiled warmly at her. "Rebecca, the Gift isn't a solution; it is merely one of the blessings bestowed upon us by Divine. And the greatest blessing for every woman is a child."

Lana couldn't help but roll her eyes. Why did all these religious discussions inevitably lead to the same conclusion? She glanced around the room, noting that all the women present were either wives or daughters, serving as a stark reminder that certain doors to life's other miracles seemed firmly closed to them. It appeared that only men had the freedom to pursue both a family and a fulfilling career.

Mrs. Turner fixed Lana with a sharp gaze. "Lana, I know you have a desire to help others. You could lend a hand at our church. Who knows, perhaps there you will meet a good man who could become your husband."

Lana fidgeted with a fork in her hand. "Thank you, but I'm good for now."

"You'll be turning twenty in the spring," Mrs. Turner persisted. "Who will want to marry you then?"

Lana's breath grew heavier. "As the wisdom of Divine teaches us, everyone has their own path. What if you focus on yours, and I'll tend to mine?"

"This is precisely what I'm trying to convey," Mrs. Turner said, spearing a piece of her pork chop with her fork. "It's my duty to guide you towards the right path. Perhaps you wouldn't be so agitated if you ceased wasting time on reading your nonsense novels and instead adhered to the expectations of a respectable woman."

Lana gritted her teeth. If she wasn't being scrutinized by onlookers, she might have responded with a sharp retort. Feeling her hand tremble, Lana was surprised when Charles reached out and took hold of it, causing her heart to skip a beat. His gesture helped to alleviate some of the tension in the air.

With a charming smile, Charles addressed Mrs. Turner. "Speaking of decency, do you know why there are so many criminals?"

Mrs. Turner's eyes sparkled as she responded. "Because they opt for the path of least resistance. Destruction is far easier than creation."

Charles gazed at her intently. "It's a bit more complex than that. Every criminal is someone who recognizes the flaws in the existing system and chooses to disregard rules that don't serve them. The perceived absurdity of religious doctrines has left many feeling inadequate, powerless, and excluded from society. Consequently, they opt out of participating in it."

Mrs. Turner smirked. "So, are you against religion, Mr. Braun?"

"Not at all," Charles replied. "I have faith in the wisdom of Divine. However, I oppose those who manipulate religious beliefs to instill misery in others. I don't believe that life should be dictated by a rigid set of rules, such as marrying at a certain age or having a specific number of children. Life is far more intricate than that."

Mrs. Turner sat frozen, a fork suspended in her hand, as she absorbed Charles' words.

Lana observed Charles with numb excitement. He was truly an extraordinary man, unafraid to defend her in front of his new acquaintances and their families. She couldn't help but wonder about his motives. Was he speaking out to impress her father? Deep down, Lana hoped that his actions stemmed from lingering romantic feelings towards her.

Lowering her gaze, Lana felt the warmth of Charles's hand still resting on hers. Perhaps he had spoken up for her because he cared for her. Lana closed her eyes, allowing her mind to connect with his. A wave of warmth washed over her, enveloping her body in a bright, white light. She felt herself sinking into this radiant glow, akin to a soft loaf of bread soaking in warm milk. In this connected state, loving Charles didn't seem as daunting; it felt truly remarkable.

Taking a deep breath, Lana opened her eyes to find Charles withdrawing his hand. "Is everything alright?" he asked.

"Yes, thank you for your support," Lana replied with a smile.

Her father cast a curious glance at Lana and Charles. "It's comforting to have someone who shares your life philosophy, isn't it?"

Lana nodded. "It is. What about you, father? What are your beliefs?"

He glanced at the Turners. "I've never been particularly religious. I believe that the best thing parents can do for their children is to allow them to make their own choices, even if it goes against our idea of their happiness." He then turned his gaze to Lana. "I know how much you wanted to assist with the secretary position at a Guardian House, and today I've decided to let you work there three days a week. What do you think?"

She stared at him in disbelief. "Really?"

"Yes," he confirmed. "So, what do you say? Can you start on Wednesday?"

"I would be thrilled to!" Lana exclaimed, pressing her hands to her chest. "This means so much to me. Thank you, father."

"You're welcome."

Becca chimed in with a smile. "Congratulations, Lana."

Lieutenant Turner chuckled. "Who knows, perhaps you'll be the one to bring order to the chaos in our archives."

"For sure," Lana chuckled, overwhelmed with joy. She then turned back to her father. "You never supported this idea before. Why the change of heart?"

He glanced at Charles. "Well... Let's say I received some sound advice from a wise consultant. It will be beneficial for you to gain work experience now. It will aid in your future job prospects once you decide on your studies. And as your father, I can provide you with that opportunity."

The dinner proceeded in a relaxed and pleasant atmosphere. Conversations flowed, laughter filled the air, and everyone enjoyed their meal. As dessert was served, Lana felt completely at ease, savoring her favorite ice cream. She couldn't help but ponder who this mysterious consultant was and how grateful she was for the timely advice that had come her way.

Charles leaned in closer to Lana, lowering his voice to a whisper. "See? I told you I would help you achieve your dreams."

She looked at him curiously. "What do you mean?"

"I spoke to your father and convinced him to allow you to work in the archives," Charles revealed.

"You?!" Lana stared at him in disbelief, her heart racing. "But... how?!"

He smiled mysteriously. "Let's discuss this in private. After dinner, when the men start playing cards, I'll excuse myself and wait for you outside."

"Sure. We have a lovely gazebo in the garden," Lana suggested. "Meet me there."

15

❦

Dandelion

Lana walked to the garden, wrapped in her shawl. The last weekend of November was the time when naked trees started shining pale blue, surrounded by a thin blanket of snow. It created a special atmosphere filled with anticipation of the upcoming winter ball and New Year celebrations.

The trail leading to the garden was covered with a thin veil of snow, with traces left by his boots. Lana stepped on the trail, and her shoes got soaked instantly. No way she would go back and change them to something more comfortable. She couldn't wait a second longer to see Charles. Her heart fluttered in her chest at the thought of meeting him. He was waiting for her, and she wouldn't reject him anymore.

The path to the gazebo was dark, so Lana held her palms out and let the energy of her Light leak from her fingertips. A bright yellow sphere shone in her hand, lighting up the garden trail.

The gazebo was lit up with an orange glow, revealing the silhouette of a man. Charles turned to her as she walked up the stairs. In his palm, he held a glowing orange sphere – his Light. Lana had never seen his Light before, and its bright color reminded her of the sweet taste of oranges that she enjoyed on the hottest days of the fast-passing summer.

As she neared him, Lana greeted him with a smile. "Hey."

He smiled back. "Hi. You have a pretty Light."

"Thanks. I like yours, too."

He moved closer and gently took her Light in his free hand. "When I was a kid, we had so many dandelions in our yard. I loved them so much!"

"Why? It's a weed."

"That's what everyone said. But it's different for me. When I was a kid, I picked them up in spring and gave them to my mother to bring her some joy. They were so bright and yellow, and she loved them." He gave her a sly look. "She also told me that flowers are the key to a woman's heart."

Her heartbeats moved to her stomach. Undoubtedly, he talked about all the flowers he had brought her. *Or not?* Now, Lana was confused about his intentions. She hoped he would start speaking because she couldn't utter a word. She didn't know why he asked her to talk in private, and honestly, she didn't care. She just wanted him to make a move. Then, she could embrace the new chance for a relationship. *Please, say something. Turn me off or ask me to be with you. Just end this uncertainty.*

Goosebumps covered her body, and she wrapped her shawl tighter around her shoulders. Charles placed both their Lights on the bench and took off his coat. He covered her shoulders, and his warm breath on her neck made a wave of heat rush over her body.

"Can I call you Dandelion?" he murmured.

Call me whatever you want. She breathed out. "Why?"

"Because when I look at you, it brings joy into my heart."

Her feet turned soft. Lana stepped back and leaned over the railing to avoid losing her balance. "Fine."

Charles gave her a serious look. "You might want to know why I spoke to your father about giving you this job."

"It would be nice to know that."

"Because when we talked in the library about that investigation, I saw something in you... A sparkle of sincere interest. I guess I know what your secret is."

Lana widened her eyes, unable to believe that he would crack it so easily. But so far, he had never been wrong in his assumptions about her.

He stepped closer and locked his eyes with hers. "You just want to help people."

She nodded. Well, in general, it was a correct guess.

"So, I asked your father if he could send you to help with the archives," he kept whispering, quickening her heartbeat. "He was against it, but I found a way to persuade him."

"You told him about the importance of work experience," she recalled.

"Exactly. I hope you'll use this opportunity wisely."

"I will."

"Good." He stepped back and picked up his Light, intending to walk away.

Will he just leave? Lana stopped breathing. There weren't any reasons why he would want to stay for a bit longer. After all, she was the one who turned him off and the one who foolishly couldn't stop desiring him.

He gave her a worried look. "Gee, you look so pale!"

She wrapped tightly in his coat. "I'm just a bit cold."

"Then you shall go home and take a warm bath."

On her unbending feet, she moved closer and opened the coat, pressing her shaking body to his warm torso. He seemed to have an inner flame, like people with the Gift of Fire. But he was a Gift

Reader, a person who happened to blind all her senses. And she couldn't just let him go.

"I'm so sorry," she whispered.

A surprised expression crossed his face. "For what?"

"For that kiss. I mean, almost a kiss. When my father almost walked on us in the library. I could have put you in a tricky situation."

He chuckled. "Don't apologize for that. I had to contain myself better. It's just…"

"What?"

The sadness in his eyes made her heart sink. "When you're so close, it's too hard for me to think of you as a friend."

"For me, too," she confessed. "I think it was a mistake to push you away."

"Agreed."

She smiled. "So we still have a chance?"

"If you want to."

"Can we date secretly?" she asked. "I know, it's silly, but –"

"You aren't ready for a big commitment, I know," he said, stroking her cheek. "I didn't know how strict your community is until recently, but now I fully understand. I don't want you to obey them. If it makes you comfortable, we can see each other without telling anyone and see where it goes. Until we are ready for the next move."

Her heart trembled. "What if we get caught?"

He chuckled. "Then we must do our best to keep a low profile. What do you think?"

"I guess it will be the most romantic crime ever committed in this town."

They talked until midnight, and when the time crystal on Lana's bracelet turned red, Charles escorted her home. The music still played through the windows, but most guests had left. Before Lana walked out to see Charles, she told everyone that she had a headache and would be resting in her room. Hopefully, no one noticed their absence.

On the porch, she turned to Charles and handed him his coat. The air was chilly, but the fire in her chest was enough to keep her warm as she said goodbye. Before leaving, he kissed her forehead. "See you soon, Dandelion."

16

Forbidden Potion

Becca wrapped herself in her coat, glancing around the crowded street. Even on weekdays, West End was busy. The evening was dark and cold, but the tree barks around shone bright blue, revealing the faces of passing pedestrians. Not wanting to be recognized, Becca pressed against the wall. The last thing she needed was if someone saw her in this criminal area and reported it to her parents.

The woman in the black cloak came closer. Her big hood shadowed her face, but Becca could distinguish her petite frame. "Lana?!"

Lana pressed her index finger to Becca's lips. "Don't say my name here! We must keep a low profile, remember?"

Becca nodded in obedience, and Lana withdrew her hand. *Interesting, where did she learn such a peculiar expression?* Becca wondered. She kept this question to herself. Most likely, it was that guardian that she fell into.

"Are you sure we must go to that potion store together?" Becca asked as they resumed their walk along the street. "I mean... Everyone in this town knows who you are because of your father. What if the seller reports on us?"

"She won't," Lana assured. "I doubt she would be happy to deal with the guardians."

"I wish I had your courage."

Lana gave her a puzzled look, her wide-open brown eyes gleaming in the dark. "Are you kidding? You are the one who agreed to be the bait. It takes guts!"

Becca shrugged. "I don't know... When I talked to Mr. Burke alone, he seemed quite sincere. Why are we so sure it's him who hurt Mina?"

"Don't you see? This is exactly how it works – firstly, he ensures you feel safe around him. He works hard to gain your trust, waiting for the proper moment. And when you are vulnerable, he stabs you right in your heart." Lana raised her hand and clenched her fist. "And you are finished."

Becca's heartbeat quickened. She wished never to become another victim on someone's list. She glanced at the shabby stairs leading to the black basement door. It was decorated with a modest wooden plate, saying *Potions for all needs.* Dark purple curtains on the basement window were closed shut, and only a trembling candlelight inside indicated that visitors were welcomed.

Lana pulled her elbow. "Ready?"

Becca took a deep breath. In and out. "Yes. Let's do it."

The room was lit up by two candles located at two sides of the antique desk. An elderly woman with only five teeth in her wide mouth smiled as they walked in. Her voice was as squeaky as the old stairs they had just used. "How can I help you, young ladies?"

Lana took her hood off. "I'm looking for a special potion."

The woman frowned. "I know you. You are a Captain's daughter."

Becca leaned closer to Lana, lowering her voice to whisper. "I've told you so! She'll kick us out!"

"Just follow my lead." Lana winked at her and came closer to the desk, where the space was well lit-up. "Listen, it was risky enough for me to come here. But I came. Because I really need your help. As for my father... He should never know I was here."

The woman winced, still not convinced. "How did you know about this place?"

"My friend said I can find you here."

"Which friend?"

Becca stepped into the circle of light. "Me."

The woman laughed, sending shivers down Becca's spine. "Just look at you – the daughters of a Guardian Captain and a church priest. What the hell are you doing here?"

Despite her uneasiness, Becca was ready with the proper answer. "Do you think it's easy to be her daughter? With all this..." She waved her hands, expressing deep resentment. "Stupid rules!"

Lana landed her hand on her shoulder, masterfully playing her role and calming her down. "Please, Becca. Not here." She turned to the woman. "As I learned recently, Becca's mother complained about your potions multiple times. And it caught my interest. You see, I have a situation with my inevitable marriage, and my father is quite insistent. Soon, I'll turn twenty, and my fate will be decided against my will. I have no wish of getting stuck with a husband I don't love and a child I don't want. That's why I came here. I need your help."

The woman smiled at her with all five of her teeth. "I think I can help you with that. Alright, have a seat."

They came closer and lowered onto the chairs for visitors. Becca finally could relax and look around. Even though it was a dark room, the bottles on the shelves gleamed in the candlelight. The smells of various different herbs filled the room, reminding her of a summer field abundant with blooming wildflowers. *Maybe our mission isn't so difficult after all? Lana knows what she's doing. Doesn't she?*

Lana placed her palms on her lap. "So, can I get your Prevention potion?"

"Of course." The woman pulled the top shelf of her desk out and quickly found a small bottle. As she put it in front of them, the thick brown liquid inside gleamed like an expensive whiskey that Becca's father kept under locked glass doors.

Lana took it and weighed it in her hand, probably just to make an impression of a picky buyer.

"It's a standard amount, girl," the woman explained with a dry chuckle. "One bottle can last for up to a year. Of course, if you don't plan to satisfy your husband too often. In that case, you might need two bottles."

Becca's heart sank as she imagined the situation Lana could be put into. Having passed a bridal age a while ago, her father had full rights to assign a fiancée for her. It was fortunate that he was a kind and understanding man. She wished her own father would be the same when she turned sixteen.

Lana kept twisting the potion in her hands. "I think one bottle is enough for now. How should I take it?"

"Daily. When your moon cycle starts, you must start taking one drop every evening. It's better to do it before you go to bed, so your body will absorb it while you're asleep. On the days of intercourse, take two drops before you fall asleep."

"Got it." Lana carefully placed the potion back on the desk. "How much?"

"Fifteen bronze coins."

Lana nodded and took her purse out. But instead of bronze, she extracted a silver coin. The woman's eyes gleamed with greed as she saw the money. Lana gave her a teasing look. "If you help me with one more thing, you can keep the change. But it must be a secret."

The woman didn't take her eyes off the coin. "Be sure that all the secrets spoken here stay in this room."

Lana glanced at Becca. "Why don't you ask your question yourself?"

Becca nodded in understanding and shifted her eyes to the woman. "You probably heard of what happened last week with one of my schoolmates."

The woman gave her a compassionate look. "I'm so sorry about that. It must be a tragedy for her parents."

"True. This is why I joined Lana today – to talk to you about Forgetting potions. As an expert, you might have a better idea of how someone could acquire it in our town."

"You think these girls suffered from a Forgetting potion, huh?"

"Just one of them," Lana said. "Another one was most likely put under the Sleeping potion or a strong sedative. As for her sister, I read her, and I saw her memory erased."

"Alright. First of all, I don't sell such potions here." The woman crossed her hands in defense. "But as you were speaking frankly today, I can give you valuable advice."

"I'm listening."

She put her elbows on the desk and brought her palms together. "With my Gift of Persuasion, I've made plenty of different potions in my life. And I know that preparing a Forgetting potion takes a lot of energy. After making it once, I was drained! This is why such a potion is very expensive. On the black market, people charge a golden coin for 30 drops! I hope it explains why I don't sell this kind of potion here... You see, my clients mostly have modest income."

Her explanation made perfect sense to Becca. West End mostly consisted of old one-story buildings with cracked facades, and locals couldn't just throw their last money for such things. As she learned from her own father, criminals here committed crimes in a sloppy way and left enough evidence to be easily caught.

"So your point is that the suspect is someone rich?" Lana clarified.

The woman nodded. "Most likely. Otherwise, he had to save money for a long time just for the sake of buying this potion."

Becca stood up, relieved. "Thank Divine! Then it's not our chemistry teacher!"

Lana gave her a sharp look, and Becca sat back down.

"A chemistry teacher, then?" The woman got intrigued. "That's a different story! He could actually make this crime happen."

"How?" Becca asked in a dull voice.

She shrugged. "Accidentally. He might've intended to give her a bigger dose of Sleeping potion. In this case, he could rape her while she was unconscious."

"She wasn't dreaming!" Lana pointed out. "It was a gap in memory, and all the side effects match the potion intake!"

"Hold on!" The woman raised her index finger. "There are several kinds of Sleeping potions. As you might know, some of them can be used along with a persuasive spell, and that's why their usage is strictly regulated by the law. For example, a doctor can put a patient to sleep for the time of surgery and then wake them up using a trigger action."

"Which is not our case," Lana said.

"Agreed. All other potions are usually just very strong sedatives, and their cooking and usage aren't regulated so carefully. There are many recipes like that, such as Calming potions, Stress-relief potions, and so on... You must take a lot of it to have serious side effects. But here is one thing – if they're mixed with alcohol, it might cause permanent memory loss. As you know, we all respond differently to medications, cosmetics, and even food. Some people simply consume it, but others acquire allergies. The same happens with taking potions – some people are more sensitive to certain mixtures than others. That's why all the doctors recommend starting with a standard dose, then decreasing or increasing the portion depending on bodily reaction. I guess this is what happened. The victim is a young girl, and her mind isn't that resilient."

Lana nodded in understanding. "Thank you for this advice. Now I have a better idea of what happened there."

They were strolling along the central park. The fresh layer of snow shimmered under the calm blue tree light, and rare pedestrians gave them friendly nods.

"So what's your theory, detective?" Becca teased her when there was no one around.

"Burke is guilty," Lana stated. "He is the one who teaches his students to prepare Calming potions. In case you forgot, you just got his product."

Becca didn't object. She really had a bottle of recently made potion at home. She kept it on her nightstand in case of insomnia, and she even used it once when she found herself staring at the ceiling, thinking of her day spent with her new friend Mira instead of falling asleep. Somehow, they started growing more attached to each other.

"It's a perfect criminal scheme," Lana continued, "Burke simply buys the ingredients and writes them off the balance when the class is over. As many of the potions aren't good for using, he says he pours them into the drain! No one would be able to calculate how many potions he had prepared for his dirty needs."

"I don't know... For me, he seemed like a fine man."

"All of them do," Lana said. "Until they take their masks off."

Becca raised her eyes to the starry skies, hoping to come up with a better answer. Then, an interesting thought hit her. "What a strange coincidence. That same day you met that teacher from the architecture university, and this crime was committed by another teacher. Isn't it strange?"

Lana gave her a perplexed look. "You think it was Maynard?!"

She shrugged. "Who knows? Right now, I think that everything is possible."

"I thought of it," Lana said. "I even had a theory that it was a Hypnotic Gift, not a potion."

"Really?" Becca asked, a glimmer of hope in her voice.

"Yes. That theory didn't work, though. After talking to my father, I discovered that Maynard's Gift is Telekinesis. To exclude the other suspects, I also checked the *Gift Registration Book* that I found in the Guardian House library. It's where we keep records on everyone's Gifts in our town. I checked the records on people who have a power of mental influence. As it appeared, we have only two people in Triville with such magic: that potion seller we've just met who has the Gift of persuasion and myself, a mind-reader. As you understand, we both have no motives."

Becca didn't give up. "Alright, then it certainly was a potion. But it doesn't exclude Maynard. He could meet the drunk girls in the street close to their home and give them the poisoned drinks. Then he just repeated his crime and left the town."

"It's a good point," Lana admitted. "He is back in the capital and out of our reach, but I'll ask Charles to keep an eye on him. If he attempts to repeat his crime, we'll arrest and interrogate him. Then, we'll know the truth."

"Can we leave Mr. Burke alone, then?"

"No. Even if the criminal is someone else, we still need to focus on Burke. He isn't as good as he tries to appear, Becca. After all, he gave alcohol to school girls, and Mira fell asleep in his house. Did you forget that?"

Becca didn't give up. "Maybe it's what she remembers. As that potion seller said, some people are less resilient towards substances, and Mira might simply forget how she walked home. Or to the place where they met a real criminal."

Lana stopped in the middle of the road and exhaled a vapor into the frosty air. "Okay, I got your point. Gee, you might have been a good detective."

Becca smiled. It was the second time people said she was really good at something, and it was encouraging. "Thanks. All I want is justice for Mira's family."

"Then we must focus on finding the truth," Lana said. "You are still bait, so just keep visiting him every Friday and try to get closer. Meanwhile, I'll keep working on developing our plan on how to expose him."

Becca nodded. "Fine. By the way, what are you going to do with the potion you've got?"

Lana gave her a sly look. "I'll keep it to myself for now."

Becca paused. She was aware that Lana was seeing that guardian secretly, but sleeping with him was another thing. "Are you... sure?"

"If my memory serves, it was you who advised me to jump from the cliff and see what happens next. This potion is my safety net."

"I hope you know what you're doing."

17

A Pleasant Mess

The cramped basement room was stuffed with piles of papers. Case folders, covered with dust, were scattered all over the place – on the desk, on the floor, and even on the single chair. A narrow basement window under the ceiling barely lit up the space.

Standing at the threshold, Lana bit her lower lip in hesitation. When Lieutenant Turner, her father's best friend, had told her about the chaos in the archives, he wasn't exaggerating. This room, indeed, was in dreadful condition.

The easiest thing would be to close the door shut and never touch it. Lana could refuse her new job politely, and she didn't doubt her father would understand. However, it also meant that she would never have access to the Guardian House anymore, which was her only chance to access its resources. If she had stepped back now, her desire to help Mina would have been abandoned and locked in the depths of her soul, just like the file cases in this room.

"I must breathe new life into this place," Lana said aloud.

She stepped inside, maneuvering between the piles of papers. At the small desk, she placed her palms together and conjured a Light ball. It illuminated the dusty room like a shy sunrise. Lana placed her Light on the tallest paper tower and rolled up her sleeves. It was a lot of work, but now she saw a perspective – the shelves were only partially occupied, and she could start by cleaning them. Then, she would organize the case files in alphabetical order. As for the really old files, she could place them in boxes and store them on the bottom shelves.

As evening approached, all the cleaning work was completed, but the filing process had just begun. Lana was on a ladder, arranging the folders on the top shelves, when the door opened with a quiet squeak. She shifted her eyes to the visitor and was delighted to see Charles standing there.

"Wow!" he whispered, glancing around. "You are really good at cleaning up the mess."

"I hope so," she responded with an exhausted but sincere smile. Interestingly, her father loved to refer to his guardian duty as 'cleaning up the mess.' She doubted Charles knew this, but she was pleased by the compliment.

He came closer and offered her a hand, allowing Lana to climb back to the floor safely. The heat of his palm ignited her senses, making her feet feel too soft. She stumbled over the last step and fell into his embrace.

Charles caught her and wrapped his arms around her. "I missed you, Dandelion."

She smiled and kissed his enticing, hot lips. His tongue explored her mouth, sending waves of excitement through her. As his grip tightened, she surrendered to his movements, ready to lose herself in him.

The kiss abruptly ended as Charles pulled away. His breath was as heavy as hers, and Lana found it surprisingly alluring. Damn, she had initially doubted whether it was a mistake to buy that contraceptive potion. Now she knew it was the right decision – the more time she spent alone with this man, the more their passion intensified. She couldn't wait to start taking the potion with her new moon cycle.

Lana had no doubt that one day she wouldn't be able to resist the temptation. Since they had decided to become a couple, they secretly met after dinner and sometimes walked in quiet places under the cover of the night. Once, on a very cold night, Charles even invited her to his beautiful house. There, they sat by the fireplace, sipping cocoa and sharing stories between kisses. It was a really cozy evening that she wished to repeat.

"So, what are our plans for tonight?" He asked in a slightly hoarse voice.

Lana brought both her palms to her racing heart. "I think I'd better go home and get some rest."

"How boring," he teased her. "If I knew you would give all your energy to work, I would never have convinced your father to assign you to this duty."

"It's just for another couple of days." She glanced at the endless piles that she had stacked close to the wall to free up some space. "It should be done by the end of the week. Then, I'll have a more sustainable workload."

He extended his hand and stroked her cheek, causing her skin to pleasantly tickle under his touch.

With her eyes blurred, Lana tried to focus. "Charles…"

"Hmm…?" He responded in a velvety voice.

"I need to tell you something important."

"What's that?"

Lana hesitated. She still had to solve the mystery of the criminal who erased memories, and she needed Charles' help in devising a plan to catch him. As her attachment to Charles grew stronger, she also started trusting him more. On the other hand, she couldn't confess that secret. After all, it wasn't hers to share with the guardian. So, Lana had to be inventive. "I think I need your help again. With that game."

He withdrew his hand. "Is it about that case that you refer to as 'a game'?"

She stared at him in silence. He had caught her in a lie, and she had no idea what to expect from him next.

Charles met her gaze. "You talk about this crime too frequently, so today I checked the store with illegal potions. Just in case. And you know what? That woman who sells them confessed that she saw you at her chambers. Moreover, you were inquiring about the criminal who might have purchased a Forgetting potion."

What a snitch! Lana shook her head in disappointment. She should never have trusted that woman. "Why did you check on her? I told you it wasn't a real case."

"Yes, you did," he said with a grin. "And I'm sorry to say this, but you're the worst liar I've ever met!"

Lana opened her mouth to retort but couldn't come up with a response. It seemed that lying wasn't her forte, and Charles had just confirmed it.

He waved his hand dismissively. "Whatever. I realized that this case is quite real, so I need to know more details now."

"Why?"

"Because I'm a guardian, and since I've learned about this crime, it's my duty to investigate it. Plus, I have all the necessary skills to catch this suspect."

"Why didn't you just arrest him, then?" She asked, crossing her arms.

"Because you were right. We don't have any concrete proof against him. Only rumors that circulate around this town."

"You heard about it, too?"

"Everyone in this town knows about that incident with the schoolgirl who lost her memories."

Lana gave him a stern look. "What now? Are you going to report me to my father for visiting that store on the west end?"

"Of course not," he said calmly, causing her to soften her temper. "I see you, Dandelion. You started this investigation on your own because you wanted to help that girl. You knew that no one would step up for her, and we don't have any solid evidence against her abuser. Am I right?"

She widened her eyes in surprise. "Hey, I am the mind-reader here."

He laughed. "If you pay attention to small details, there is no need to read a person."

"You're very attentive," she remarked.

He smiled at her compliment. "I just wonder... What were you thinking? Even if you manage to prove that the teacher is poisoning his students, you won't be able to make an arrest. You'll only put yourself in danger."

"I planned to find proof and give it to my father."

"Which proof are you talking about? You have nothing against this man."

"Not yet," Lana corrected him. As he had already seen through her facade, there was no point in pretending any longer. "I have a plan."

His expression turned concerned. "You have what?"

"Becca," she explained. "She joined his extracurricular activities in chemistry, and she's currently working on seducing him."

Charles stared at her for several long moments, speechless. Then he turned and started pacing the room. Lana pressed her back against the shelves, giving him some space as the room was too small for both of them. She needed to give him time to process this information.

Finally, he stopped by her side. "I think we can be useful to each other."

She opened her eyes wide. "What do you mean?"

His voice softened. "I really like you, Lana, but I honestly think you are making a big mistake. I just wanted to suggest another way of helping this girl."

"Which one?"

He gave her a sly look. "I think I have a couple of ideas that might work. But let's not discuss it here."

Lana smiled, anticipating another romantic evening at his house. This time, they would be fully open with each other. She glanced around. "Well, I guess we can call it a day here."

"So we can even have dinner together?"

"Why not?" She moved her index finger along his chest. "I can tell my father that I decided to take a long walk after such hard work. But I need to be home by nine, though."

18

Lost in Lies

"Are you one hundred percent sure about this?" Becca asked. They sat in the living room of Lana's house, but she couldn't enjoy her tea and freshly baked biscuits. Not after she learned about the plan that Lana suggested.

"Yes. The only way to find out the truth is to frame Burke," Lana assured her. "His guilt is very hard to prove now, but we can make the guardians arrest him as a suspect. There, I can read him and make sure that he is a criminal. If he is innocent, then we'll let him go."

"Like there are no other ways of reading him," Becca said, not hiding her disappointment. "You can visit the school anytime to confront him."

Lana exhaled a sigh and put her untouched teacup back on the table. "Becca, it's not that easy. I was able to read the first guy, Maynard, only because he didn't know about my Gift! If Burke is guilty, he can escape the town when I try to touch him. Plus, the Winter Ball will be soon, and then a long study break. We can't just waste all this time!"

"Okay... suppose Mr. Burke must be arrested. How exactly would you frame him?"

"By using his tactics against him."

"Sounds promising," Becca remarked sarcastically. "And for how long must I attend his class and tempt fate?"

"Just a couple more times," Lana said cheerfully. "The day X will be at the Winter ball."

"Winter ball?"

"Yes. It's the most opportune time," Lana explained. "You'll be celebrating at school, and I will have most of the guardian team at our house. As you know, their Chief can't host guests this year for the celebration."

"Yes, I've heard his wife is seriously ill," Becca recalled. "My mom mentioned it. She said the Chief is really down these days, so it's good that your father is assisting him in every way."

"Yeah. And I'm helping him organize the evening." Lana smiled. "I think we make a good team."

"Little does he know you're pulling off your plan behind his back," Becca said, furrowing her brow.

"Right, about that," Lana returned to their discussion. "The point is, everyone will be preoccupied that night, but we can easily carry out our plan."

Becca gave her a disappointed look. "Actually, I was looking forward to enjoying the evening with my school friends."

"You'll have time for that as well," Lana assured her. "But ultimately, everyone must be held accountable for their actions, right?"

Becca let out a heavy sigh. When Lana referenced the church priest's words, it was difficult to argue with her. After all, they were on a mission to uncover the criminal who had harmed Mina.

Becca had to constantly remind herself that the risks they were taking were justified. She must believe that justice would prevail.

"Fine," Becca agreed after a moment of tense silence. "What is our exact plan?"

The sound of footsteps echoed from behind her, prompting Becca to turn her head. Molly, the maid, approached to refill their teacups, her face bright and curious as usual.

"We're fine for now," Lana informed her in a firm tone.

Molly nodded in understanding and retreated.

Lana sighed. "This house has too many prying ears. Let's take a walk instead, and I'll fill you in on all the details."

"You mean, on my way to the chemistry extracurricular class?" Becca clarified. It was Friday, and she now regretted stopping by Lana's during her break between classes. Instead of offering sensible advice, Lana had proposed a reckless plan. *Was it that conniving guardian who had suggested such nonsense?* Becca didn't particularly like Charles, especially after getting to know him better. In her opinion, he seemed too manipulative. However, she kept her reservations to herself. She couldn't upset her best friend, who was infatuated and oblivious to his peculiar behavior.

"Trust me, the plan is solid," Lana said, rising to her feet. "Let's go now. Otherwise, you'll be late."

Becca checked her time crystal, noting its yellowish-green hue indicating it was around two-thirty. Her class would commence in less than half an hour. She stood up. "Fine. But please, promise me that we won't get into trouble."

"Don't worry. I'll take the blame if anything goes awry."

In the school lab, Becca observed the potion quietly simmering in a metal cup. The flame from the burner flickered beneath it, leaving new black marks on its surface. The scents of eucalyptus and linden wafted through the room from the boiling liquid. She deliberately chose this intricate Cough and Flu potion – its preparation took approximately two hours, and the other students had already departed by the time it was halfway done.

"Rebecca?" Mr. Burke's voice called out from behind her.

She turned to face his fatigued expression. The room was dim, with the sun having nearly set. The days were growing shorter, nearing the winter solstice, and people were becoming weary more quickly due to the lack of daylight.

"Yes, sir?" She batted her eyes innocently.

He yawned. "I just realized this potion is taking much longer than expected. If you'd like to leave, feel free to do so. You've done a commendable job, and I'll complete the brewing process tomorrow."

She mustered a look of frustration. "Oh... I apologize for keeping you waiting... I selected this potion because my younger brother, Kyle, fell ill recently, and I wanted to do something thoughtful for him," Becca explained.

She wasn't fabricating this detail. Her brother had caught a cold after the snowball fight in his schoolyard. It had been a week since then, and although his fever had subsided, he continued to cough, causing Becca concern for his health. Once the potion was prepared, it would be beneficial for him.

Mr. Burke narrowed his eyes. "Aren't your parents providing him with medication?"

"They do," she affirmed with a nod. "But, as I mentioned, I wanted to create something with my own hands. I've heard that potions and meals made with love possess a special healing quality."

"You're truly kind." His smile warmed her heart. At that moment, she found it difficult to believe that this man could be a criminal. "I wish all the girls in your class were like you."

"They're all fine," Becca dismissed with a wave of her hand. "I even managed to reach Mira's heart."

"With your kindness?"

She chuckled. "It was indeed an original approach, and it proved effective."

"Perhaps because she isn't the ringleader of their group."

She blinked. "What do you mean?"

He shook his head, appearing uneasy. "Nothing. I think I'm just exhausted, and it slipped out. It's inappropriate for me to discuss such matters. Can you please forget what I said?"

"What if I can't forget?" She gave him a sharp look. "I can't simply erase it from my memory, especially after everything that happened to Mina."

Becca never expected to muster such courage within herself. Perhaps it was Mira's influence – since they had embarked on this investigation, they had grown closer and now conversed daily, even after classes. Becca was eager to uncover the truth about Burke. If he was guilty, he might become enraged and reveal his true nature.

Alternatively, he could feign innocence and later employ his poisoning scheme on you, her inner voice warned in a chilling tone. Becca swallowed nervously. *Have I just provoked him?*

"Alright then." Mr. Burke clapped his hands. "Let's address this matter once and for all."

Becca was rendered speechless as she awaited his explanation. The only sound breaking the silence was the bubbling of the potion.

He pulled a chair closer to her desk and seated himself. "On the night of the incident, I encountered both of those girls near my house."

Becca continued to stare at him. If he was about to confess to his crime, she feared she might become his next victim. Glancing out of the window, which was rapidly darkening, she anticipated Lana's imminent arrival to hide beneath it. They had arranged the next phase of their plan at four-thirty. Becca just needed to stall for time. She could pose questions or attempt to appear understanding.

If things took a turn for the worse, she could potentially disarm him by throwing a boiling potion at his feet. His momentary hesitation could provide her with an opportunity to escape through the open door. If he attempted to impede her exit using his Telekinesis magic, she could try to break the window by hurling something heavy at the glass. Lana would then realize that something was amiss and rush to her aid.

Feeling reassured by this plan, Becca locked eyes with him. "What happened to the twins after you encountered them?"

"They were clearly up to something. I was on my way from the pub, and they began taunting me because I was a bit tipsy. So, I invited them to my house to teach them a lesson."

Becca swallowed nervously. His confession seemed to come too easily. "I'm pretty sure they learned their lesson."

"I doubt it," he replied, his eyes filled with sorrow. "I didn't do much, it seems. After they left my place, they went elsewhere and encountered their troubles."

"Wait... they left?" This contradicted what Mira had previously told her. According to Mira, she had fallen asleep on his couch. *One of them must be lying.*

He nodded solemnly. "Yes. At my home, I offered them some tea and gave them a lecture. They hardly paid attention, though. Afterwards, I escorted them back to their neighborhood to ensure their safety." He hung his head in remorse. "That area is considered safe, so I didn't bother checking if they walked inside their house. If only I had known that they would be attacked!"

"What time did you split?"

"It was around a quarter past midnight. Why do you ask?"

"It's nothing," she muttered. "I just want to offer my support. I don't believe this is your fault, so please don't blame yourself."

He looked at her with gratitude. "Thank you, Becca."

"You're welcome," she responded with a small smile before redirecting her attention to her brewing station. Becca's mind was consumed with thoughts, her focus drifting from her potion-making task.

Considering the information she had just received, Mr. Burke was an adept liar or he was telling the truth. If the latter was the case, it didn't add up. Who else could have administered a concoction of Forgetting potion and provided the alcohol to the girls? Why did Mira have no recollection after having a drink at Burke's house? Additionally, the time he mentioned was after most people had returned from the circus show, indicating that the town streets were deserted, devoid of witnesses. As she could recall, the circus show had concluded twenty minutes before midnight, and Stan had escorted her home afterward.

Regardless of Mr. Burke's motives for deceiving her, it suggested that he wasn't planning to harm her imminently. However, she needed to remain cautious and fulfill her role in the mission to apprehend him.

"You know, it's getting quite late," Becca remarked, gesturing towards the darkened window. "If you'd like, you can head home. I'll lock up and leave the key at the reception desk."

Mr. Burke glanced at a burner. "For safety reasons, I need to ensure all the flames are extinguished before I depart."

"Don't you trust me?"

"I do, but..." He trailed off, rubbing the back of his neck. "Actually, you've done it numerous times, and I'm confident you won't accidentally set the lab ablaze."

She chuckled. "Everything will be fine. Don't worry."

"Are you sure?"

"Absolutely."

As Mr. Burke finally departed, Becca made her way to the window frame and pushed it open. The chilly winter breeze rushed into the classroom, causing her skin to prickle with goosebumps. The window on the second floor offered a view of the snow-covered backyard. The moon cast a bright glow, revealing Lana's figure as she lurked beneath one of the trees. In early December, the trees sparkled with a magnificent light-blue hue, illuminating Lana's silhouette.

"Lana!" Becca called out softly.

"She speaks..." Lana responded with a chuckle, moving closer to the window and theatrically extending her hand towards Becca. "Oh, speak again, bright angel!"

Becca shot her a tired look. "Seriously?! I'm risking my life here, and she's quoting the balcony scene from a romantic tragedy!"

Lana placed her hand over her heart, still in a cheerful mood. "A rose by any other name would smell as sweet. Oh, Becca, please reveal the stolen key!"

Becca rolled her eyes. Lana had a knack for injecting humor into even the most tense situations. While it was usually a source of relaxation, at that moment, it only heightened her anxiety. She eagerly awaited the conclusion of their mission. Raising her hand, Becca revealed a small key glinting in the cold moonlight.

"Wait!" Lana cautioned. "Wrap it in cloth. Otherwise, it might get lost in the snow."

Becca complied, using her shawl to tightly encase the key before tossing it into the snowy yard. Lana retrieved it swiftly.

Leaning against the windowsill, Becca rested her chin on her hand. "I wonder how you're going to return it to me."

Lana unwrapped the key and tucked it into her coat pocket. "Easily. While I create a duplicate, you'll need to find a long knit, preferably woolen. It's thick enough to hold the key weight. You'll toss me one end of it, and I'll secure your original key to it. You can then pull it up and act as if nothing out of the ordinary has occurred."

"With your inventiveness, you could be a skilled criminal," Becca teased her.

"Or the one who catches them," Lana replied with a wink before darting off.

19

Winter Ball

The stalks of the night plants wrapped around the tall pillars of the hall room. The flowers glowed with blue and white lights, creating an enchanting atmosphere. It was exactly what Lana aimed for – an illusion of a fairytale. Yes, reality was full of tragedies, but at least this ball could be an escape for people who grew weary of the ugliness of real life.

Lana stood at the top of the stairs, watching the guests entering the hall room. They passed their coats to the doorman, revealing their gorgeous outfits. According to tradition, all the ladies wore long ball dresses in various shades of blue, with their necks and ears adorned with sparkling topazes, aquamarines, and sapphires. The gentlemen were clad in white costumes, adding brightness to the room.

This ball was held every year on December 21st to celebrate the beginning of true winter. As Lana saw it, people simply needed this entertainment to brighten up the darkest and coldest months of the year. She lifted the hem of her long turquoise dress and descended the stairs. Molly, her servant, stood nearby, now dressed in a lovely dark-blue dress that fell to her knees, with a white apron tied around her waist. She carried a tray of snacks – tarts filled with salmon marinated in garlic-lemon sauce.

"Great job with the food service, Molly," Lana complimented her. "Check the west side of the hall; it looks like people are getting hungry there."

"Of course," Molly replied with a meek smile.

"Perfect. And one more thing before you go." Lana glanced around discreetly, ensuring no one was listening in. "Close to seven in the evening, I need to slip away."

Her face became intrigued. "Another rendezvous with Charles?"

Lana nodded. "I'll be gone for about an hour, then return. If my father inquires..."

"I'll say I saw you at the opposite end of the hall." Molly smiled knowingly. "Don't worry. There are too many guests today for anyone to notice your absence."

"Thank you!"

After briefing Molly, Lana mingled with the crowd, ensuring that all the guests were content. This was what she enjoyed about organizing parties – she could use her creativity to make the world a bit brighter. Unlike her clandestine mission, she no longer felt ashamed of striving to improve the lives of the people in Triville.

She only needed to oversee the beginning of the evening. Once the guests were served, they relaxed and enjoyed the night with their friends and colleagues. Lana planned to seize this opportunity to slip away from the ballroom and complete her mission with Charles. Speaking of whom, where was he?

"Dandelion," his velvety voice called out from behind.

Lana turned to face him. Today, Charles was dressed in a white parade uniform adorned with a golden dragon on his shoulder.

His dazzling smile perfectly complemented his attire. She stood in awe, unable to believe that this handsome man was her beloved.

He stepped closer and kissed her hand. "I can't wait to dance with you."

As his lips brushed against the back of her palm, her heart fluttered. "Do we really have time for this?"

"Let's make time," he insisted, his hand still clasping hers, causing her head to spin. "I believe we both deserve it."

Lana hesitated. Their public display of affection would lead to assumptions about their relationship, especially from her father.

Seizing the moment, Charles guided Lana to the center of the ballroom. The music began to play, and more couples joined them on the dance floor. The melodious strains of violins filled the hall. While guests sipped champagne and engaged in lively conversations, Lana scanned the room for her father. She breathed a sigh of relief when she didn't spot him. He could arrive at any moment, though.

"Charles, everyone's watching us," she whispered.

He chuckled. "So what? You worked hard to organize this event in your home. Why not relax and enjoy a dance?"

"They might assume we are together."

"Well, one day Captain Morris will discover our relationship," Charles stated matter-of-factly. "I believe he's already beginning to suspect something, so it might be best to inform him sooner rather than later."

"Not today."

He looked disappointed. "Why not? It's been nearly three weeks since we started dating, and I see no reason to continue keeping it a secret. I feel like a schoolboy sneaking around. We can't even go out for dinner like a normal couple!"

Lana had a ready excuse. "Today is not the right time. What if something goes awry with our mission? He could deduce that you assisted me and terminate your employment."

"Fair point," Charles conceded. "What about tomorrow?"

Lana locked eyes with him. "In this community, we can't simply announce that we are 'dating.' I can't bear the thought of people mocking my father, insinuating that his only daughter is a slut."

He winced at her frank words. "I never intended to make such an impression. We could consider a formal engagement. It's a significant step, but –"

Lana gently placed her index finger on his lips, halting his proposal. The idea of marriage felt overwhelming at that moment. "Let's revisit this topic later when I'm not so preoccupied with our clandestine activities."

Charles grinned. "Are you referring to our mission or our forbidden romance?"

Lana chuckled, grateful for his presence and discretion. "Okay, if you insist... I promise to think about it and provide you with an answer tomorrow."

"Great," Charles replied, content with her response. "Now, let's review your role in our plan."

Lana refocused on their mission to apprehend Burke. "I will head to the school shortly and place the Calming potion in the teacher's drawer. I already have it in my purse."

"Good. Take your time. Your energy traces will dissipate within 24 hours, and I intentionally won't verify it tonight when I get there. Therefore, no one will be able to trace your movements."

"And tomorrow morning, I'll delve into Burke's memories and find the truth."

As the music faded, Charles leaned in close to her ear. "Good luck, Dandelion."

"Thank you," Lana replied, glancing at the dark-blue glow of the time crystal on her bracelet. It was already seven in the evening. She needed to act swiftly to avoid jeopardizing their entire plan.

As they returned to the guests, Lana found her father standing by a pillar.

He smiled at her. "You've orchestrated a splendid celebration, Lana."

She returned his smile, attempting to appear casual. "Thank you. I hope everyone is enjoying the evening."

He nodded, observing them both. "I can't recall the last time I saw you dance like that."

Her cheeks flushed with heat. Apparently, her father had just witnessed her and Charles dancing, and now he was teasing them. "Well, I suppose my dancing lessons have finally paid off."

"I'm glad to hear that," her father remarked, shifting his gaze to Charles. "Could you spare a moment for a private conversation?"

"May I?" Charles sought confirmation from Lana with a questioning look.

It was only then that Lana realized they were still holding hands, and she quickly released his palm. "Go ahead," she said nervously. "I should check on the guests, anyway."

Charles smiled. "I'll catch up with you later."

Lana waved a hand over her blushing cheeks and hurried towards the exit doors.

20

The Mission

In a dimly lit school corridor, Lana moved stealthily along the wall. The distant strains of music echoed from the hall room at the far end, evoking a sense of nostalgia for her own school days. Lana's chest warmed with pleasant memories of her youth. Back then, she was filled with hope and believed all her dreams would materialize once she reached adulthood. After getting the ability to read minds, she had been exposed to the true ugliness of human nature. It was a harsh experience. However, understanding how cruel people could be, she developed a new ultimate goal – to change the order of things.

Her father had instilled in her the belief that she could always choose not to succumb to the darkness. Lana strived to be a better person despite the challenges she faced. While she may be bending the rules at present, it was all in service of a greater cause – the apprehension of Burke. It was now her responsibility to orchestrate his next 'attempted crime' to bring about his arrest. There was no other way to resolve this complex case.

The staircase leading to the second floor was far from the hall room. Lana pushed open the double doors to the stairwell and paused. A small paper cup of fruit punch sat on the windowsill, emitting the sweet aroma of berries. She smiled, grateful that Becca had done her part and left it for her.

Lana picked up the cup and began her ascent to the second floor, heading towards the lab. With the key she had recently obtained with Becca's assistance, Lana unlocked the door and pushed it open. A smile played on her lips as she entered the dimly lit room, still amazed at how smoothly everything was progressing. However, luck could be fickle, so she needed to act swiftly, especially after the unexpected delay. She was already twenty minutes behind schedule, and Becca could arrive at the lab at any moment.

Moving along the desks equipped with small cooking stations, burners, and glass vessels of various sizes, Lana reached the teacher's desk. She set down the paper cup of punch on the corner. Her hands trembled as she opened her small clutch, revealing two bottles inside – both containing potions.

The first bottle held her contraceptive potion, which she had started taking about two weeks ago, realizing that her relationship with Charles might progress further than she had anticipated. The second bottle bore a yellow paper sticker with the label *'Rebecca'* written in Burke's handwriting. This was the crucial potion she needed for their plan. Lana had to add precisely ten drops to the drink, as Becca had instructed her earlier.

Pulling a chair closer, Lana placed her clutch on it to keep it out of the way. Carefully tilting the bottle over the cup, she began counting the drops. *One, two... ten... twelve to be sure.*

Lana's palm was sweaty as she finished adding the drops. She sealed the potion vessel and placed it on the edge of the desk, taking a moment to catch her breath. However, as she removed her hand, the yellow sticker stuck to her palm.

"Damn it!" Lana muttered. The stubbornly sticky paper refused to come off easily, but she couldn't waste time trying to remove it. With her time crystal now glowing a dark-purple hue, she knew she had to act quickly.

In a rush, Lana stepped back, frantically searching the dark room for tweezers or any suitable tool. Unfortunately, luck seemed to have abandoned her at that precise moment. As she hurriedly moved, she stumbled over the chair, causing it to crash to the floor with a loud noise.

The sound reverberated through the room, and Lana was certain it had alerted everyone in the building. Her temples throbbed with anxiety, realizing she needed to make a swift exit. She had to get out of there as quickly as possible.

Lana retreated to the teacher's desk, attempting to locate where her clutch had fallen. In her haste, she accidentally nudged the potion bottle with her elbow, causing it to bounce and then roll to the floor, coming to a stop against the wall.

Her eyes widened in fear as she touched her flushed cheeks, shocked by the chaos she had just created. A sense of foreboding crept over her. Undoubtedly, this mishap was a punishment for her actions. However, her rational mind reminded her that she couldn't afford to dwell on despair – she needed to think quickly to avoid getting caught.

"Think, Lana, think," she muttered to herself, trying to calm her racing heart. Taking three deep breaths, she blinked rapidly, attempting to regain her focus on resolving the situation. The silver lining was that the potion bottle remained intact, and the paper cup with the punch was still undisturbed. This gave her a glimmer of hope as she strategized her next move.

She brought her palms together and conjured a sphere of yellow Light, placing it on the floor to illuminate the space better. It was a risky move, as the Light could potentially be seen from outside, but Lana was more concerned about the risk of being caught in the act.

Feeling a tingling sensation on her cheek, Lana realized that the paper sticker was no longer on her palms – it must have transferred to her face. She delicately touched the tip of the sticker and carefully peeled it off, ensuring it remained undamaged. Placing the sticker on the rim of the cup, Lana then crawled to retrieve the potion bottle.

On the floor, she found two bottles, causing a surge of panic to rise within her. Taking a deep breath to steady herself, Lana picked up her clutch and inspected its contents. Unfortunately, all she found was the lab key she had recently used, indicating that her own Preventive potion had also rolled away. Gathering both bottles, she brought them closer, attempting to discern which one was which.

The two bottles appeared almost identical, both containing brownish-yellow potions that had been minimally used. Lana's mind went into calculation mode. She recalled taking around fifteen drops from her bottle while using only twelve drops from Becca's. Therefore, Becca's bottle should be slightly fuller than her own.

Confident in her deduction, Lana concealed her own bottle back in her clutch and stood up. She retrieved the sticker and affixed it to the correct potion bottle. Opening a drawer in the teacher's desk, she found papers and some test blanks. She placed the potion on top of them.

Lana rubbed her hands together and smiled. *The mission is complete.* The trap for Burke was now set, and all that remained was to exit the school safely. She picked up her clutch and stepped on the sphere of Light, causing it to burst into shining sparkles and vanish. With the door left unlocked, Lana made her way back to the corridor, ready to leave the scene behind her.

In the stairwell, Lana nearly collided with two students. Becca, dressed in her elegant ball gown, stood by the window. A young man in a snow-white costume faced her. When Becca noticed Lana, she gave her a puzzled look, drawing her partner's attention. The man began to turn his head, on the verge of spotting Lana.

Cursing under her breath, Lana quickly leaned back and concealed herself on the other side of the wall. Panic surged through her as she surveyed her surroundings. The corridor was long, illuminated by moonlight streaming in through the tall windows. They were too close, and there was nowhere for her to hide. *I won't slip by unnoticed.*

Pressing her back against the cold wall, Lana counted her heartbeats, disbelief washing over her. The fear of being caught gripped her as she braced herself for the inevitable.

21

Catch Me if You Can

"What was that?" Stan turned back to Becca in confusion. They were at the stairwell, talking, and Becca was about to accomplish the most responsible part of their mission. Now, she had just figured out that Lana hadn't even left the school building. Instead, she had almost bumped into Stan!

It was fortunate that she had hidden behind the wall before he noticed her. *Did Lana actually do her job of arranging the lab?* Becca breathed heavily, thinking. She had left a paper cup with a punch at the stairwell of the lower floor, exactly as planned. When Becca checked it again just ten minutes ago, it was gone, which meant that Lana had picked it up and was most likely on her way back.

"Becks?" Stan's worried face demanded an answer.

"Sorry, I've just lost my train of thought..." Becca gave him an apologetic look. Inside, she cursed their mission once more. It was risky enough to use Stan in catching Burke, and if he found out that Lana was here, he would tell everything to the guardians. Then, their mission would fail, ruining Becca's reputation as an exemplary student that she had worked so hard to maintain. *How foolish!*

"You were saying that Mr. Burke asked you to come check the lab with him," Stan reminded her.

"Right." Becca nodded, focusing on the role she had to play. "You see, sometimes I stay longer to help him clean the lab, and I just remembered that I might have forgotten to lock the door when we had the last lesson."

He gave her a look full of understanding. "You want me to check it with you?"

She lowered her eyes. "Yes... I mean... Stan, can I tell you something?"

He moved closer and took her hand. "Of course. You can tell me everything. What's bothering you?"

"Burke..." She kept her voice low, trying to appear ashamed of the topic, which was partially true. "When I told him I forgot to lock the door, he acted so weird."

"What do you mean?" He narrowed his eyes, becoming over-protective. "Was he rude to you?"

She let out a heavy sigh. "Not exactly. I spoke to him recently. Didn't you notice his reaction?"

He nodded, recalling the conversation. "Yes, I saw his concern when you two talked in the ballroom. What exactly happened?"

She glanced down the stairs before continuing. Burke was about to show up, so she had to hurry to convince Stan. To do this, she had to lie to him. "He asked me to come here alone and wait for him! Isn't that strange?"

"It is."

Becca rubbed her bare shoulders. "A couple of weeks ago, when I stayed late to brew a complicated potion, he confessed that he met Mina on the night when she was..." Becca paused, unsure how to continue.

"When Mina was assaulted?" He helped her finish the sentence.

Becca nodded, her eyes filled with genuine anxiety. "I'm so afraid he might do something to me!"

"He won't," he reassured her, coming closer to hug her. "I'll be with you the whole time."

She looked up at him. "Can you just lurk in a dark corner of the room? Or behind a curtain? I'm not sure if he's really dangerous, and I don't want him to think badly of me... I just want you to be nearby."

"Of course," he assured her.

Becca smiled. Now, she had Stan involved as they had planned. There was only one unresolved issue – Lana. Becca was confident they could pass her unnoticed if Lana stayed on the left side of the entrance. People usually never look back once they enter a room. She had used such a trick multiple times herself when playing hide-and-seek with her younger brother.

"Let's go, then," Stan urged her.

Becca nodded and took his hand.

Together, they walked into the corridor. As the door to the lab was on the right, Stan turned right without looking around and not noticing Lana, exactly as Becca had expected. As Becca walked by his side, she glanced back to throw Lana a dirty look. Lana smiled apologetically, still pressed against the wall. Becca shifted her eyes to the stairwell entrance, silently urging Lana to escape. Then she turned back to Stan.

"What?" Stan gave her a worried look. Then he narrowed his eyes in suspicion and slightly turned his chin to the place where Becca had just looked.

Before his eyes found Lana, Becca raised her hand and placed it on his cheek, preventing him from turning his head. *Was it too pushy?*

Her heart raced as his attentive eyes studied hers, silently waiting for an explanation. *If I only had an excuse for such a weird gesture!* Nevertheless, Becca had to say something before Stan realized that something was wrong.

"You look so handsome tonight," she said in a trembling voice. She stood with her mouth partially open, trying to think of how to fix the awkwardness of this situation.

Apparently, her words weren't as nonsensical to him. Stan smiled at her words and leaned in to kiss Becca. He hugged her gently, and she closed her eyes, savoring the moment.

She had never kissed anyone before, and this unusual sensation sent tingles across her skin. As his hands gripped her waist, she relaxed, thinking of the moment she would tell Mira about it. *Would she be jealous?*

The sound of heavy steps on the stairs brought them back to reality.

"It's Burke!" Stan whispered, releasing his grip. "Hurry!"

They sprinted to the lab. Becca's shoes clicked on the wooden floor, making it difficult to move silently. At the chemistry lab, Stan pulled the door, and it easily opened.

Becca quickly hid Stan behind the curtain, her hands shaking with overwhelming anxiety. As soon as she finished arranging the curtain, the door behind her opened soundlessly. Becca knew that Mr. Burke had entered because of the bright lilac Light that filled the room.

She turned to greet her teacher with a forced smile. "Mr. Burke! How are you?"

His face, illuminated by the Light sphere in his hand, looked concerned. "I heard you running in the corridor. Has something happened?"

She swallowed nervously. It was fortunate that he didn't inquire about her presence there. And he didn't seem to notice Stan. Mr. Burke had come to the lab for a different reason that Stan was unaware of – because Becca had informed him that she had seen a student adding jimsonweed to the drinks. She had also mentioned that she might have forgotten to lock the doors, so she asked Burke to check if anyone could steal the herb from the lab. He had agreed, but he never asked her to accompany him.

After their conversation, Becca left the ballroom with Stan. It was Mira's task to distract Mr. Burke by asking him questions about her 'outrageously low chemistry marks.' Mira's role was to hold him for ten minutes, giving Becca time to convince Stan to accompany her to the lab and hide him before drinking her poisoned punch.

"Rebecca?" Mr. Burke called out again.

She stared at him, realizing that one wrong move could cause everything to crumble like a house of cards. "Nothing happened," she finally replied. "I was just concerned for you."

"Why?"

She waved her hand dismissively. "Well, two heads are better than one in solving problems. And quicker."

"Yeah," he agreed, scanning the room. "You were right – someone was here recently."

"You think so?"

Mr. Burke pointed to the side of his desk, where a chair had been moved. "See? Was it like that when you left the room?"

She shook her head.

He frowned. "Interesting. Let's look for evidence."

He walked to his desk, and Becca followed him, her heart sinking. Seizing the moment when Mr. Burke was placing the chair back in its original position, Becca shifted her gaze to the paper cup resting on the corner of his desk. The original plan was to drink from this cup when Burke was in the corridor, causing her to fall asleep and allowing Stan to call for help to apprehend him without needing to speak.

However, with the change in timing, Becca had to improvise. She discreetly moved the cup behind her back so that Mr. Burke wouldn't see it. If he noticed, he might try to prevent her from drinking it, fearing it was poisoned. Which it was.

"What's that?" His voice startled Becca. Mr. Burke sat on the floor with a puzzled expression, holding something sparkling in his hand.

Becca leaned closer, observing a hairpin with a small turquoise flower on it. *Unbelievable!* Considering that Lana wore a dress of the same color, the hairpin definitely belonged to her. Becca made a mental note to advise Lana never to break the law again. She was just too clumsy for it!

Mr. Burke eyed her with suspicion. "Do you know who it belongs to?"

"Maybe. Just give me a minute to remember who wore this accessory," Becca replied, touching her forehead and pretending to be deep in thought.

Mr. Burke nodded and walked to check the shelves in the storage room.

Seizing the opportunity, Becca turned back to the teacher's desk. Her punch beckoned to her, promising to transport her from the awkward crime scene to a dreamland where everything was easy and not her concern. Without hesitation, she raised the cup and finished it in two gulps.

Just in time, as Mr. Burke returned to the room, visibly relieved. "All the dangerous ingredients are secured," he announced.

"Great." Becca managed a weak smile. Her feet felt like jelly, and her head was spinning. *How many drops did Lana add?* She took two steps forward before losing her balance. Mr. Burke caught her, preventing her from hitting her head on the hard floor. She was grateful for his quick reflexes and smiled, looking at his blurred face.

He held her empty cup in his free hand. "What have you done?"

"I'm so sorry," she whispered. Then, her heavy eyelids closed, and the Calming potion dulled all her senses.

22

In The Dark

Lana moved along the dark corridor of the first floor, her heart beating heavily with each step. She wrapped herself in her long black coat, hoping the shadows would conceal her from any unexpected encounters. After everything had gone wrong, the last thing she needed was to face another potential witness. She had been fortunate enough to evade Stan and Mr. Burke on the second floor without being noticed.

As she reached the end of the corridor, a girl suddenly appeared from around the corner and collided with her. The girl fell to the floor, landing on her bum. The hem of her blue dress sparkled as she illuminated the area with her shining pinkish Light, looking around in confusion.

It was Mira. Lana breathed a sigh of relief and stepped out of the shadows.

Mira eyed her disapprovingly. "Weren't you supposed to leave already?"

"It took a bit longer than I planned," Lana explained in a whisper. She extended her hand to Mira, and the girl took it.

A touch. It was the perfect opportunity for Lana to read her without wasting time on absurdly long real-time dialogues. She just wanted to ensure that everything had gone smoothly with Mira's part of the plan to delay Burke and if she needed any help.

As Mira rose to her feet, Lana closed her eyes and quickly scanned her memory in search of the most emotional event of the last hour. To her surprise, her consciousness shifted to the moment when Mira stood at the pillar, watching Becca dancing with Stan. A bitter taste of unrequited love filled her soul from within. She wished for only one thing – to be the person who could freely dance, hug, and kiss... Becca. *Wait. Is Mira in love with Becca?!*

"Lana?" Mira called. "Are you alright?"

Lana nodded, blinking rapidly to dispel her shock. "Ah... Yeah, I'm fine. Just a bit worried. Are you okay with continuing the mission?"

"I'll be alright," Mira said with a shrug. "As usual."

"Perfect." Lana breathed out and walked away before Mira could realize that she had just been read.

Her horse galloped back to the empty street where her house stood. There, Lana could finally slow down her pace. The fresh air and fast ride helped her refresh and shake off the shock from her recent discovery about Mira's feelings. Once again, she had learned someone's deepest secret, but this one was surprisingly beautiful.

It seemed that Becca was more popular than Lana had imagined. She hadn't had enough time to delve into Mira's memories further, and now she was curious about how long her forbidden love had been brewing. Perhaps it had started from the moment

Becca agreed to help Mira seek justice for her sister, or maybe it had begun long before that. What if all the bullying had been a way to gain Becca's attention? Regardless, Lana was pleased that she had played a role in bringing them together.

Lost in her thoughts, Lana arrived at the crossroad where Charles was already waiting for her. He stood under the glowing blue pine, his face decorated with charming dimples.

"Sorry for the delay," Lana said, passing him the reins. "It's all done."

Charles patted his horse's mane before turning to her. "Great job!"

Lana glanced back. They were at the top of the hill, so she could clearly see the school building. Mira was supposed to burst into the room and start panicking when she saw Becca unconscious. Given her feelings for Becca, it wouldn't be difficult for her to act convincingly. Then Mira would send a Light signal to the guardians using her Light. This signal would indicate to Charles that he could start riding there. This plan would give them a few minutes alone before he departed.

Lana moved closer and hugged him. "Please, tell me everything will be alright."

"Everything will go smoothly, Dandelion," he assured, caressing her cheek. "The main thing is that you accomplished your part. Now, I just need to get there and apprehend the suspect."

"I don't doubt that you can finish this operation. But what about *us*?" Lana had to ask him about the 'private talk' with her father. Until now, she had pushed her worries aside, focusing on her part of the mission. Now that it was over, a new wave of anxiety washed over her. "You talked to my father after he saw us dancing. What was it about?"

"Oh, that..." Charles hesitated. "Let's not discuss it now."

"Charles?!" She clutched onto his coat, feeling the ground slipping away from under her feet. "What does he know?"

A gleam of pink Light illuminated his somber face. Then, a distant bang followed. Lana turned her head. In the dark sky above the school, Mira's Light was melting into hissing sparkles.

"I gotta go," Charles said as he moved away from her embrace and mounted his horse.

She waved her hand, silently wishing him good luck.

It took Lana another half an hour of walking along the streets before she mustered the courage to return home. She was too afraid to face her own father and discuss the situation with Charles. She could already envision him grumbling about Charles being too young and unsuitable for her. If her father forbade her from seeing him, she would rather leave home than give up on her love.

Would Charles be willing to welcome her into his home under such circumstances? And if he did, wouldn't it jeopardize his career? Lana shook her head in exhaustion. It was clear she wouldn't find all the answers in her head. She needed to talk to Charles.

Perhaps she would spend the night on the street, but it was too cold for that. Eventually, the chill seeped under her winter coat, and her hands began to shake uncontrollably. Lana had to return home.

Inside, the ball was in full swing – guests danced in the ballroom, their laughter mingling with the sounds of piano and violins. The clinking of glasses and loud chatter filled the air, creating a lively atmosphere. Hoping to blend in with the crowd, Lana navigated her way through the guests, careful to avoid crossing paths with her father.

She spotted him near the stairs, engaged in conversation with his friend, Lieutenant Turner. As Lana emerged from the crowd, her father's gaze immediately locked onto her. His furrowed eyebrows and piercing eyes seemed to see right through her.

Lana shivered. She couldn't tell if she was trembling from the cold or fear – perhaps both. Anyhow, she was grateful for her long ball dress that concealed her shaking knees. Trying to look content, Lana offered him a weak smile. "Father."

"Where have you been?" He inquired, approaching her. He briefly touched her hand before pulling away. "Are you made of ice?! What happened? And why were you outside for so long?"

She glanced at Lieutenant Turner, silently hoping that he would intervene and assist her in answering at least one of her father's questions. With that, Lana could make her way to her room to warm up and compose herself.

However, Lieutenant Turner appeared preoccupied. A young guardian approached him and began whispering something in his ear. As the conversation concluded, Turner's expression stretched, his blue eyes widening in shock. "She did what?" he exclaimed, causing Lana's father to startle and redirect his attention to the commotion. Turner shook his head, attempting to clarify the situation. "Sorry. It's about Becca. She ingested a potion and collapsed in the classroom, so I must leave immediately."

Lana's father grew concerned. "I'll accompany you."

"There's no need," Lieutenant Turner said. "You better check on that Charles guy. He apprehended a teacher who was with Becca. They are currently at the Guardian House."

Lana's father cast her an anxious glance. "Please warm up and attend to the guests. I'll be back late tonight."

She nodded silently, acknowledging this brief respite. It meant she had the entire night before the sky began to fall.

23

Burning in the Flames

The wood cracked in the fireplace, enveloped by merciless flames. With her eyes wide open, Lana admired the lovemaking scene of two elements of nature. The flame kissed the wood with passion, soaking in its heat and savoring every pulsation. Their fiery dance would last for hours until they both reached their culmination and turned to ashes.

Fidgeting on a fluffy carpet, Lana drew closer to the heat. Under her soft shawl, she still wore her ball dress. After the ball ended and the last guests departed, she couldn't bring herself to retire to her bed. Unable to wait at home for her father's return, she asked Molly to cover for her and sought refuge at Charles's house.

Charles was not yet home, likely preoccupied with their mission. Lana used the key hidden under the flower pot at the entrance to let herself in. As she looked around, the flickering firelight illuminated the curtains and white walls adorned with beautiful landscape pictures, creating a serene ambiance.

Among all the rooms in his house, this one was Lana's favorite – cozy and filled with warm memories from the days they started dating and getting to know each other. Lana sighed, uncertain if this would be her last night with Charles. Regardless, she was determined to make the most of it on her own terms.

As the entrance door quietly opened, Charles walked in, his face registering surprise at seeing Lana. "What are you doing here?" he asked, unable to hide his smile.

Lana stood up. "Waiting for you. Isn't it obvious?"

Charles chuckled. "I see. You couldn't bear to stay at home and wait for the news."

She gave him a sad look. "Is it bad?"

"Of course not," he reassured. "Everything went smoothly. I found a potion in Burke's desk and placed him under arrest for the night."

"My father..." Lana's voice trailed off. "We never anticipated his interference so soon."

Charles shrugged. "It was fine. I was at the Guardian House, and he arrived shortly after me. I shared my suspicions with him, and he handed the potion over to the experts for analysis."

"Then he's not angry with you?" Lana asked, her hope wavering.

"Of course not. We must separate personal feelings from our professional duties. It's crucial for our work as guardians. If we let personal conflicts interfere, we won't be able to catch any criminals."

She took his hand. "Okay, if you keep me in suspense any longer, I might..."

"What will you do?" His expression teased her.

"I'll die," she blurted out. "From a heart attack. Can you tell me already? Does he know about us?"

"Well, he suspects that something's going on because of how close we are."

"And...?"

"And that's all. I simply told him that I like you. A lot."

A smile blossomed on her lips. "Do you?"

"No, I'm just messing with you to win your father's favor," Charles replied wearily.

Lana playfully punched his shoulder. "I knew it!"

"Hey!" Charles stepped back, feigning injury and holding his shoulder as if seriously hurt. "Easy! I'm just an honest man making a confession! Please, don't beat me up."

Lana's eyes locked with his. "Don't you ever dare mess with me!"

"Fine," he raised both hands in surrender. "But seriously, we both need to talk to him tomorrow."

"And what if he says 'no'?"

"Then, Dandelion, we'll continue secretly dating until we're old and gray," Charles replied with a grin.

She snickered. "Sounds like a plan."

"Not a bad one, huh?" Charles pulled her closer and kissed her.

Lana melted into his kiss, slowly relaxing and pondering what the future might hold – growing old together with this man. Her imagination painted a picture of her elderly self, sitting by a crackling fireplace with a gray-haired man reminiscent of Charles. They held hands, surrounded by file cases they had solved together. The image filled her heart with warmth.

As their kiss deepened and intensified, the warmth of their love spread through Lana's belly. When Charles attempted to pull away, she caught his hand. "Don't go."

Gazing at Lana, Charles breathed heavily, his eyes shimmering in the firelight with the intensity of a lover. Lana removed her shawl and let it fall to the floor. Stepping closer, she placed her hands on his muscular shoulders. "I want you," she whispered, feeling his inner heat despite the barrier of their clothes.

Charles kissed her with newfound passion, his hands slowly trailing along her spine, deftly unlacing her tight corsage. Her dress slid to the floor with a quiet rustle, reminiscent of dried leaves shedding from branches, unveiling her nakedness like a tree stripped bare. Clad only in her underwear, she stood before him, biting her lip in anticipation.

He slowly unbuttoned his white jacket, his gaze fixed on her form. As he tossed the jacket onto a chair, Lana assisted him in removing his shirt, her hands trembling. She touched his chest, feeling his heart pounding in rhythm with her own.

Gently laying her on the carpet, he trailed his tongue over her breasts, eliciting a pleasurable arch of her back. Moving his kisses lower, he reached the heat at the base of her belly, where her desire burned the brightest. His warmth melted her, rendering her pliant in his hands. As her blood boiled, she moved in unison with his skilled mouth, the intense inner flame obliterating all other thoughts.

Breathless, motionless, and struggling to comprehend what had transpired, Lana slowly opened her eyes. The fire still blazed, indicating only a few minutes had elapsed. Nearby, Charles lay watching her as she regained her senses.

"We can stop here," he spoke softly. "Before it goes too far."

Lana gave him a dazed look, her hand sliding to his groin. Though he remained clothed in his pants, the bulge was evident, yearning for release. "I don't want to stop. I want all of you."

Charles stood up. "I'll be back in a moment."

Lana propped herself up on her elbow, pondering what could be more pressing for him than their intimacy. She refrained from asking, not wanting to disrupt the moment's beauty. Considering he had just returned from work, she assumed he might need to visit the washroom. "I'll be waiting," Lana promised before he departed.

The warmth of the fireplace enveloped Lana's body as she reclined, listening to the gentle crackling of the flames. She had never felt so relaxed. Despite hearing numerous tales of the embarrassment associated with intimacy, she found herself surprisingly content. Perhaps those who found it shameful lacked the special connection Lana shared with Charles.

Not keeping her waiting for long, Charles soon reappeared at the entrance doors, now fully undressed. Lana's mouth half-opened in awe, relishing the pleasant tingles that danced across her skin at the sight of his naked form. He joined her on the carpet, allowing her to acclimate to their closeness.

Their lips met once more, and she ran her foot along his leg, silently inviting him inside. Charles positioned her on her back and moved atop her. Their hips aligned, and she groaned beneath his hot, powerful body. Immersed in his passion, Lana was prepared to burn alongside him in the night, free of regrets and thoughts of the impending morning.

24

Simple Truth

When Becca was pulled back from her dreamland, she found herself lying on a soft mattress. The daylight tickled her eyelashes, and she opened them. Someone's soft hand was holding hers, making her feel safe. She smiled and turned to her visitor, only to be surprised to see Mira sitting on a chair beside her, holding her hand and watching her with attentive gray eyes.

"Morning," Becca greeted with a smile.

Mira hesitated before letting go of her hand. "Hey! Welcome back, sleeping beauty."

Becca chuckled and tried to sit up, but her body still felt weak.

Mira helped by placing more cushions behind her back. "Is it comfy now?"

"Yes, thanks," Becca replied, looking around. She was in her own bedroom. It was a good sign – apparently, she had been brought here right after the accident so she could properly recover after taking the potion.

Mira fidgeted on her chair. "You probably wonder what the heck I'm doing here."

"Sort of," Becca admitted.

"That morning, when I woke up after being poisoned, it was so scary," she said, her voice laced with sadness. "I was on the brink of a panic attack because I was completely disoriented. I had no idea what happened and how I got there!"

"So you were worrying about me?" Becca smiled, amazed by her attentiveness. "I knew you had a heart!"

Mira gave her an offended look. "Of course I do."

"Okay." Becca laughed. "I'll keep it in mind."

Then Mira explained what had happened after Becca fell asleep – from the moment she sent a Light signal to Burke's arrest. Interestingly, when Mira wasn't with her sister or preoccupied with her doubts, she seemed completely different – kind and funny. The one Becca had started to really like.

They were discussing the enchanting dresses they had seen at the school ball when Lana walked into the room. They fell silent, preparing themselves to face the truth, whatever it may be.

As there were no extra chairs in Becca's bedroom, Lana took a seat in the corner of the bed. Her brown eyes sparkled with a light that Becca had never noticed before. "I have two pieces of news for you," Lana began. "One is good, and one is bad. Which do you want to hear first?"

"Let's start with the bad one," Mira suggested.

"Agreed," Becca said, turning her gaze to Lana. "Go ahead."

"Burke is innocent," Lana said, lowering her eyes. "I checked on him this morning. He simply gave the girls some tea at his home and lectured them. Then, he followed them to their neighborhood to make sure they were safe."

A smile began to blossom on Becca's face. Deep down, she had always hoped that Mr. Burke was a good man, and knowing that he had told the truth brought her immense relief. Now, they could proceed with the 'after-plan B' to complete this operation.

According to this plan, Becca would have to say that she saw a punch on the desk and foolishly drank it as she was thirsty. It would be portrayed as an innocent school prank, with someone placing the poisoned cup in the opened lab. With too many students in the hall room, it would be impossible to pinpoint the culprit, as anyone could have used homemade sedatives. As for Mr. Burke, everyone would believe it was a simple misunderstanding, and life in Triville would return to normal.

"Does it mean we imprisoned him for nothing?!" Mira's voice snapped Becca out of her daze.

Lana nodded. "I'm so sorry. If only I believed he was a good man, I would never have dragged all of you into this tricky and dangerous adventure. I should have tried to see him in a different light."

"The thing is, you didn't believe it until you knew for sure," Becca reminded her. "You were worried about Mina, and this mission was the only way to uncover the truth. We all did our best. Now, we'll proceed with the prank version, and hopefully, by spring, everyone will have forgotten about it."

"Agreed," Mira added. "But if that's the bad news, what's the good news then?"

Lana gave them a sad look. "We now know who the poisoner is."

"Who?" the girls asked simultaneously.

"Maynard. The guy I'd read just before all this tragedy happened," Lana explained, shaking her head as she stared into the space in front of her. "He probably got angry and did what he did."

"It doesn't make any sense. I fell asleep –" Mira started.

"You did," Lana agreed. "Or at least that's what you remember. You might have encountered this man near your house and unknowingly consumed a poisoned drink."

Mira crossed her arms, visibly unconvinced. "I wouldn't accept anything from a stranger."

Lana sighed. "I don't know exactly what happened that night, Mira. And we may never find out. The only thing I can confirm is that Maynard was eventually arrested in Middle Lake."

"How do you know?" Becca inquired.

"Charles told me," Lana explained. "I informed him about that crime, and Charles used his connections to have Maynard placed on a list of suspects. Maynard was apprehended last week. Thank goodness he didn't commit another crime before the authorities intervened. He is currently being interrogated, but he has not implicated Mina as his victim. It's possible that he will never confess to it."

Mira lowered her gaze, her chest rising and falling heavily as she breathed.

Becca reached for her hand and gave it a gentle squeeze. "I understand that it's difficult to accept the uncertainty. But that criminal caused a lot of harm, and he will face the consequences for his actions."

"True," Lana agreed. "Based on Maynard's confession, he'll be sentenced to at least a decade on Death Island. There, he will lose his magic. So, justice has been served. He won't escape the consequences any longer."

Mira wiped her tears with the back of her hand. "Thank you, girls, for being by my side throughout all of this and for everything we've experienced together."

"Always." Lana smiled. "You know what? Even though this mission is complete, we can still uphold our tradition. What if the three of us meet every Friday for a cup of tea?"

"So you'll share details of your forbidden romance?" Becca asked with a laugh.

"Without discussing men," Lana clarified. "Just some girl time for us. To talk about what matters to us and support each other."

"I would love that," Mira agreed.

Becca gave her a close look – something had changed in Mira since they started talking more. She seemed more relaxed, and her face was now animated. After everything they had been through, it felt comforting to have her by her side. Becca smiled at her. "I would love it, too."

25

A Drop in the Ocean

"Can you explain this?" Her father's voice echoed in Lana's ears as she stood at his desk, staring at her hair clip – a small turquoise flower that had once adorned her head during the winter ball. It had matched her dress so perfectly! If only she had known that the darn clip would fall off while she was at school, staging a crime scene, she would never have worn it.

"I don't have all day for you to come up with another lie." Her father's demanding gaze caused Lana to take a step back.

"I really don't know what to say," she mumbled.

"How about you tell the truth?"

Lana looked around, searching for a quick escape. Her father's home office was not very large, just a simple room with a massive maple desk and a row of shelves covering one wall. On the dark wooden floor, there was a small space for a plush carpet and a comfortable chair for her father's visitors. The door was only ten steps away from Lana, allowing her to keep stepping aside until she reached it.

She took a step towards the door, but her father thwarted her plan by raising his hand and pointing to the chair. "Sit!" he commanded.

Reluctantly, Lana obeyed. She remained silent, unsure of what to say next to maintain her dignity.

"Fine. If you don't speak, then I will," her father declared, clasping his hands together. "Last night, you were with Charles, weren't you?"

Her heart sank. He was a perceptive guardian indeed. Lana had done her best to keep her romance with Charles a secret, especially their last night together. The memory of their time together caused her cheeks to burn. If it was to be their only night, she vowed to cherish it in her heart forever.

"Your silence confirms my suspicions," he concluded.

"Please, don't dismiss him. It was my idea, and he behaved like a true gentleman all the time."

He frowned. "All the time?! How long have you been secretly walking out with him?"

Walking out? Lana took a sharp breath. *Is that all he knows about us?* "For a while," she replied quietly, careful not to reveal too much.

"What nonsense! And you used Molly to cover up your... What exactly is it? A close friendship or something more?"

Lana shrugged. "I just like him. A lot." It wasn't the most convincing response, but she recalled Charles saying the same thing about her the night before.

Her father narrowed his eyes. "So you liked him enough to follow him to the school as soon as you both saw a Light signal?"

What does he mean? She nodded, silently agreeing with his assessment. Whatever conclusions he drew, she was sure they would be more palatable than the truth.

"What were you thinking? You could have been hurt!"

"Nothing bad happened."

"Perhaps not this time, but Lana, you can't just show up at a crime scene and tamper with the evidence! Your energy traces could compromise everything in that lab!"

Lana blinked, finally understanding her father's perspective. It seemed that the previous night, he had arrived at the staged crime scene and discovered her presence. Perhaps he had used a special Revealing spell to detect energy traces. Every mage left an invisible trace wherever they went, which typically dissipated after 24 hours. Lana's father was knowledgeable about such matters. However, he had not realized she was there *before* Burke and Becca arrived, not *after*.

"Okay, you caught me." Lana raised both hands in surrender. "I was just concerned for Becca, that's all. There was a school ball happening, and we went to check on her. Then I came back home."

Her father appeared upset but somewhat relieved. "Is there anything else you want to tell me?"

She bit her lip. Her father would soon discover her morning visit to the Guardian House. It was better to come clean about it before the truth shattered his heart. "Okay. Last night, I couldn't calm down and sleep. I was so worried about Becca!"

He continued to gaze at her, waiting patiently for her to reveal the whole truth.

Taking a deep breath, Lana confessed, "Then morning came, and I went to the Guardian House to read Burke."

Her father's breath grew heavier at this admission.

Moving closer, Lana placed her hands on the desk. "This time, I had to do it. One of the girls had been raped before, and knowing that it was this man..." She paused, fighting back tears. "This man who had taught me when I was her age... I could never forgive myself if I stood by and did nothing!"

He shook his head but didn't argue. "And what did you discover by reading him?"

"He is innocent," Lana stated firmly.

"If that's the case, then why did he have a potion labeled for Rebecca?"

Lana had a ready explanation for this. "He probably kept it from their extracurricular lesson. As I later found out, on their first lesson, Becca made this Calming potion, and she simply forgot it in his lab."

He frowned. "I have no idea what you're talking about, but there wasn't a Calming potion."

"What do you mean?"

He softened his voice, explaining, "I received the results of the analysis. This is the same potion used to prevent... unwanted pregnancies."

Lana's head spun as she recalled the events of the previous night. When she had accidentally dropped both bottles of potions in the lab, she must have placed the wrong one in the drawer. It perfectly explained why she had slept so soundly and why it had been so difficult for her to wake up that morning. Charles had to give her two cups of coffee before she could focus on her mind-reading task.

If this was indeed what had happened, it meant two things, and Lana wasn't sure which one scared her more. Firstly, she might end up with an unexpected child in the next year, and she wasn't even certain if she wanted to spend the rest of her life with Charles. Secondly, due to her carelessness, an innocent man could now be wrongly imprisoned. *Good job, Lana,* her inner voice mocked sarcastically.

Lana stood up. "Excuse me, father. I need to do something. It's urgent."

"What exactly?"

"If only I knew," she replied before walking away.

The lights of the evening town blurred in front of Lana's eyes as she paced the library of the Guardian House. Her hands waved frantically, her voice trembling as she explained the predicament she had put them in.

Charles sat calmly on a sofa, listening attentively without interruption. "So, you drank the wrong potion?" he asked as Lana finished her speech.

She nodded, tears streaming down her face as she wiped them away with both palms. "I don't know how it happened. I'm so scared right now!"

"Oh, Dandelion... I didn't even know you were taking a Prevention potion."

She gasped. "Of course I am! Do you think it's easy being a woman here? Constantly worrying about your impending bridal age expiration date? About being forced into a marriage with a man you don't even like?"

"Hey, I thought you liked me," he joked.

She didn't crack a smile. "I do like you. But I'm just not ready for such a commitment, okay? Yes, I'm almost twenty, but the mere thought of that burden suffocates me! Maybe one day I'll be ready, but not now."

He stood up and tried to hug her, but Lana pulled away and walked to the window.

She pressed her burning forehead against the cold glass. "What am I going to do now?"

He stood nearby. "Firstly, stop freaking out. Please."

"Oh, sure. And where was this brilliant idea of yours before?" she retorted in a gloomy tone.

He chuckled. "Look, Dandelion, nothing will happen. I've taken care of it."

"How?"

He gave her a sincere smile. "I took a Prevention potion as well."

She stared at him, speechless.

He continued, "Last night, I took it before the real action began. Men can also take it, but we need to do so 20 minutes before we finish."

This was where he left off the previous night, Lana realized. "Why didn't you tell me?"

"You didn't tell me either," he pointed out. "Honestly, I hadn't planned it, but after visiting that underground store, I bought a potion for myself. We were getting closer, and I wanted to avoid any complications. I couldn't rely on you because you aren't as knowledgeable in these matters."

"So, you're not ready for commitment either?" Lana asked.

"I think we can take our time and enjoy being together. If that's what you want."

"Of course, I want that," she replied calmly. "Gee, it's such a relief to have clarity."

He smiled. "It is. I know the topic of contraception isn't the most comfortable to discuss, but I believe we should talk about everything we plan together. Maybe we need to trust each other more."

She hugged him tightly. "From now on, let's be honest with each other."

He gently stroked her hair. "Agreed."

"Now, we only have one problem left. Burke."

"Not really. He was recently released from temporary custody with an apology."

She looked up at him in surprise. "For real?"

"Yes. We couldn't hold him for more than 24 hours as there was no direct evidence of his crime apart from that Prevention potion."

Lana glanced at her turquoise time crystal. "But it's only six o'clock. Why was he released so early?"

"Because of Mira. This girl came to the Guardian House in the afternoon and took all the blame for the school prank. Of course, she didn't know that she confessed to having the illegal Prevention potion. But when she realized what had happened, she explained that she had bought it after what had happened to her sister. Also, she voiced her suspicions about Burke. In her written explanation letter, she stated that 'it was wrong to frame an innocent man, even though the guardians didn't do anything to find the real culprit.'"

"That's a strong stance," Lana remarked.

He nodded. "I'm relieved this girl dared to admit our mistakes and take responsibility. Not many people would take such a risk."

"Will she get into trouble now?"

"Not really," Charles reassured her. "Mira was a victim of neglect, and we can't hold her accountable for this desperate act. However, her situation served as a wake-up call for the guardian team, who failed to act for her sister. I hope they'll be more diligent in their duties now."

"We've all learned a valuable lesson from this," Lana said, relaxing in his embrace. "I hope things will return to normal now."

He gave her a mischievous look. "And the next time you mix up potions, we might end up with a cute baby."

She playfully poked his shoulder. "Oh, shut up!"

He laughed, filling her heart with joy.

26

A Lucky Charm

The spring arrived in Triville, bringing warmer weather and longer days. Becca stood in the churchyard, relishing the gentle kisses of the sun on her face. It was Friday, and the spring charity fair event was in full swing – by five in the evening, most of the boxes had been emptied by eager buyers looking for second-hand treasures.

This annual event held a special place in Becca's heart, and she always made sure to participate. As winter came to an end, she would sift through her wardrobe, parting with clothes that no longer fit but were still in good condition. The idea that someone else would find joy in wearing these clothes brought her immense satisfaction. Additionally, the church raised funds by selling these items, which were then used to support the local shelter for the less fortunate.

This year, Becca had also decided to part ways with her collection of plush toys that no longer held her interest. She was on the brink of becoming a senior student, so these toys would be better appreciated by younger girls who could truly enjoy playing with them.

"Can I have this toy?" a thin voice asked.

Becca looked down at the girl with beautiful golden hair and dark blue eyes. Though she didn't see her often, Becca recognized her immediately. Elisa Palmer. At eleven years old, Elisa was the same age as Becca's younger brother, Kyle. Becca had observed Elisa during her visits to their house, watching the children play in the backyard.

"Which toy do you want, sweetie?" Becca asked, leaning over to open a box filled with her old plush toys, including dolls, ponies, and soft teddy bears.

Elisa gave her a suspicious look. "When people call me 'sweetie,' they usually want something from me."

Becca chuckled. "What could I possibly want from you?"

"Isn't it obvious? You want to sell me something at a higher price."

"Well, all the money we make goes to charity anyway," Becca explained.

Elisa crossed her arms. "Oh, please. I know where most of that money really ends up."

"What do you mean?"

"I mean that only a small portion of the donations actually goes to charity. The rest is pocketed by the church leaders," Elisa stated, her dark blue eyes filled with annoyance. "Don't you know that?"

Becca shook her head in disbelief. Clearly, someone had filled Elisa's mind with these unfounded accusations.

"My father told me that," Elisa revealed.

"I see," Becca replied, trying to mask her growing unease. Elisa's father, Joseph Palmer, was known as one of the most troublesome men in the West End of Triville. Becca knew this because her father often spoke of Palmer's questionable actions. These included bar fights, inappropriate behavior towards women when intoxicated, and multiple instances of domestic violence. The latter was frequently reported by concerned neighbors who were troubled by the disturbances coming from the Palmer household. Surprisingly, Mrs. Palmer never lodged any complaints against her husband.

"What?" Elisa furrowed her brow. "Do you think my father is a liar?"

"No one said that..."

"You're giving me that judgmental look."

Becca shook her head. "It's not about you."

"Then it's about my father," Elisa deduced. "Isn't it?"

Becca sighed. "Listen, I know how much you love your family. But sometimes, the people we love the most can hurt us."

Elisa lowered her eyes. "I know. And I can't do anything about it."

Becca knelt to be at eye level with her. "I understand your feelings, so you can always count on me. If things escalate and you feel scared, just let me know. Or seek out Lana at the Guardian House and share your concerns with her. I promise we'll do our best to help you."

"I'll remember that," Elisa replied, meeting Becca's gaze. "Now, will you give me a free toy?"

"Alright, since you're such a smart girl, I'll give you a good discount," Becca promised. She may not be able to change Elisa's family situation, but at least she could bring a smile to her face.

Elisa's face lit up. "That would be nice!"

"Okay, which one do you want?"

Elisa selected a snow-white teddy bear and hugged it tightly to her chest. Becca's heart trembled. *How could I part with this particular teddy bear?* It had been one of her very first toys and a constant companion during sleepless nights. Becca had always found solace in hugging this fluffy bear, regardless of what challenges life threw her way.

"Is this your favorite one?" Elisa asked. "If it is, you should keep it."

Becca offered her a warm smile. "No, you keep it. You've chosen a truly special bear. My mother cast a Comforting spell on it when I was a child, and this bear has been a source of comfort throughout my life."

Elisa looked skeptical. "Even I know those spells only last for a few nights. The magic has faded by now!"

Becca shook her head. "Not when the object holds special significance for you. Even after my mother stopped enchanting this toy, it continued to bring me comfort."

Elisa turned the bear in her hands, examining its ears and the buttons of its eyes. "So, it's like an anchor, then."

"You're familiar with the concept of mental anchors?"

"Of course," Elisa confirmed. "My mom often sings a song she learned in her youth. She believes that people are drawn to melodies that evoke the best moments of their lives. Sometimes, the smallest things hold important memories, like this bear."

Becca smiled, impressed by Elisa's insight. The girl's curiosity about the world around her hinted at a potential for a happier future than her parents.

"Why are you selling it?" Elisa inquired after finishing her inspection of the bear.

Becca shrugged. "I feel it's time to embark on a new chapter in my life. I want to pass it on as a lucky charm to someone who could use a little support. Someone like you."

Elisa sighed. "Well, you certainly have a knack for selling."

"And you have a talent for bargaining."

"Thanks. So, how much?"

Becca chuckled. "It's just two bronze coins. But you can have it for one."

"Deal." Elisa retrieved a bronze coin from her pocket and handed it to Becca.

The time crystal on her bracelet turned blue, signaling the end of the day. Becca gathered two boxes that were still full, intending to take them inside the church for storage. As she ascended the stairs, one of the boxes slipped and began to slide away.

"Gotcha!" Stan laughed, quickly placing his hand on the side of the box to stop it. He then lifted the top box, revealing his smiling face to Becca.

"Oh, you finally decided to show up," Becca remarked, frowning at him. Stan had promised to help her earlier in the afternoon, but he had only arrived after the fair had ended.

"Better late than never," Stan quipped as they made their way into the church building.

Inside, the soft light streaming in through the tall windows illuminated the sacred hall. Becca cherished the serene atmosphere of the church, particularly during this time of day. The gentle sun-rays bathed the wooden benches and illuminated the figures of six stone saints. Their pale faces glowed in the yellowish light, giving them a radiant and contented appearance. Each saint symbolized a fundamental value that served as a pillar of life and harmony – safety, health, love, family, dignity, and truthfulness.

Becca often found solace in sitting alone in the spacious hall, gazing at the saintly figures and pondering their untold stories. The official records provided only limited information about their lives, focusing mainly on their adventures and accomplishments. Details about their personal lives were scarce. As Becca's mother had once remarked, personal matters were just that – personal and not for public consumption. Thus, Becca let her imagination roam, envisioning how these saints might navigate the challenges she faced and striving to emulate their virtues in her own life.

They entered a small chamber at the far end of the hall, and Becca set her box down. "You promised to come in the afternoon," she reminded Stan, "I ended up doing all the work alone."

"Sorry... I couldn't make it earlier. My biology tutor was really tough on me," Stan explained, his puppy-dog eyes melting away Becca's disappointment. She couldn't stay mad at him for long. Stan was always dedicated to his studies, striving to become a doctor. That commitment meant he often had tutors helping him after regular school hours. Becca could only support him on his path.

"I understand," she replied in a composed tone.

"Thank you." His warm eyes met hers. "So, now we can walk around the town. How about eating some ice-cream?"

"Not tonight. I have plans with the girls."

"Again?" Stan sounded disappointed. "We hardly get to see each other with all your constant meetups."

Becca sighed. "I know, Stan. I don't like how our schedules clash either. But I can't do anything about it."

"You see Mira every day in class. And Lana after school! I'm sure they'll understand if you skip your tea party just this once," Stan reasoned, reaching out to touch Becca's hand. "Come on, the weather is lovely, and all I want is to spend this evening with you."

"Really?" Becca narrowed her eyes, still unsure.

"Of course," he whispered, leaning in to kiss her on the lips.

Becca couldn't deny that she enjoyed his kisses. Ever since their first kiss at the winter ball, she cherished every moment their lips met. He embraced her waist, providing support as her legs grew weak.

"Seriously?! In church?!" Mira's loud voice shattered the moment, causing Becca to pull away from Stan.

She stepped back, breathing heavily. Mira stood at the threshold of the chamber, her hands outstretched between the door frame. A wave of shame washed over Becca. Among all the buildings in Triville, the church – where her mother served, no less – was the most inappropriate place to make out.

To Becca's surprise, Stan remained composed and unflustered. He frowned at Mira. "I hope you have a good reason for interrupting us."

Mira met his gaze with intensity. "Oh, I do have a reason. But it's none of your concern."

"What do you mean?" Stan moved closer, their faces mere inches apart.

Undaunted, Mira maintained eye contact. "I mean your time is up," she declared, turning to Becca. "Let's go. The meeting is about to start."

Becca felt torn, unsure of what to do. On one hand, she had a girls' meeting to attend, and Lana had promised to teach them a protective spell. On the other hand, Stan had just arrived, and sending him away would be too rude.

Stan looked at her with a questioning expression. "Seriously?! You're going to choose her over me?"

"Why not?" Mira interjected playfully. "I don't make her abandon her other friends or disregard her commitments. Besides, you two were supposed to spend the whole day together. Wasn't that enough?"

Stan's face turned red, leaving Becca uncertain whether it was due to the room's warmth, embarrassment, or anger. She had never seen him like this before.

"Okay, let's calm down, guys," Becca implored, gesturing to dissipate the tension and cool the atmosphere. "Mira is right. I made a commitment, and we have a master class scheduled."

Mira nodded in agreement. "Exactly. I came to check if you needed more assistance, so we can head to Lana's place together."

"Thank you," Becca replied with a smile.

"Unbelievable," Stan muttered, his frown deepening. "So I guess I'm dismissed."

Mira stepped aside, allowing Stan to storm out of the room. Becca hesitated, unsure whether to follow him or give him some space. After all, Stan had promised to help her in the afternoon, but he hadn't shown up. It wasn't her fault that their time together had been limited to a single kiss.

"Don't worry about him," Mira reassured. "If he truly cared for you, he would respect your time. Clearly, he doesn't."

"If you weren't my good friend, I might think you're jealous of him," Becca remarked, giving Mira a suspicious look. "Should I be concerned?"

Mira blushed slightly. "No, nothing to worry about. I just love you and want you to be with the right person."

Becca's eyes widened. "Did you just say the 'L' word?"

Mira fell silent.

"Aww..." Becca hugged her shoulders. "I love you, too."

27

Self-Defence Framework

A flower-scented spring air filled the spacious bedroom. Lana sat at the head of her bed, fully prepared to cast a spell. Mira and Becca had recently arrived and took their spots at the foot of the bed, their eyes wide open as they listened to her instructions.

"So, you place your palms close to each other but not touching," Lana explained as she lifted her hands. "Then, you close your eyes and imagine something that makes you feel safe. Let that feeling flow through your fingers along with your Light."

Lana closed her eyes, thinking of her favorite book. This story was her sanctuary – all the characters and places in that world seemed to be created just for her. Her fingertips tingled as she pushed her energy out, and a pleasantly cold mist began to form between her palms.

When she opened her eyes, she held a ball of milky-gray mist in her hands. Mira also held a similar ball, a Paralyzing spell. Becca's hands, however, were empty.

"Can that calming thing be a person?" Becca asked, fidgeting with the bed cover.

Mira shot her an annoyed look. "Are you still thinking about Stan?"

"I didn't mean *him*."

"Then who is it?" Mira pressed.

Becca let out a heavy sigh but remained silent.

"That's what I thought," Mira concluded, furrowing her brow.

Lana gave them both an annoyed look. "Girls, can we please focus?"

"Sorry," Mira apologized. "I just think Becca is putting too much emphasis on this guy."

"Here we go." Lana dropped her hands, causing her spell to dissipate on the bed, leaving a circle of frost on her blanket. "Do we really need to discuss this now?"

"Of course not," Becca waved her hand dismissively. "We promised not to talk about boyfriends here. I just thought that if someone makes you feel safe –"

"Then you become foolish and end up getting hurt," Mira interjected. "That's why we should never base our mental anchors on people."

"She's right," Lana confirmed. "Relationship dynamics can change at any moment."

Becca looked around helplessly. "Why are you both so against him?"

Lana sighed. Over the past four months since the winter ball, she had done her best to keep Mira's secret. She hoped their connection with Becca would deepen and any misunderstandings would fade away. However, Mira's jealousy often got in the way and only worsened things.

Giving Becca a reassuring smile, Lana said, "No one is against you and Stan. I just mean that relationships are constantly evolving. Even if you love someone deeply and feel calm, there may still be moments of misunderstanding. And if you feel anger towards your mental anchor, it could affect the quality of your spell."

"I never get angry with him!" Becca argued.

"Passion can also impact your spell. Strong desire is another opposite of calm," Lana explained.

Becca blushed. "I… I've never considered that before."

"And you better not even consider it," Mira warned, holding up a spell in her hand.

"Why not? Maybe we'll end up getting married," Becca retorted.

Mira turned to Lana, seeking her support.

"Let's clarify this once and for all," Lana said, rubbing her frozen hands as her fingertips remained numb from casting the spell. "You must choose an *object*, not a *person*. It could be your favorite book or a place. Something simple that evokes only the specific emotion needed for the spell."

"Got it," Becca said, lifting her hands and closing her eyes. However, she only managed to cast her Light – a baby-blue with navy sparkles inside.

Mira shook her head. "It's clear that you struggle to protect yourself."

"It's a good thing she has *you*," Lana said, offering a supportive smile.

Becca rolled her eyes. "Why do we even need this spell? It numbs your magic channels after casting it, and I don't like that feeling."

"Because this town isn't as safe as it appears," Lana reminded them. "Honestly, I believe every girl should know the basics of self-defense just to be able to protect herself."

"I agree," Mira said somberly. "Knowing how to cast this spell makes me feel more secure. Just imagine if it were taught in schools! It could prevent so many assaults."

"I'm not sure," Becca said, standing up and walking to the window. The breeze from the open frame brushed against her face, but she remained unfazed.

Lana gave her an attentive look. Indeed, Becca was preoccupied with something. "What's wrong?" Lana inquired. "Please, tell us."

Becca turned to face them. "Today, I met a girl from a wretched family."

"Which girl?" Mira asked, intrigued.

"The one who often plays with my Kyle," Becca explained. "Her name is Elisa Palmer."

Lana nodded in recognition. Since she had started working as a secretary at the Guardian House, she had witnessed Mr. Palmer's arrest on at least four occasions.

He was typically locked in a cell for the night and released once he sobered up. Each time, he would promise that it was the last time, only to repeat the cycle when he received his monthly welfare check, inevitably getting into trouble again.

"Her father is that alcoholic from the West End?" Mira asked for clarification. Her Paralyzing spell had dissipated, leaving her sitting on the bed with her hands in her lap.

Becca nodded. "Yes, he's from the West End. I gave Elisa my old plush toy that I used as a calming anchor to comfort her. But I'm really worried. Whenever her father gets drunk, he abuses his wife... And it's not going to end well for Elisa."

"Unfortunately, you can't save everyone," Mira said, her regret evident in her voice.

"It doesn't mean I can't try."

Lana stood up. "Becca is right. I'm part of the team now, so I'll find a way to help."

"Seriously?!" Mira looked at her skeptically. "Firstly, you're just a secretary there, not a guardian. And secondly, it seems like you haven't learned anything from life. No offense."

"None taken," Lana replied, undeterred. "The incident with Burke taught me a valuable lesson. I vowed not to meddle in people's lives or falsely accuse anyone, regardless of how suspicious they may appear."

Mira folded her arms. "So, what's your plan then?"

Lana paced the room, formulating a strategy. Her mind raced when it came to apprehending criminals. "I'll conduct a research on Palmer. I should have his case file in my archive. Then, I'll consult the *Book of Law* to determine the extent of his offenses and how many more are needed to ensure he is held accountable."

Becca's eyes widened. "Accountable?"

Lana nodded firmly. "He's harming his wife, putting the child in danger. Do you think it's better to let him continue ruining their lives?"

"Of course not. But we can't take matters into our own hands. It's not the right approach."

"Agreed," Lana concurred. "After I conduct the research, we'll use the information to confront him."

Becca looked puzzled. "Confront him how?"

Lana's eyes lit up as she had an idea. "We can compile a list of his offenses and use it as leverage to threaten him with imprisonment. It might compel him to change his behavior."

"We could also encourage Palmer to seek professional help," Mira added. "I know there's a support group in the capital for individuals struggling with alcoholism."

Becca visibly relaxed. "With you both, I feel confident we can make a difference."

Lana smiled. "Together, we are unstoppable."

28

A Secret

The night sky was covered with heavy clouds, ready to burst with rain at any moment. Strong gusts of wind made the glass windows of the Guardian House tremble. Lana pushed against the heavy entrance door, but it refused to budge. "Damn it!"

Today, she had a simple, straightforward plan – to enter the building pretending that she had decided to treat the guardian on duty with homemade baking, then quickly check the archive and find the case folder on Joseph Palmer. However, the first part didn't go as planned. It turned out that the guardian at the entrance was absent, and the front doors were locked. Usually, they assigned someone to open the doors and check who came in, and in his absence, the doors were supposed to be kept open.

Lana gripped a wicker basket filled with fresh muffins and walked down the stairs. No, she couldn't give up so easily. *How can I get in?* Lana turned to the dark building, which loomed over her like a solid rock that could easily squash her.

Then, her eyes landed on the window leading to the basement. *Of course!* A spark of hope ignited in her chest. Since Lana started working here as a secretary, people often complained about her bad habit of leaving the basement window unlocked. Now, it might work to her benefit. She approached and moved the frame, which slid aside smoothly. *Good job, Lana!* With a smile, she squeezed herself inside.

Landing on a pile of papers wasn't pleasant, and she also dropped the wicker basket filled with baking. A part of her muffins rolled all over the floor. *Whatever*, she thought. She was inside, and she couldn't wait to start her search.

Unfortunately, she failed to find the case folder on Palmer in the archive. It simply wasn't there. And that could only mean one thing – someone had worked on Palmer's case today. Whoever had taken the case folder hadn't returned it to the archive; instead, it was resting on his desk.

Lana walked into the dark corridor and began pulling on the doorknobs to peek inside. Unfortunately, she had no luck – all the desks were empty of paperwork.

The corridor on the third floor led her to the last door – the library, which also served as an observation room. Here, the guardian on duty was supposed to be. Lana hated the idea of facing someone, but she could still give her basket away and ask the man to open the front door for her. She hoped that whoever he was, he would be happy to see the food and not question her too much about the way she had entered the building.

She knocked three times, waiting for the steps to approach. Then the door opened, revealing Charles. His face brightened in surprise. "Lana? What are you doing here?"

It was unusual to see him there. Charles had never mentioned that he was working this weekend. In fact, they had a date planned for Sunday. Regardless, now wasn't the time to question him. She raised her hand with the basket and smiled. "I brought you a treat!"

"Well, thank you! I can't believe you figured out that I took Carl's shift today." He hesitated. "Unless you came to see him."

"Of course not. My father told me you're here," she lied. "But I can walk away so that I won't distract you from work."

"Please, don't." He stepped back, inviting her inside.

Lana walked to the desk and placed her basket on it. This desk was empty, too. *Where the heck is this case folder, then?*

"It seems I left the front door open," Charles said as he came closer. "This is how you walked in, right?"

"Yeah, exactly." Lana hated lying to him for the second time today, but she didn't want him to figure out how she got into the building. "It's alright. It is supposed to be this way if there is a guardian on duty."

"Everything is so simple in small towns," he said with relief in his voice. "In the place where I grew up, people use three different locks on their entrance door to prevent robbery."

She chuckled. Perhaps that's why Charles had the habit of keeping all the doors shut. "You'll get used to it one day."

"Maybe. If I stay in Triville," he said gloomily.

Her heart sank. "What do you mean? Are you leaving?!"

He shrugged. "This is what I wanted to discuss with you for a while, but I never wanted to ruin the moment."

"What happened?!" She touched his unshaven cheek. Only now, in the dull candlelight, she noticed how tired he was – with dark circles under his eyes and his skin dehydrated and dull. Charles often worked overtime, explaining that he had a goal to buy his own place instead of renting that distant house at the edge of town. *Is he tired from the low-paid work here?* If so, she could always ask her father to give him a raise.

He took her hand in his. "I can't forget one thing – just before we met, you wanted to become an architect. And you even talked your father into studying in the capital."

Lana nodded, recollecting the events of that evening when Charles had come to their home for the very first time. Back then, Lana really had such a talk with her father, and studying was her backup plan. It was only because her father refused to make her a secretary at the Guardian House. As soon as Lana received this job, she completely forgot about that other decision.

Lana locked eyes with him. "Maybe I wanted it once. But I'm here now, and I like it much more."

"Oh, please." His voice was full of sadness. "I talked to your father the other day, and he told me about your deal. I knew you were supposed to leave Triville this summer. And I..."

"You asked him to make me a secretary. And I'm so grateful for that."

"You shouldn't be." He averted his eyes. "I explained it as a chance to add some practice to your resume. But honestly, I only wanted to be closer to you. To buy some time so we can get to know each other better."

She shrugged. "Well, your plan worked perfectly. So what?"

"It's just not right. The closer summer gets, the more I realize that I might ruin your dream because of my selfishness." He breathed out. "When we had our first kiss, you pushed me away. Do you remember why?"

Lana looked at him without blinking. "I said we can't date or marry as it would ruin my dream to help people. But I didn't mean the architecture profession."

"Then what did you talk about?"

Lana smiled. Maybe she had never confessed it to anyone, but now she felt safe to tell him everything she had dreamed of since she was a teenager. "I'm sorry that I refused you first. I did it only because I wanted to impress my father so he would make me a part of the team. All I want is to be here and help people in need. And not just as a secretary. As a detective."

His face became puzzled. "So that actually was your dream you were afraid to talk about?"

"You would have laughed at me back then." She lowered her eyes. "I know it's silly and forbidden by law. Women can't enter this field and become guardians."

"You're right about the law. But who told you it's silly?"

"My father. He wants me to choose a proper path in life that would suit our community."

He narrowed his eyes. "So, all you want is to keep helping people here, in Triville?"

"Exactly."

"And you aren't planning to leave me?" He caressed her hand, making her skin tickle. When Charles touched her like that, she never could resist this temptation.

Lana gave him a warm look. "I'll stay here. And you?"

"Then me, too," he said before his lips crushed on hers.

Charles easily lifted her by her waist and placed her bum on the desk. His hot lips traveled lower, kissing a sensitive spot on her bare neck, making Lana forget of anything. His hands gently slid by her back, then to her hips, lifting the hem of her dress. When he stepped back to remove his belt, Lana shook her feet, letting her shoes fall on the floor.

His pants slid down, and he gripped her, moved by his unstoppable desire. Lana could feel the heat coming from under his shirt. Her naked foot slid along his hip, pushing him deeper inside. Their bodies moved synchronically. Their hearts raced in the same rhythm. Lana moaned, captivated by his heat until her consciousness burst into millions of shining sparkles.

The storm rampaged against the expansive library windows, causing the glass to rattle. The skies turned completely black, with only occasional flashes of lightning illuminating the room. Charles stood by the window, hastily pulling on his pants. Another bolt of lightning pierced the sky, casting his silhouette against the glass.

He frowned at the storm. "How am I supposed to see the Light signal now?"

Lana adjusted the hem of her dress, ensuring it wasn't too wrinkled from their activities. "Do you think someone would really commit a crime in this weather?"

"In case you forgot, most crimes happen indoors."

Lana approached him. Together, they gazed out at the dark yard, the only light coming from the smashed mint-green glow of the tree trunks.

Charles turned to her. "You shouldn't go outside now. Let's satisfy our hunger."

She gave him a playful look. "Are we talking about another round of love-making?"

"You are so insatiable." He pecked her forehead. "But that's not what I meant. I hope the muffins you brought are still good to eat."

She glanced at the wicker basket pushed into the far corner of the desk. "Sure. They are tasty even when they're cold."

"Then stay here, and I'll make us some coffee." He smiled at her before leaving.

Lana grabbed the muffins, walked to the sofa, and took a seat. Her summer dress no longer provided any warmth, so she grabbed the comforter from the corner to wrap around her upper body. To her surprise, she noticed a white case folder resting on the sofa handle. Lana narrowed her eyes, trying to read its title, when the lightning exploded again, revealing the name - *Joseph Palmer.*

Lana flinched. *What is it doing here?* With trembling hands, she took the case folder and opened it. As she had expected, there were multiple records of Palmer's arrests with attached interrogation reports. The records were mostly brief but detailed the same scenario – heavy drinking followed by assaults. There were also arrests made due to *'Loud noises coming from Palmer's home.'* His wife's name was Agnes, as Lana discovered, and she was surprisingly protective when their concerned neighbors called the authorities to intervene.

Among the paperwork, Lana found a witness testimonial filled out by Agnes herself. Apparently, the woman had completed it at the local hospital, as the form was signed by the doctor who took her statement. With her mouth agape, Lana read the lines:

"I admit, my husband can be brutal at times. As his wife, I fully accept him the way he is. Every night, I pray to Divine to give me enough strength to go through all our difficult days together. And I'm truly grateful for all the good days. This time, I pray for my swift healing and another chance to see my daughter. I confirm that I have no regrets about my marriage, and I have nothing to complain about.

This testimonial is signed by me,
Agnes Palmer."

Lana re-read the text twice, but it still made no sense. It appeared that Agnes had been influenced by their community's rules, which advised women to never fight back and to be obedient, regardless of the circumstances. There seemed to be no chance that she would ever see her marriage as toxic. Lana could only attempt to comprehend this decision. After all, Agnes Palmer was an adult woman. However, there was a concern that Lana couldn't ignore – it involved a child. What would become of Elisa if these abusive episodes continued?

The entrance door squeaked, and Lana quickly closed the folder, placing it back on the sofa handle. She still felt uneasy about everything she had just learned.

Charles walked in, carrying two cups of steaming coffee from the kitchen. "Here we go." He smiled as he placed the hot drinks on the coffee table. "Now, we can enjoy this night together. And this time, I mean not just food."

"I can't stay for too long," Lana said, raising her coffee cup.

"Why not? Everyone knows we are... actually, what is our official status?"

"Good friends," she reminded him. "That's why spending the night under the same roof is questionable."

He took her hand. "We can't hide forever, Dandelion. And honestly, I bet Captain Morris understands what's going on between us. It's just a matter of time before he questions my intentions towards you."

"Intentions... Damn, we should figure something out, then."

"Like what?"

"Well... we can pretend we had an argument and stopped talking. It will ease my father's worries."

He laughed. "What are you always afraid of? We know each other quite well, so we can get officially engaged. Don't you agree?"

Without knowing how to respond, Lana stood up and walked to the window. This was the conversation she hoped to avoid. Since the incident at the winter ball with the potion mix-up, Charles had stopped being so insistent. Her father had also changed; seeing Charles so close to Lana, he had stopped being preoccupied with the idea of getting her married to one of his friends. And now, it was time for Lana to make a decision. She needed to gather her thoughts. *If I only knew what to do...*

Lana raised her eyes to the black sky, hoping that Divine would send her a sign. As her best friend Becca had assured her, it always worked.

The lightning flashed, illuminating the front yard and a spacious porch. There, a stranger in a raincoat was desperately knocking on the entrance doors. The sound of the knocks was barely audible on such a stormy night, which is why they had not heard it before.

"Dandelion," Charles called out as he approached and hugged her from behind. "You can't avoid this conversation forever."

"It's not that." She pointed to the yard. "There is someone. A visitor."

"Where?"

"By the doors." She turned to him. "The door is locked, so she can't get inside."

"You said it was open."

She let out an irritated sigh. "I don't know, okay? I might have locked it when I came in. Let's go downstairs and see."

"Hold on." He stepped to the window, narrowing his eyes. "Actually, it's that poor girl. We arrested her father recently, and her mother probably sent her here to try to get him released faster. Again. What terrible parents!"

Lana's heart skipped a beat. When someone arrested a man, they usually took his case folder from the archives to make a record. That's why she found Joseph Palmer's case file here, in this very room. "Are you saying it's Elisa Palmer?"

He widened his eyes. "Do you know this family?"

"Not too well. But I can talk to her now. To calm her."

"You'll have to wait until morning." He crossed his arms. "Because I'm not opening the door."

She widened her eyes. "You're going to leave this child outside in such nasty weather? She might catch pneumonia!"

"Maybe then her foolish father would think twice before getting drunk again."

She gasped. "Seriously?! You're just going to stand here and watch that child like this?"

"Of course not." He came closer, his breath brushing against her flushed face. "I would rather look at you."

"Unbelievable." She stepped back. "If you don't let her in, then I'm not staying here."

He rolled his eyes. "Fine. Let's see why she came. But I warned you about her, so don't complain if she starts begging for her dad's release!"

Lana didn't listen. She was already running to the corridor.

29

A Plush Proof

The candlelight cast a warm glow in the library. Elisa sat on a sofa, wrapped in a comforter, holding a cup of herbal tea that Lana had prepared for her. Charles fidgeted with a plush teddy bear in his hands, frowning at the spots of blood on it.

"So, this is your evidence against your father?" Charles inquired.

Elisa nodded. "After their fight, Mom cleaned the floor as usual, but she didn't notice how my toy fell into a puddle of her blood. I hid it after my dad was arrested."

Charles let out a deep sigh and placed the toy on his desk. He rubbed his temples, grappling with the complexities of his role as a guardian. "Sweetie, we can't imprison a person based solely on this."

She looked at him with disappointment. "Why not?"

"It's circumstantial evidence," he explained. "To imprison someone, we need solid proof that they have broken the law. We need witnesses."

"I'm the witness!"

He shook his head. "You're a child, so no one will believe you. I mean, I believe you now, but in court, they won't listen to you. We need an adult witness."

Elisa turned her head to Lana. "You have a mind-reading Gift. Can you read the bear?"

Lana shook her head with regret. "Unfortunately, I can only read humans. Well, sometimes animals. But not objects. Your mom should come here and give her testimony. There is no other way."

Elisa set her mug down and gave Lana a stern look. "You've got to be kidding! Yesterday, I talked to Becca, and she said that you would help. I even brought the proof to make your job easier. Here is the proof!" She then shifted her gaze to Charles. "And you are a guardian, so do your job!"

His eyebrows twitched in response.

This girl sent shivers down Lana's spine, and she could only imagine what Charles was feeling at that moment. She needed to calm Elisa down.

"Elisa, listen," Lana said in a soothing voice. "This teddy bear can't be our evidence for one simple reason – it's impossible to prove how it got stained with blood. If your mom officially complains –"

"She never complains!" Tears welled up in Elisa's dark blue eyes, shimmering like sapphires in the candlelight. "One day, he'll kill her. I know it!"

Lana's heart sank. "You're right. She won't file a complaint. But you can."

Elisa blinked. "What?"

"What?" Charles echoed.

Lana leaned in closer to Charles and lowered her voice. "This might be a case of child abuse. If we have Elisa's testimony stating that he beats his daughter, we can legally visit them. I can read her mother, and then I'll see how to help her."

He gave her a puzzled look. "If Elisa says he assaulted her, it won't necessarily lead to a positive outcome. The girl might end up being separated from her family. Have you seen the shelter in Middle Lake city? It's a shithole!"

Lana was determined not to give up. "Shouldn't we do everything we can to help her? And, by the way, it's your responsibility as a guardian to protect her now."

He frowned, deep in thought.

"And I'll assist in bringing this case to court," Lana assured him. "If you advocate for this child, it will reflect positively on your record."

"Fine," he agreed after a moment of contemplation. "But we need a solid plan, then."

She smiled and turned to Elisa. "Can you write?"

Elisa rolled her eyes. "I'm eleven. Of course, I can write. Just give me a piece of paper and a pen."

Charles retrieved a testimonial form from the drawer and handed it to Elisa. Lana provided her with a pen.

After Elisa finished writing, Charles took the paper and skimmed it. "Good. We'll inspect your house sometime next week."

"Next week?" Lana widened her eyes. "It's an urgent matter, so we must go now!"

He shook his head. "I've already told you – we need a solid plan. It takes time to prepare everything. Besides, I'm on duty tonight and can't leave unless there's a Light signal."

Elisa yawned. "Lana, it's okay. I don't really want to go home right now."

"Won't your parents worry?"

Elisa gave her a sharp look. "Are you kidding? In case you forgot, my dad is here, in the cell in the basement. And my mom took a Calming potion to help her rest after all the bruises she got. She won't even notice my absence."

Lana let out a heavy sigh. "I'm so sorry. You know what, you can stay here, at my father's office."

She turned to Charles. "Can I?"

He nodded. "If Lana isn't worried about her father finding out, I don't see any problem."

"Let me handle my father," Lana assured. She stood up and took Elisa's hand. "Now, let's go. You need to get some rest before my father arrives for work."

"Like I can fall asleep now," Elisa grumbled.

It was around midnight when Lana returned to the library. Charles was seated at the table, engrossed in a book Lana had lent him a month ago. It was her favorite book, and she was surprised he had almost finished it.

"How is the kid?" Charles inquired as she entered.

"Asleep," Lana replied.

He chuckled. "Ah, kids. They can sleep through anything, even after all the emotional turmoil."

"I had to give her three drops of Sleeping potion," Lana added.

He closed the book. "Where did you find it?"

"In Lieutenant Turner's office."

Charles placed the book on the desk, his expression turning serious. "Don't you find it strange that he keeps a restricted Sleeping potion by his desk?"

Lana shrugged. "Everyone knows Turner has insomnia."

"But he should keep it in his nightstand, not in the office," Charles pointed out.

She moved closer and sat on his lap. "Charlie, this job can make you paranoid at times. Please, let go of this unfounded suspicion towards my father's best friend, and let's focus on our plan."

His arm wrapped around her back. "I've been thinking about it. All we need is a piece of pie."

"If you're still hungry, I can bring more baked goods or something more substantial," Lana offered.

"That's not what I meant. We'll need a pie for our mission, scheduled for next Saturday."

"In a week?" Lana furrowed her brow. "Why do we have to wait so long?"

"Because alcoholics often drink with their friends on Friday night and try to act normal with their families on Saturday morning. It's a small window before they start behaving aggressively again. We need to catch him during that time and provoke him before he makes his next mistake."

She had to admit, it was a clever plan. "Alright, I'll ask Molly to bake it."

"It has to be you alone. No one else should know about this pie except us," he emphasized.

She smiled knowingly. "Ah, we need to keep a low profile."

"Exactly. Because we'll add a drop of a special potion to make him talk."

"It's a brilliant plan," Lana praised him. "I can't believe you're doing this for me."

"Well, honestly, it's not just for you."

She looked into his eyes, waiting for an explanation.

He gently stroked her hair, causing Lana to relax in his touch. "Well... It's my duty as a guardian to help those in need. When I see someone in trouble, I feel compelled to intervene."

"Just like that?"

"Yes," he assured her. "And since you've entrusted me with your secret, I feel I should be completely honest with you. Do you remember when you first read me?"

Lana nodded, recalling the night of their first date. They had shared a kiss on the bridge of wishes, and she had glimpsed into his thoughts. "Yes, I saw how you had an argument with your colleagues just before leaving your previous job."

He gave her a somber look. "That's correct. However, I never told you the real reason why I left like that."

Curious, Lana tilted her head, eager to listen.

"Unfortunately, ever since my time at the Guardian Academy, all my teachers saw me as a coach. I gladly took on this role because I wanted to understand how other Gifts functioned. And I didn't even realize how I became stuck in that position," he explained.

"I thought that was what you wanted."

He nodded. "Yes, initially. But as time passed, I realized that my true passion lay in unraveling the patterns of criminals. I enjoyed delving into case files and constructing theories on how crimes were committed. However, my former boss never allowed me to participate in investigations, which left me feeling frustrated. I had no other option but to resign. I moved to this small town in hopes of starting anew. Ironically, I could only find a job as a coach. Now, Captain Morris only sees my teaching abilities and wants me to focus on developing Gifts for others to enhance their detective skills."

"Well, Triville is a small town, and we don't have many intriguing cases here," Lana remarked.

"Small towns can often hide very dark secrets," he said, giving her a mysterious smile. "That's why I came here – I was seeking an opportunity to do more than just be a coach."

"I understand. You want to become a detective."

He placed his hand on her shoulder. "We share the same goal, Dandelion. I see your determination to help Elisa, and now I share that desire."

The warmth of his touch melted her heart. "Do you think we can make a good team?"

"Why not? I believe we can work together effectively to prevent crimes," he affirmed, giving her an attentive look. "Let's keep this partnership between the two of us."

"I can't keep secrets from Becca, though."

After a moment of consideration, Charles replied, "Alright. If you trust her with secrets, then I trust her too. We'll involve her once we have the plan details sorted out."

"I promise. And I'll make the best pie ever!"

He chuckled. "Look at you – you're really improving your cooking skills!"

"Anything for you!" Lana replied with a smile. Maybe baking wasn't her forte, but she could always rely on her best friend for help.

30

Lie To Me

Becca was in her kitchen, busy cooking. Placing strips of dough on the pie, she explained each step to Lana. "You must cover the topping, but make sure to leave some space so the jam inside won't spill out."

"Uh-huh." Lana nodded, visibly bored by the activity. She twisted a glass of water, taking sips and daydreaming as Becca shared her family recipe.

"And voila, it's done!" Becca finished the pie and shook off the flour from her hands. "Now, we just need to bake it. Did you pre-heat the oven?"

Lana blinked. "Should it be preheated?"

"Seriously?! You don't even know such basic things?" Becca frowned. "How are you going to cook for your man once you are married?"

"Well... we always had a housemaid who is taking care of such things."

"Charles isn't too rich," Becca reminded her.

"I know that." Lana rolled her eyes. "I'll find a solution."

Becca shook her head and walked to the oven to turn it on. She placed the pie on the top rack so it would be warm when the oven was ready. Now, it was time to try the main ingredient that Charles had given her last night – a potion of Sincerity.

Their team tried to keep this mission secret – last night, Becca and Mira walked to the West End together when it got dark. Meanwhile, Charles had obtained the potion from the store that Becca had once visited. They quickly made the exchange, ensuring that no one witnessed their meeting. When Becca brought the potion bottle home, she hid it on the top shelf so no one would accidentally find it.

She climbed onto a stool and took the bottle with the transparent liquid.

Lana's face brightened. "Is it going to work?"

"This is what we need to check," Becca said, twisting the bottle in her hand. The liquid was as thick as sugar syrup, and it must be sweet. She hoped that it would work just fine, but before the mission, they had to run a test just to know what they might expect in case Lana or Charles had to take it during their mission. "So, are you ready for a trial round?"

"Of course I am!" Her dark-brown eyes sparkled with excitement. "How shall we drink it?"

"Watch." Becca pulled open a drawer and extracted a small syringe. Her mother usually used it to fill muffins with cream or jam. Now, Becca was about to use it in a different way. Carefully, not to spill the potion, she collected several drops of the liquid into the syringe. Then she took a loaf of bread and cut two small pieces. She inserted the syringe into the soft dough and poured some liquid into it.

When it was ready, she gave one of the bread pieces to Lana. Then, she raised her piece as if she was making a toast. "For the truth!"

"For the truth!" Lana chuckled and placed the bread into her mouth.

As Becca chewed her piece, she took a small notebook to make her recordings. As she knew, the potion must start working fast, in a minute or two after intake. She had no idea how long the effect would last, and that's why they had to test it.

"One in the afternoon," Becca said as she made a written note. *"The experiment has begun."*

Lana checked her time crystal. "It is several minutes past two, actually."

Becca gave her a curious look, then got back to writing. *"The liquid has started working on the subject. Let's see how long it will last."*

"Seriously?" Lana lifted her eyebrow. "It's already working?"

"Let's check." Becca put her pencil down. "For the sake of the experiment, I shall ask you some personal questions. Just to check if the potion works and you can talk openly. Please, don't get offended."

"I'll try." Lana gave her a small smile. "I bet you have a lot of questions about Charles."

"Of course I do. Honestly, I don't trust this man." Becca's eyes widened as she said these words. She covered her mouth with her palm but kept talking. "I mean that I want you to be happy, but sometimes I think that Charles is not the man you would be happy with."

"Interesting." Lana drummed her fingers on the tablecloth. "Well, it's only your opinion. Also, I understand that you are forced to speak frankly right now, so no offense. What did you want to ask?"

"Do you love Charles?"

"Of course, I love him." Her voice was calm. "I never loved anyone this way before. He is kind, understanding, funny, and such a terrific lover –"

"Enough!" Becca raised her hand before Lana could go into details. "As I assume, you just can't stop supplying me with information."

"It's like a rush." Lana winced as she scratched her chest. "I just can't keep anything to myself right now."

Becca nodded and made another note.

"This is it?" Lana asked. "Should I question *you* now?"

"Hold on." Becca gave her a hesitant look. If Lana answered the next question, it would mean that the potion had managed to melt all her barriers. Also, the answer might upset Lana. But she had to ask. For the sake of science and for her own good. "If you love him that much, why don't you want to marry him?"

"You know how many times I asked myself that?" Lana exhaled a nervous sigh. "I never was brave enough to admit it, but... it's all because of my parents. After my mom left, I constantly asked myself, 'Why?'" Her eyes watered, and she wiped them with the back of her palm. "Was she so unhappy with my father?! I mean, he is a kind, good man. How could she just leave both of us? Her child, her husband? Like she was sick and tired of playing her role of a mother and wife..."

"Lana, I'm so sorry." Becca rushed to give her a hug. If she only knew how deep the truth can cut, she would never have given this potion to her.

"And now..." Lana sobbed in her embrace. "I constantly think that I can be just the same. What if I get tired of being a housewife? What if I won't bear this existence and just leave everyone behind, and it would hurt them as much?!"

"Hush..." Becca patted her back. "You aren't like this."

"What if I am?" She couldn't stop crying. "You said I won't be happy with Charles, and you are under a damn Sincerity potion!"

"I just worried for you as a friend," Becca reassured her. "I'm just human, and I might be wrong about Charles. Here is another truth for you – he might seem arrogant, but he supports you in your wildest dreams. In case you forgot, you are on this mission with him! You're a team, and you help people the way you always wanted to. He loves you that much."

"He never even said he loves me!" She dropped her head in her hands, her shoulders shaking uncontrollably. "Damn, Becca! This potion you gave me is too strong! How do I turn it off?"

"I don't know." She helplessly looked around. The bag of ground coffee beans was on the counter. As she knew from her father, this drink helped him sober up after he had too much to drink during evenings with his friends. "Actually, I can make some coffee."

"I love your coffee." She nodded in agreement, her voice quiet. "Especially the one with orange zest."

"I know." Becca smiled, relaxing.

As she placed the pie in the warm oven and started preparing the coffee in a cezve, Lana calmed down completely. She even stood up and moved to the kitchen sink to splash some water on her puffy face.

"Damn, I forgot when I was so... relieved," Lana confessed.

"You didn't look relieved," Becca said carefully, trying not to trigger another mood shift from Lana. "You were such a mess. I got really scared!"

"It opened my eyes!" Lana's eyes shimmered with excitement now. "Now I know exactly where the problem is, and it means I can fix it."

"Let's take it easy," Becca suggested.

"Come on, it's your turn to tell the truth now!" Lana walked closer and poked her shoulder. "Do you love Stan?"

"No." Becca gave her a confused look, trying to take control over her speech. Her tongue was loose despite her best efforts. "I don't love him."

Lana kept glaring at her with uncovered interest, silently waiting for continuation.

Becca frowned, unable to believe her own words. "I was attracted to him in the beginning, and kissing him is fun but..."

"But...?" Lana softly pressed her.

"Mira is right. He is fully focused on his studies, and we don't really communicate as much. And when we meet, we just hug, kiss, and that's it. Honestly, sometimes I wish I would date Mira instead." She stepped back, shocked by the conclusions that her poisoned brain supplied her. "Alright. We must have a really strong coffee now."

Lana nodded and took a pencil. *"The potion is slowing down after ten minutes. The object is able to stop the speech flow, gaining some control."*

"Thank Divine!" Becca breathed out. "I was about to say that I love her."

Lana gave her a puzzled look. "You what?"

"Please, don't make me repeat that." Becca hugged her head as if it would stop her from spilling another scary truth. To her regret, this time she wasn't able to stop herself. "On that day when I ran a charity event, we met, and... I felt a jolt when she said that she loves me."

"She did say that?!" Lana kept eyeing her, a pencil in her hand pointed at Becca. "What did you do with it?"

"After that, I couldn't shake this feeling off. I mean, Stan never told this to me, and I was thinking and thinking... and I decided it was foolish. I'm pretty sure Mira meant it as a friend, so..."

The coffee started hissing, risking spilling on the hot oven. Lana jumped to the stove and took it, preventing the incident.

"At least you can cook coffee." Becca chuckled. "And this is a good start for your family life."

"That's true," Lana agreed, laughing. She took the coffee cups from the shelf and started filling them with a heavenly-smelling dark liquid.

Becca took the pencil to make the last notes. *"When the object is distracted, the truth flow can stop."*

"Or when all the important truth is told," Lana added.

Becca took a coffee cup and took a sip. It was well-made, and she hoped it would sober them up quickly. Lana was enjoying her coffee, too, not attempting to talk. Perhaps, they both desperately needed a moment of silence. Becca closed her eyes, listening to the rustle of the curtains brushing against her window, and the calm heat coming from the oven.

When all the truth was spoken out, everything around seemed serene.

"See, this is the relief I told you about," Lana whispered.

"Interesting. We never shared anything so deeply hidden."

"Because we never took such a potion. This thing is really good. Now I understand why the guardians use it for interrogations!"

"Actually, they use a Truthful potion," Becca clarified. "The one that we tried is a much lighter version of it."

"What is the difference?"

"The Truthful one is designed to break through all the mental barriers. It's like a sharp knife cutting through butter. If the person has too many mental blocks or strong egos, the potion can cause severe brain damage.”

“Oh.”

“I know… My dad says the criminals would rather confess their crimes than agree to intake it.”

Lana massaged her temples. “What about the one we just took? Does it have side effects like that?”

“The potion of Sincerity only empowers our emotions, making them too strong to bear. So, that’s why we got this irresistible urge to speak it out. It’s often used in therapy when the patient wants to solve a problem but can’t find the root of it. The potion helps awaken all the suppressed feelings.”

“Like we just did.”

“Exactly,” Becca confirmed. “And as you see, there is no such thing as absolute truth. Everyone has opinions affected by our hopes, expectations, and doubts. But when we speak the doubts out, we can be open to changing our truth.”

Lana placed her cup on the table but kept holding it with both hands. “Is it still a potion, or you’re just speaking like a guru?”

“It’s easy to check. Try to lie to me.”

She laughed. “After everything I told you today, I can’t even think of a proper lie.”

“Say that the sky is green,” Becca suggested.

“I would rather say that Mira loves you, too,” Lana revealed. “And not as a friend. I once read her mind, so I got to know that.”

Becca’s heart skipped a beat. “For real?”

Lana shifted her eyes to the ceiling, her voice mysterious. “By the way, the sky is green today. Didn’t you notice?”

“Lana!” She could barely sit on the edge of her chair. “You can’t trick me like that! Did you read her mind or not?”

Lana gave her a sly look. "I would answer, but... I just don't want to ruin this moment of truth for you. You have to figure it out on your own."

"I hate you!" She grumbled, finishing her coffee.

"Good thing I know it's a lie." Lana checked her time crystal. "So, the experiment was successfully completed within 15 minutes. I guess we are ready for the real mission."

Becca shifted her eyes to the oven. The pie, stuffed with blueberry jam, took on an attractive brownish color. The smells started to waft through the air, making her mouth water. It was only a matter of minutes to fill it with her potion, using her syringe. Then, even the most secretive criminal wouldn't be able to resist showing his true face.

31

A Piece of Cake

Blossoming trees made even the creepiest parts of the West End look pretty. Holding a fresh-baked blueberry pie in her hands, Lana strolled along the street with Charles, enjoying their conversation and the warm weather. Today, she wore her favorite summer dress, and her hair was styled into two plaits adorned with seasonal flowers.

"When I gave the potion of Sincerity to Becca, she promised to ensure that it would work," Charles said. "Did she conduct tests on it in a school lab?"

"We tested it at her home, and trust me, it works just fine."

He grinned. "So, did you confess your biggest sin?"

"Well… the potion helped me uncover the fears hidden deep inside," Lana said, giving him a warm look. "After I confronted them, it felt like a huge weight was lifted off my chest. Now, I feel liberated from all my doubts."

"Which doubts?"

Lana smiled mysteriously. She could finally be completely honest with Charles, and she looked forward to the moment when their mission would be completed. Then, they could discuss their future openly. Because now, she was ready to embrace it.

"I think I'm ready to make an important decision," Lana announced.

He became intrigued. "Okay... Should I start worrying?"

"No. I think you'll like it," she said cheerfully.

Meanwhile, they arrived at the Palmers' household – a small one-story house with a bright red roof. The windows were dirty from the outside, but the blossoming currant bush added a touch of beauty to the scene.

"Well, let's rehearse the plan," Charles suggested as they stood by the shabby white door with cracked paint.

Lana took a deep breath before outlining their plan. "I'll give this pie to Agnes, so she'll suggest we have tea with them. I'll tell her I'm allergic to blueberries and won't eat it, but you will have a piece to avoid suspicion."

"And what if they start asking me uncomfortable questions?"

"Then I'll change the subject, and you won't reveal too much."

"Perfect." He smiled. "I guess we're ready."

"We are."

Charles knocked on the door, and they fell silent, waiting for someone to answer. Lana checked the blueberry pie in her hands. It smelled heavenly, and she adjusted the towel around it to keep it warm.

Heavy footsteps approached, and the door swung open. A man in his forties with a wrinkled face gave Charles an annoyed look. "Can I help you, Sergeant?"

Lana's heart raced. It was him, Joseph Palmer, the man whose case folder she had read at the Guardian House. And now he stood before her. Lana glanced at Charles.

His voice was firm. "Mr. Joseph Palmer?"

Joseph frowned, the wrinkles on his forehead deepening. "What's with all the formalities? You were the one who arrested me at least twice, so you know exactly who I am."

Charles grinned. "Good that you remember me. Especially considering your condition when you were brought to our humble abode."

Joseph's expression turned weary. "What's your problem?"

"There was a complaint lodged against you," Charles explained. "We are here to conduct an inspection."

Joseph's face displayed a puzzled expression. "What inspection? Do you have a warrant?"

Charles gave him a scornful look. "A warrant is permission for a search, in case you didn't know. We are here for a different purpose."

Lana offered an apologetic smile. "Please excuse us. Sergeant Braun means that we are here to assess the dynamics within your family."

He scowled. "What is this about?"

"Don't worry," Lana reassured in a soft tone, attempting to diffuse the tension. Charles was playing the role of a bad guardian, while she was meant to be the good one. It was a tactic to expedite their objectives. She gestured slightly, allowing the aroma of the blueberry pie to waft through the air. "We simply wish to have tea and engage in conversation. Just to ensure the well-being and safety of your daughter."

"And if not, we will refer your daughter's case to the social workers in Middle Lake," Charles cautioned. "I suggest you cooperate to avoid any complications."

"Okay." Joseph turned to Lana. "And who are you?"

"Lana Morris, the Captain's daughter," she explained, slightly surprised that Joseph didn't recognize her. "I often volunteer to assist families in your neighborhood. I came to see if you need any help."

He scoffed. "Well, we always need money. Can you help with that?"

"Rest assured, I'll do my utmost to support your family," Lana replied, meeting his gaze.

A woman's voice echoed from within the house. "Joseph, who is it?"

He glanced back. "Put on a kettle, Agnes. We have visitors."

Charles and Lana exchanged silent glances. His eyes sparkled. *Well done.* The ice had been broken. Now, the most crucial part lay ahead – to execute their plan successfully.

While Agnes, the mistress of the house, was busy preparing tea, Lana assisted her in the living room. She laid a cloth on the round table and smoothed out the folds. Charles stood against the wall, studying the family portraits. As he had mentioned to Lana earlier, he enjoyed examining old photos to gain insight into people's backgrounds and potential hidden aspects.

"You came." Elisa approached Lana and embraced her.

Lana returned the smile. "Of course! As I promised."

Elisa glanced towards the kitchen door, her expression tinged with concern. "What if something goes wrong?"

Lana placed a comforting hand on Elisa's shoulder. "It will be fine. We are professionals. Besides, the situation can't worsen from where it stands now."

Elisa sighed. "What if I end up in a shelter?"

Lana's heart sank. Elisa had likely overheard their conversation just before entering the house. Unfortunately, this intelligent girl was trapped in a difficult family situation; the least Lana could do was to be honest with her.

Lana sat down on a chair and locked eyes with Elisa. "Listen, I can't promise that your father will stop drinking. It may never happen."

Elisa lowered her gaze. "I understand... Will you really have him arrested?"

"We'll do our best to make an arrest today and bring this case to court."

"What if someone takes me away from home? What will I do all alone?" Her eyes welled up with tears.

Lana gently touched her shoulder. "Elisa, my dear. You are incredibly brave. The bravest person I know. I didn't expect you to seek help at the Guardian House, but you did. That's why I'll be brave and help you. If things go awry, I'll locate you wherever you are and ensure your safety."

Her eyes widened. "Using a Searching spell?"

"Exactly."

She hesitated. "But... How? Will you need my blood for the spell?"

"The guardians only need blood when all other methods fail to locate a missing person. For instance, if the energy trail has dissipated. But that's not the case here. All personal belongings can retain your energy for many years, making it easier for me to locate you through them. If you have something that you cherish and frequently wear, it will be effective."

"Like this?" Elisa reached up to her curly golden hair, revealing a beautiful hairpin adorned with three pearls.

"Is it a family heirloom?" Lana inquired, admiring its beauty. *It must be of a high value.*

"Sort of. It belonged to my grandmother. When she passed away, my aunt Rachel gave it to me," Elisa explained.

Lana raised her eyebrows. "You have an aunt? I wasn't aware of her."

"She lives in the capital, in our grandmother's old house. The last time I saw her, I was seven." Elisa sighed. "It was before my father began drinking, and my mother ceased communication with her."

"So, your mother and her sister... I guess they didn't see each other for a long time."

Elisa nodded. "I miss her greatly."

Lana discreetly tucked the hairpin into her pocket. "Let's discuss it once this mission is concluded."

Elisa smiled. "Of course."

Agnes entered the living room carrying a tray. Her sleeves were rolled up, revealing bruises on her wrists that caught Lana's attention. A memory of the report from Joseph Palmer's case flashed in Lana's mind. She vividly remembered a line from the report penned by one of the guardians: *"The suspect confessed to tying his wife, Mrs. Agnes Palmer, to a pipe with power ropes to prevent her from using her Telekinesis Gift. He claimed his wife had requested it herself."*

As Agnes gestured, the teacups floated gracefully to their designated spots around the table, landing with precision. Lana couldn't help but flinch. Agnes was unable to use her Gift to defend herself, but she displayed proficiency in utilizing it to serve dishes.

Once the table was set, Agnes placed a sliced pie in the center. Lana took a seat beside Charles. When Becca had baked this pie, she had infused a potion of Sincerity into the filling.

As they had discovered earlier, the potion infused in the pie had a temporary effect. It would begin to take action after two to three minutes and last for approximately twenty minutes. The potion's duration could be halved if they had opted for coffee, but Agnes had only offered tea, much to their advantage. Lana had to make the most of this time.

The strategy was well-devised. Charles's role was to incite Joseph and alert the guardians to intervene when he displayed aggressive behavior towards either Lana or Charles.

With bated breath, Lana observed as Joseph consumed his portion of the pie. After about two minutes had passed, she discreetly nudged Charles's leg under the table. It was their signal that the mission was underway.

Charles dabbed his lips with a paper napkin and cast a curious glance at Agnes. "It seems you have a pleasant atmosphere here. Is it always like this?"

"Absolutely," Agnes affirmed, then turned to Elisa, awaiting her confirmation. "Isn't that right, dear?"

Staring at her untouched pie, Elisa let out a heavy exhale through her nose. "Whatever you say."

Agnes chuckled. "Don't worry about Elisa. I believe all families have their challenges, and we are no exception."

Joseph nodded gravely. "This kid certainly has a strong will! Last Sunday, she ventured out early and returned in the afternoon! She didn't even think to inform us."

Elisa gave him a look tinged with sympathy. "I apologize if I caused any trouble. I couldn't sleep, so I went out to meet a friend."

Agnes stirred her tea with a spoon. "Which friend?"

Elisa glanced at Lana, seeking guidance. She couldn't disclose the truth, and Lana understood this, having spent that morning with Elisa, outlining the tasks for their mission. Lana played her part well for now, leaving her slice of pie untouched on the plate.

Lana smiled at Agnes. "She is referring to me. Elisa came to the Guardian House that morning after her father's arrest." She turned to Joseph. "By the way, do you recall the reason for your arrest?"

"Don't answer!" Agnes interjected, swiftly raising her hand and placing it over her husband's mouth, preventing him from speaking.

Lana blinked in disbelief. Could Agnes possibly be aware of the potion? And most importantly, how could she protect her husband after all he had done to her?!

Agnes grinned mischievously. "What, did you think I'm too foolish not to detect a potion in this pie?"

Lana turned to Charles, who remained composed before the Palmers, the effects of the potion gradually taking hold within him. "This is exactly what we had hoped for," Charles acknowledged with a subtle nod.

Lana buried her face in her hands. Her father's words echoed in her mind, *"Don't set a trap for others. You may end up ensnared yourself."* How right he had been!

Joseph regarded his wife with a puzzled expression. "What's happening? I'm really worried now."

"They need to leave," Agnes said in a firm tone. "That's what's happening."

Charles concurred, "Indeed. It's best we depart now. The situation is becoming too precarious –"

"Can't you see?" Lana locked eyes with Joseph. With their initial plan foiled, she had to think on her feet. "We'll depart shortly, allowing you to continue abusing your wife and traumatizing your daughter. But when your actions ruin their lives –"

"How dare you come into my home and accuse me?!" His voice thundered in Lana's ears.

Charles rose from his seat, but Lana grasped his hand, preventing him from making any further unnecessary disclosures. Time was of the essence.

"What if we refuse to leave?" Lana asked. "Will you resort to violence against me as well?"

His face flushed with anger. "I'll ensure your inappropriate behavior is reported to your father!"

Charles leaned in close to Lana's ear. "We need to leave. I'm afraid of him."

Lana rolled her eyes. If Charles was so fearful, why had he involved himself in this case to begin with? His wavering resolve was jeopardizing all their efforts. Fortunately, Lana remained resolute and unswayed by fear.

Lana seized her slice of pie and hurled it at Joseph. He attempted to evade it, but the pie splattered on his shirt. Lana snatched the remnants of Charles' pie. "Want more, you bastard?"

Joseph raised his hand, his eyes ablaze with green fire. Lana recalled from his case files that he possessed an Acid Gift. His mere touch could inflict severe burns. Provoking him was a significant risk, but it was the only way to achieve their goal.

Elisa's voice pierced the heavy silence like a delicate violin. "Daddy, please stop."

His tone was cutting. "Go to your room. Now."

Elisa glanced at her mother, and Agnes nodded in agreement. "Listen to your father. Go."

As Elisa vanished behind the door, Agnes rose to her feet, raising both hands, prepared to utilize her own Telekinesis Gift.

"Just attempt to harm me," Lana cautioned. "And I –"

Before Lana could complete her sentence, Agnes intervened. With a swift motion of her hands, she propelled both Lana and Charles towards the exit door. Surprisingly, her actions were precise and gentle, ensuring they were not harmed during their expulsion.

Maintaining her hold on them through her telekinetic power, Agnes escorted Lana and Charles until they landed on the verdant grass of the front yard.

"Thank you for the pie and the lesson," Agnes remarked before firmly shutting the door behind them.

32

Three Words

When her ability to speak returned, Lana sat up and inspected her body. Unfortunately, there were no visible traces of abuse. She didn't even have any proof against Agnes and her husband. They had absolutely nothing on them to make an arrest!

Charles still lay on the grass, his eyes looking up at the white clouds floating by the darkening skies.

Lana fell on her back by his side. "We officially screwed up."

His voice was calm. "I know. Probably Agnes overheard your talk with Elisa. You had to be more careful and quieter."

Lana rolled her eyes. It was all she needed – Charles' fogged brain, marinated in that damn potion. She glanced at the time crystal – it was purple. *Eight in the evening.* Well, the potion's effect would last for at least ten more minutes.

"Charles, I'm so sorry. I let you down."

"It wasn't your fault. Agnes appeared to be smarter than we thought."

"Not too smart in terms of protecting her daughter," Lana retorted.

"Maybe she is in love? When people love someone, they do desperate things just for the sake of being close to them."

Lana turned to him. Charles was so vulnerable now, which meant she could ask him whatever she wanted, taking advantage of his condition. Not that she would go too deep. She only needed to hear those three words he never told her.

"I love you," she whispered.

He moaned and covered his face. "Lana, please. I need more time for this talk."

"Why?"

"Because it's not that easy for me – to fall in love."

This confession made her heart sink. It was absolutely not what Lana expected to hear... she was almost certain Charles loved her. *What if I was wrong all along?* Lana shook her head, chasing away the silly doubts. No, it didn't make any sense. If he never really loved her, he wouldn't support her all this time. Perhaps he was just upset with her. After all, Lana had never accepted his proposal, which might have affected his feelings.

Charles sat up. "What I wanted to say... I'm slowly growing more attached to you. I just can't say such words if I don't mean it. Do you understand?"

She nodded. "I'm so sorry I pushed you like this. Did I upset you?"

"Yes, you did." He rubbed his forehead as if trying to erase the leftovers of the potion. "Sorry... I would find a way to say it gently, but I can't help it right now, so everything I say comes out too harsh!"

"Fine. I won't ask you anything, then. Not before the potion evaporates."

He glanced at her time crystal. "Shit... my night shift will start in fifty-five minutes! I need to sober up!"

She rose and gave him a hand so he could stand up.

"Where are we going now?" He looked worried.

She smiled. "Chill. We just need a good coffee shop."

The central street was busy in the evening. May, the warmest spring month, was in bloom, and people strolled along the blossoming valleys, discussing the latest rumors and enjoying the nice weather. Under the shade of an orchard, there was a bench where Lana and Charles could sit, hidden from people's curious glances.

He drank his coffee from a paper cup, and she just watched him, trying to gauge when he would be in the right condition to explain himself. After his confession about not being in love, she couldn't pretend like everything was still alright. It just wasn't.

"How do you feel?" Lana asked.

"My head hurts," he grumbled, touching his forehead. "Probably after the potion. But I'll be alright."

At least he didn't get into details, Lana noted. It meant that the potion was starting to wear off. She glanced around. The night was approaching, and the windows in houses lit up one by one. The bark on the trees around started glowing with a gentle shade of green. The beauty of spring was so frail, just like human trust.

Damn, I must switch my focus to work; otherwise, we'll end up arguing. As Charles had once said to her, the guardians would never catch any criminals if they let their misunderstandings affect their work. She must act professionally now, even after her discovery of his true feelings.

Lana gave him a sad look. "Agnes just kicked us off like two shabby cats. What a terrible character!"

He finished the coffee and placed the empty cup on a bench. "She won this round. But it doesn't mean that our plan failed."

"What do you mean?"

"Agnes cracked our plan and protected her husband from prison. But she won't be able to do it forever. Tonight, we did an important thing – we ignited his anger. Now, we need to wait until he explodes."

"That's why you are on duty in the West End tonight? You think he'll do something to her?"

"He might. And when it happens, I'll be ready to make an arrest."

The thought of Joseph Palmer hurting his family made her uneasy. Lana took his empty paper cup and crumpled it. "We can't leave it like that."

He gave her a weary look. "Lana, please. You did enough already."

"Not really. Charles, I read about people who like it when others hurt them. It's a kind of mental disorder."

Charles raised his eyebrows. "You mean Agnes? Think she really likes to be hurt?"

"I don't care if she likes it or not. She can play whatever games she wants with her husband when nobody watches. But involving a child in this madness... it's unacceptable."

"Agreed. Unfortunately, we don't have enough proof except for Elisa's written complaint. She's just a child, and even if we bring it to court, no one would take her testimony seriously."

"What if I get another testimony from an adult person?"

"It would work. But from whom? No one really knows what's going on. We already asked their neighbors – they just heard some noise and screaming from that house. But they never saw anything."

"I'll find Elisa's aunt."

Charles widened his eyes. "Would she agree to be involved?"

"I think yes. Just think of it – she gave Elisa an expensive family heirloom, which means she really cares about her niece. Also, when two sisters stop talking for years, it might mean that one disapproves of the other. And we both understand what is the subject of their contradiction."

"Joseph Palmer is the reason they stopped talking," Charles voiced her thoughts. "It might work. How would you find her?"

"She lives in the capital, Middle Lake."

"Too far to cast a Searching spell."

Lana gave him a sly look. "No magic needed here. I got to know her name – Rachel. I can find her maiden name in our records, as Agnes has the same one. I also know the city where she lives, so –"

"You can send her a letter through our post office."

"Exactly." Lana smiled. "If Rachel agrees to give a testimony against Joseph, Elisa will be protected from him."

"I must admit, it's a much better plan than mine." Charles stood up and checked his time crystal, which was tied to the rope that he carried in the chest pocket of his uniform shirt. "Okay, I need to run now. I'll see you tomorrow."

Lana glanced at the busy street, a sense of impending tragedy filling her heart. "We provoked Joseph today. He must be furious."

Charles shrugged. "Whatever. I'll be in the West End all this time, and if something happens, I'll be there on time to protect his family from his rage."

"Please, be careful." Lana hugged him. He smelled of coffee and baking.

"Of course, Dandelion."

33

⤷❈⤶

Disobedient Daughter

'*We can't be together. Not like that,*' Becca re-read the words that had completed her letter to Stan. Now, she had explained that they couldn't see each other any longer, and she had nothing more to add. She raised her tired eyes to the window. The dull light of sunrise was starting to climb into her room, signaling that the restless night was coming to an end. Becca exhaled a heavy sigh and took the white envelope.

After her confession under the potion of Sincerity, Becca had decided to set things right. It was obvious that her relationship with Stan had to end. Only if she could make herself stop thinking about Mira!

Now, everything made perfect sense, starting from that frosty November evening when the twins had mocked her. Yes, she was angry when Mira and her sister acted rudely and crossed the line, but it was short-lived anger.

On the day when the tragedy had happened to Mira's twin sister, Becca got to know another side of her – vulnerable and kind. It wasn't really love back then, just simple sympathy. Over the months, they grew closer, and Becca started calling it 'a special connection.' In reality, she was slowly falling for this amazing girl with a contradictory character. And she had no idea what to do about it.

Becca was afraid that if she confessed her feelings to Mira, she would be called a 'weirdo' for the rest of her life. Well, for the rest of their school life, for sure. And she had another year ahead to make it through high school. No, she couldn't put herself at such a risk. Even though Lana attempted to cheer her up by saying that she had read Mira, after giving it some thought, Becca was confident that Lana was simply trying to support her as a friend. There was no hope that Mira would ever think of her as a... girlfriend? The word, when it pertained to Mira, made Becca chuckle nervously.

Even if Mira loved her, their romance would never stand a chance. Due to their strict religious community, any relationship except for 'husband and wife' was forbidden. If someone found out about her longing, she would be in trouble.

The noise coming from the corridor startled Becca. There was a mixture of voices, fast steps, and sobbing. A lot of sobbing. Among them, Becca recognized her mother's voice, and it made her heart sink.

She jumped to her feet, rushing to the door. The thought that her mother had discovered her feelings towards the girl crossed her mind, and Becca pushed it away. No, there was no way her mother could have figured it out so quickly. Something really bad must have happened, and Becca needed to find out.

Her mother was in her bedroom. She sat on her bed, her face buried in her hands, her shoulders shaking.

Becca stepped closer, fear creeping into her chest. "What happened?"

Her mother inhaled deeply and wiped her eyes as if trying to erase the evidence of her meltdown. "I thought you were asleep. Did I wake you up?"

"Sort of," Becca mumbled. "It doesn't matter. Mother, please, you can tell me. Is it about Kyle or our father?"

She shook her head in silence.

"Then what?" Becca was ready to start shaking her. It seemed like a better choice than being kept in the dark.

"Do you remember the girl who came to play with Kyle?"

Becca's breath caught in her throat. *Elisa... Oh, no...* deep down, she worried that something might go wrong with their mission to save her. It had happened before when they tried to catch a school poisoner. They ended up imprisoning the wrong man. Unfortunately, that mistake hadn't taught them anything. Now, it was much, much worse. It must be so bad that Becca couldn't even bear to think about it. Instead, she looked her mother in the eyes, bracing herself for the impact.

"Her mother, Agnes, passed away tonight."

"What?!" Becca widened her eyes in shock. "How... What happened?"

Her mother raised her blue eyes to the ceiling, tears welling in them. "It was an honorable death. Agnes Palmer died, suffering a great deal!"

Becca swallowed. *Did it mean that Mrs. Palmer died at her husband's hand?* She was afraid to ask. This way of death was somehow considered 'honorable' in Triville, as well as in other small towns where wives were expected to be docile. Becca disagreed with this view, but her mother had a different opinion.

"Agnes was such a good, compassionate soul!" Her mother raised her hand to the ceiling as if speaking to Divine itself. "I'm devastated by this loss. It happened too soon, but now she is in a better place. She will join your great Shine!"

"What about Elisa?" Becca interjected, not wanting to hear more of that 'noble way to die' nonsense.

"What about her?" Her mother blinked, not quite understanding. "The child will live with her father, of course."

"Oh, I see," Becca said coldly. "To end up just like her mother, right?"

Her mother knitted her eyebrows. "It's not appropriate to talk like this."

"Why? Should I be grateful that our church encourages suffering?!"

"Watch your tongue," her mother warned.

Becca didn't care about her wording. She almost yelled, the tears of rage and sorrow rolling down her cheeks. "Where is Elisa now?"

Her mother shook her head in disapproval of her behavior but eventually replied. "I placed her in the church shelter for some time. Until her father is free from the Guardian House dungeon."

"I can't believe they would free him. Not after everything he did! Don't you think he might harm Elisa, too?"

"If he ever harms a child, he'll lose his parental rights," she explained. "Then her placement will be decided. In a worst-case scenario, she'll be sent to a nice orphanage in the capital, Middle Lake. Now, please go wash your face and pull yourself together."

Becca wiped her tears with the back of her palm and gave her a look full of disdain. "Not before I find Elisa and bring her here."

"She can't stay with us!"

"Why not? Isn't Divine teaching us kindness and compassion?" Becca questioned. "I saw that church shelter, mother. If I can prevent a dozen homeless men from harming her, I'll do my best to protect her. Elisa will sleep in my room, and I'll share my food with her. Is that convenient enough for you?"

"Well..." Her mother looked around, hesitant. "I need to talk to your father first."

"Fine." Becca nodded. Without waiting for her mother's response, she spun on her heels and left the room.

34

An Orphan

The streets of morning Triville were foggy, but the light streamed from the clouds, promising a bright day. Becca walked along the valley leading to her house together with Elisa, holding her thin palm in hers. The petals silently tore from the blossoming trees and fell under their feet.

Becca glanced at her – in her simple checked dress and unbrushed hair, Elisa was like a lost doll that girls forget on the bottom shelf of their closet once they grow up. Now, she was that abandoned toy. A victim of the cruel community where they both happened to live.

In her hand, Elisa held her 'proof,' as she called it for some reason – a white plush teddy bear that once belonged to Becca. Only now did Becca notice that it was marked in something brownish. *Perhaps the dirt from the shelter,* Becca decided.

"Will my mom really join the eternal Light?" Elisa asked.

"Of course, sweetie," Becca promised.

"When people call me 'Sweetie,' it's usually when they lie."

Becca stopped in the middle of the valley and leaned towards Elisa. "Listen. I have no idea what happens to us after death. But

I can tell you for sure that the way your mom suffered… It's not right."

Elisa hugged her plush bear. "She's gone now. But a part of her will always stay with me. Her blood is on this bear. This is how I'll know that she is always near."

Is it… blood? Becca widened her eyes at the plush toy but restrained from commenting on it further. It was too hard for Elisa already, and her insistence on cleaning the teddy bear would only make it worse. "Dear, people don't just disappear when they die. You'll always have the love of your mother in your heart. This bond can never be broken."

She lowered her eyes, her tears streaming down her flushing cheeks. "I miss her so much."

"Of course, you'll miss her," Becca said in a quiet voice. "It's the worst part of grieving. But when you feel uneasy, just remember – her Light is always in your heart, too. And it will give you the strength to keep living. You shall not repeat her mistakes. Instead, learn from them and make things different. To honour her, try to live your life to make this world a better place."

"How would I make it better?"

"I can't tell you exactly but there is one thing that seems to be completely unfair." Becca locked her eyes with hers. "Was it your father who… did it to her?"

She nodded.

"Then you can make sure he won't repeat this to any other woman."

"There might be others?!"

"He can remarry," Becca suggested. "And I'm afraid for you. Now, there is no one to protect you from him."

Elisa frowned. "And the court won't believe my word if I lie that he hurt me physically."

She knows the laws well. Becca sighed, trying to keep her emotions at bay. "Well, unfortunately, guardians act only *after* the crime happens, not *before.*"

"Will he kill me, too?" She asked, her eyes filled with fear.

Becca gave her a compassionate look. "I won't let it happen. You can stay at my home for as long as you want. I'll find a way to persuade my parents that you need time to recover."

"How?"

"I'm not sure yet. But I'll figure something out."

"Will you lie to them?"

Becca sighed. "I hate the idea of lying. But sometimes, there is no other way to survive because of our cruel laws. Girls like you often end up dying out of someone's cruelty. If they only dared to protect themselves, they could live a different life, full of wonders. They could set an example for the others."

"What about you?" Elisa narrowed her eyes. "Are you brave enough to stand up for yourself?"

Becca's heart pounded. It was silly to ask this girl to be brave when she acted like a coward, hiding her feelings towards Mira. Also, she never was brave enough to face Stan and end things between them. Instead, she had come to his house this morning and slipped an envelope with her goodbye message under his door. "Okay, let's make a deal. I'll be brave for you and face the person I'm afraid to talk to. And you'll be brave for me and behave in front of my parents. How does it sound?"

"It sounds good." Elisa smiled for the first time today. Then, her face became concerned as she looked over Becca's shoulder.

Becca turned back to check what it was about, only to see Stan. He was fast approaching, his face serious. Considering that this morning he had received her goodbye letter, it didn't promise to be a good meeting.

"Is it that person you were afraid to talk to?" Elisa asked.

"Sort of. I broke up with him just recently. I guess he's mad."

"I'll be near. When there is a child around, men are usually not that harsh."

She gave her an appreciative smile. "Thank you."

Stan neared them, breathing heavily, his fists clenched. "What did you mean by that letter?"

Becca stepped back, staying by Elisa's side. "I'm sorry. I just didn't want to trouble you any longer."

"Trouble me?" He was puzzled. "Becks, you never troubled me. And I'm really sorry I paid you so little attention. Why didn't you talk to me directly? We could sort it out to keep seeing each other. Why do you ruin everything we have because of this tiny misunderstanding?"

Because I don't love you. She clenched her teeth, unable to confess.

"Whatever." He waved his hand. "Let's talk now."

Becca placed her hand on Elisa's shoulder. "I'm busy now. I need to take care of Elisa first."

He shifted his eyes to Elisa, as if he had just noticed her. "Hey, little one."

Elisa frowned. "I'm not little."

Stan chuckled, clearly amused by Elisa's reaction. "Anyways. Would you mind giving us some space? I really need to talk to your friend."

"I need my friend more now!" Elisa stomped her foot. "I just lost my mother."

His eyes widened, and he helplessly looked at Becca. "I'm so sorry. I had no idea."

"Now you do," Becca said in a quiet voice. "Please, Stan. Let's not discuss it now."

"Then when?"

Becca bit her lip. She had to talk to him like a mature person, apparently. And she couldn't delay this talk for too long. As she promised Elisa, she had to resolve it, and tonight was the best time. Her mother would be away until late – she would be busy in church, preparing for the funeral ceremony for her friend, late Mrs. Palmer. And Becca's father was supposed to be on duty. "Come after ten to my place."

"Okay." He ran his hand through his hair, then looked at Elisa. "Can I talk to you for a minute?"

Elisa glanced at Becca in doubt.

Becca gave him a puzzled look. "Talk about what?"

"I just want to apologize for being so rude," he said in a plain tone.

Becca nodded. "Alright, then."

She stepped to the blossoming tree, watching Stan leading Elisa further down the alley. Then he knelt down, his voice too low to be heard. Based on the way they glanced at Becca from time to time, she was almost certain that Stan was trying to convince Elisa to side with him, so he could win her back. If only he knew that her heart didn't belong to him. And it never would. It simply belonged to the person who could easily break it. This Becca didn't doubt. If only she were as lucky as Lana.

35

Shards of Heart

Lana gripped the chair handles tightly as her father's burning gaze bore into her. In the oppressive silence, the sound of her own heart pounding filled her ears. The news of Agnes' death was still sinking in, the weight of it heavy on her mind.

It wasn't like that foolish mistake she had made before, mixing up potion bottles and framing the chemistry teacher. This time, it was a grave error that had cost a woman her life and left Elisa an orphan. *What have I done?*

Lately, Lana had been consumed with one mission – to help Elisa. Earlier that morning, before being summoned to the Guardian House, she had visited the post office to send a letter to Rachel, Elisa's aunt, urging her to come as soon as possible. And now, her world was shattered by this family tragedy. If only she had never listened to Charles and never brought that cursed pie to provoke the murderer!

She glanced over at the visitor chair beside her. Charles was seated there, but he didn't appear shocked. *Perhaps he had already learned of the murder during his night shift*, Lana surmised.

She had no idea what Charles had told her father or what was expected of her. The only thing she could surmise was that the guardians had likely investigated the crime scene and found Lana's energy traces, leaving no room for deception. There were already enough lies.

Charles gave her a sorrowful look before turning back to her father. "Captain Morris, please. It's not entirely Lana's fault."

She held her breath, wondering if her father blamed her. *If he does*, she thought, *it's deserved.*

Her father regarded her with a mix of pity and anger. "Was it your idea to lace a pie with an illegal potion and bring it to their house?"

Lana blinked, recalling the night she and Charles had devised their plan. It had been her idea to help Elisa, but it was Charles who had suggested the provocative gesture of bringing the pie. "We visited the house together, but the idea –"

"Lana did all the baking," Charles interjected, cutting off her awkward attempt at an explanation. "She simply wanted to help this girl. And I saw no harm in checking their home. I had no knowledge of the potion."

"What did you just say?" Lana gasped. It was hard to believe that Charles could lie so blatantly in front of her father. *Is he trying to save himself from being fired?* If so, it was the most hurtful thing he had ever done to her. She was so shocked that she couldn't bring herself to speak another word.

Charles avoided meeting her eyes, instead fidgeting with the collar of his shirt as a bead of sweat trickled down his neck. "Of course, it was my mistake as well," he added nervously. "It was foolish of me to involve Lana in the case. If I knew the risks, I would never allow it."

Her father's gaze shifted to Lana, the tension in the room palpable, making it difficult for her to breathe. His voice boomed like thunder. "What have I told you about your foolish detective dreams?"

"Dreams?!" Her own voice sounded foreign to her. "Father –"

He raised his hand, silencing her. "Right, I'm your father. At home. But right now, I'm your boss, and you've let me down."

Lana dropped her gaze, feeling her cheeks burn with shame. It had been foolish of her to believe that her father would ever have faith in her abilities as a detective. Now, with this grave mistake made, he wouldn't even allow her the chance to explain herself. And any explanations she offered would likely be dismissed as lies. She wished the ground would open up and swallow her whole.

"You interfered with the case," her father pressed on. "And now that woman is dead. If you hadn't visited her home yesterday and asked questions, her husband wouldn't have become so enraged."

"He could have gotten angry regardless of my presence," Lana mumbled, still unable to meet her father's eyes.

"He claims that you threw food at him!" Her father's fist slammed down on the table, causing the folders in front of him to jump. "Such behavior is unacceptable! You know what? Allowing you to work here was my biggest mistake!"

The room fell silent as Lana continued to stare at her lap, rendered speechless.

Charles' voice was barely audible. "I apologize, Captain. I thought we were making a regular visit. I had no knowledge of her plan –"

"Enough," Lana interrupted, standing up abruptly.

Both men looked at her with confusion.

"I didn't finish speaking to you," her father said.

"There's nothing more to say. You're right – I'm not a guardian, and I shouldn't remain here any longer." Without another word, Lana turned and hurried out of the office without looking back.

In the cramped basement, Lana leaned against her desk, taking deep breaths to calm herself. Her gaze fell blankly on the book resting on the surface. It was the same book she had cherished, dreaming of finding a perfect partner to solve crimes with.

Charles had likely finished reading it and returned it to her. It now struck her as peculiar that he had shown interest in the story. As Lana slowly began to comprehend what he had done to her, one question lingered in her mind – Why?

With trembling hands, she opened the book and discovered a paper note. It bore Charles' shaky handwriting. *"What a fun read, Dandelion! I definitely learned more about you and your secrets! :)"*

She slammed the book, a burning sensation pulsating in her chest. Previously, she had only imagined what a 'broken heart' meant, but now she understood it firsthand. It was as if her heart had been shattered into countless pieces, each fragment falling to the pit of her stomach and agonizing there.

The pieces of the puzzle that Lana had never noticed before began to flash before her eyes. From the moment Charles first met her at the circus and presented her with a fake rose to his subsequent visit to her home bearing a real bouquet. Now, it was clear that he had always been trying to impress her. Despite her attempts to push him away, he persisted in his efforts. Lana had naively believed that he was deeply in love with her, but now she saw it for what it truly was – an illusion.

Charles was never in love with her. And if romantic feelings were not the driving force behind his actions, then there must have been another motive for his relentless pursuit of her company. It suddenly dawned on Lana – *his career*. The answer was so simple yet profound. The more she pondered it, the more it made sense.

Charles had 'assisted' her in catching a school poisoner and had pushed for progress in the Palmer case. Just before they had devised a plan to apprehend Palmer, he had confessed his desire to become a detective. He had sought to gain recognition by solving these crimes, regardless of the cost or consequences.

A memory of their first night together sent shivers down Lana's spine. Just before she had slept with him, Charles had jokingly mentioned that he was only toying with her to gain favor with her father. *Was that the truth?* If so, it would have been incredibly convenient for him to have Lana as his fiancée. Blinded by love, she could have easily influenced her father to grant him a promotion. This was the very question she had intended to pose to her father once their engagement was finalized!

She buried her head in her hands, struggling to come to terms with her own foolishness. In her distraught state, Charles found her.

He entered the room and closed the door behind him. Lana didn't need to turn around to confirm that it was her beloved betrayer. The scent of tree nuts and coffee that emanated from him felt like a stab to her soul.

"I'm relieved you managed to keep your job," she remarked coldly.

"Lana, please listen –"

"Oh, spare me," she interrupted, her tone laced with disdain. "There's no need for pretense anymore. You know, I could easily inform my father that it was you who suggested I bake that cursed pie and provoke Joseph Palmer."

"I'm relieved you didn't say that." Charles touched her hand, causing her to shiver. "I truly appreciate that you didn't tarnish my reputation."

Lana brushed his hand away. "It's because I was left speechless after all your accusations. And neither of you gave me a chance to explain myself!"

"I'm truly sorry... I was backed into a corner. The Captain will dismiss me if he discovers the truth. I'm a guardian, and I made a serious mistake. But you... you have nothing to lose."

Nothing to lose? Lana gasped. "What about *my* dream? All I ever wanted was to work here... to help people!"

"It's just a secretary's position. You can find something similar."

Lana shook her head. "You never believed in me. You only lied."

He paused. "I just wanted to give you a task because you enjoy this job. That's what good fiancées do."

"You know what else good fiancées do?"

"What?"

"They love and respect their future wives."

He gazed at her in silence, his blue eyes shimmering in the sunlight streaming through the small ceiling window.

She let out a sigh. "We might work things out if you possessed even one of those qualities. But you don't."

Lana turned away from him, concealing the tears that welled up in her eyes. Then, she opened the door and ran.

She ran as fast as her legs could carry her, desperate to escape from the building and from the deceitful man who had claimed to be a guardian. Lana had always known that she would never fit in with them, but now she was certain that it was for the best.

36

New Life

At home, Lana collapsed onto her bed, tears streaming down her cheeks and dampening the pillow. This day had been a complete disaster. It all started in the morning when she was fired from her secretary job and broke up with Charles. After that, she visited Becca only to discover that Elisa was now staying at her place. Elisa was rightfully angry with her, making Lana feel crushed by the situation. All she wanted was for this day to be over.

She had no idea how long she lay there, lost in her thoughts. As the room darkened, the door creaked open, and her father entered.

He sat down nearby, his voice gentle and soothing, as if he were speaking to a child. "Lana, I feel terrible about our argument this morning. I know how much you wanted to help that family."

"You have no idea," she whispered.

"I think I do. I also understand that sometimes things spiral out of our control. We make mistakes, but that's how we learn and grow."

"Today, I learned a lot, then."

Her father took her hand in his large palm. "Listen, I don't know what's going on between you and Charles, and I never asked —"

"It doesn't matter anymore. It's over."

His brown eyes filled with sadness. "Why? I know that you love him."

"It only complicates things further," she said gloomily. *Shall I tell the truth and explain what really happened?* What if her father knew the price she had to pay for Charles' ambitions?

She doubted he would believe her. Right now, her father was trying to make peace with her, assuming Lana was too incompetent. He wouldn't trust her at this moment. As for Charles... she would have to find a way to approach him later, when her emotions weren't clouding her judgment. After all, they say, *'revenge is a dish best served cold.'*

"Lana?" her father called out.

She wiped her tears away. "I'm too exhausted to talk about it. Besides, you would rather believe his version of events than mine."

"I know that he might not be completely honest. But when a man must choose between his career and a woman, he will never choose the woman."

She sat up, her eyes searching his face. "So love means nothing to you?"

"It does, but... some things are bigger than us."

Lana's eyes widened in disbelief. "What could be more important than the people you love?"

"The flame of love burns out sooner or later, and passion fades with time. On the other hand, being a guardian means maintaining a good reputation for the rest of your life. Otherwise, you are a wretched man with no purpose."

Her heart raced in her chest. In any other circumstance, Lana would never have dared to ask him the question that had been weighing on her for years. Now, she no longer feared hurting him. As she had learned that day, guardian men were as solid as a rock. "Is that what happened between you and mom?"

He adjusted his mustache, carefully selecting his words. "Our paths had diverged. Melissa was just like you – she wanted to help people. I wanted her to stay at home and be a good wife. As you can see, it didn't work out."

"I heard she became an actress. I doubt that's related to helping people," Lana remarked.

He furrowed his brow. "Nobody truly knows what women want."

"Not even women themselves?"

"As far as I know, yes," he replied with a soft chuckle.

Lana glanced at her hand in his, noticing the stark contrast between them. His palm was twice as large as hers, his weathered skin rough to the touch. She had to admit, he had a wealth of life experience. *How could I let him down like this? How could I blindly trust Charles?* She had acted recklessly when she agreed to his risky mission.

No, she couldn't continue to disappoint him. She needed to mature and let go of her childish dreams that only brought trouble into his already tumultuous life. "Father, I've decided to leave Triville."

"Sweetie, you really shouldn't make this decision because of Charles. You know, I've seen how much you enjoy working on cases and solving mysteries. You were truly helpful in the archives."

"Was I?"

He nodded. "I believe you could contribute at a local library. You could immerse yourself in reading mysteries instead of getting caught up in real cases that only serve to confuse you. What do you think?"

Lana offered him a small smile. Her father was a formidable figure, and she knew he wouldn't take her seriously as long as she remained under his roof and behaved like a child. "Thank you, but I can't stay here. I don't want to see Charles anymore."

"Come on, it's just a minor disagreement between you two."

"It's not just about him. I feel like I need to mature and grow. I can't do that here, surrounded by the town's mysteries and with easy access to the Guardian House. After much thought, I've decided to go to Middle Lake and pursue a career in architecture."

"Are you sure about this decision?"

She nodded. "Do you remember when we discussed my studying at the architecture university? Is that offer still on the table?"

Her father smiled warmly. "Of course. Maynard may not be teaching anymore, but I can write a strong recommendation for whoever has taken his place. If you pass the exams, you can start in the fall."

She hugged him. "Thank you."

Concern creased his brow. "When do you plan to leave? In the summer?"

She gave him a somber look. "As soon as possible. But first, I must make sure Elisa is taken care of."

"She'll be fine. She's staying with the Turners now. As I've learned, she is too afraid of her dad. Which means she needs a more permanent placement. So, I contacted social services. They'll be coming in two days."

"I also wrote a letter today. To her aunt."

"Why?"

"Because it seems like her aunt genuinely cares for her niece. It's a better option than her living in an orphanage."

He smiled. "Well, if her aunt agrees to take her in, that would be wonderful."

37

Forget Me Not

Close to ten in the evening, Becca was tucking the blanket around Elisa, who appeared visibly exhausted but too anxious to fall asleep.

"Are you sure you're okay with me resting in your bed?" Elisa asked, clutching her plush bear. The toy still bore blood stains as she had refused to part with it for laundry. Becca hesitated to take it away forcefully, fearing it would only upset her further.

Becca glanced around her not-so-spacious bedroom. There was enough room on the floor for an extra mattress. Upon bringing Elisa in, she had informed her parents that she would sleep by her side until her placement was resolved. Given what the girl had been through, it was the least Becca could do to offer some comfort. "It's really no trouble for me. Please don't worry."

"But this is your home. And I'm just a guest."

Becca offered a reassuring smile. "I insist. I've heard that sleeping on a firm surface can help with back pain."

Elisa furrowed her brow. "You don't have any back pain."

"Aren't you quite attentive?" Becca asked, amused.

"Is that a bad thing?" Elisa looked visibly worried.

"Not at all."

Elisa shifted her gaze to the dark window, where the white curtain sheets softly brushed against the sill. "My dad always said it's not appropriate for a woman to behave like I do. Am I truly hopeless?"

Becca shook her head. It was too sad that such a bright girl harbored so many doubts due to societal prejudice. She doubted these attitudes would change, but she was determined not to let them erode Elisa's self-worth. "You shouldn't heed those who say such things. As long as you act sincerely and don't harm others, there's nothing wrong with you."

Elisa sighed. "When Lana came, she mentioned writing to my aunt Rachel. Do you think she will actually come here for me?"

"I believe she will. And if she provides an honest testimony, your father will face consequences for everything he did to you and your mother."

Tears welled up in her sapphire-blue eyes. "I really want to forget what happened."

Becca's heart sank. She reached out and gently stroked Elisa's golden curls. "Dear, you won't forget it. I wish you could, but it won't happen. You can only do your best to honor your mom's memory and try to move forward."

"There is a way to forget, actually. Stan told me."

"What are you talking about?"

Elisa lowered her eyes. "Nothing."

Becca stared at her in disbelief. *What could Stan have possibly told her?* If he mentioned the possibility of forgetting the loss of her mother, it might involve some kind of potion. *A Forgetting potion.*

Becca's mind flashed back to that November night when someone had assaulted Mina. Then, there was their reckless investigation when the school teacher was about to be imprisoned.

Eventually, they all believed that the perpetrator would never be found. However, if Stan had access to such a potion, it changed everything.

Becca stood up. "Whatever Stan told you, it's a lie."

"It isn't a lie. And it was actually our secret that I wasn't supposed to tell you."

"Too late for that. Now, you must tell me the rest."

Elisa clutched her plush bear tightly, seeking comfort from Becca's probing. "I won't! I'm not a snitch."

Becca's heart pounded. It seemed that forcing the truth out of Elisa wouldn't be effective. Besides, she wasn't skilled at interrogating others. She could only attempt a different approach. Becca took a deep breath and sat at the corner of her bed. "I'm sorry, Elisa. I shouldn't have reacted like that."

"Yes, you shouldn't have," Elisa agreed, softening slightly.

"I just got concerned about this plan," Becca continued, "because consuming a Forgetting potion could have serious consequences. Your brain is still developing as you grow up, and it's too risky for you."

"Don't worry. It's not a potion that he suggested."

"Then what?" Becca blinked, her confusion deepening.

"Okay, I'll tell you. But only because I don't want you to worry."

"Deal."

"He has a Hypnotic Gift," Elisa announced proudly, a smile lighting up her face. "So, he can erase my memories."

A Gift? Becca's eyes widened in astonishment. She couldn't believe Stan possessed the ability to erase memories with a touch. He had never mentioned his Gift to Becca or anyone else, leading her to assume that his power had not yet manifested.

Typically, everyone received their Gifts in adolescence, around the age of fifteen. These Gifts were officially registered during the doctor check-ups recommended for all young mages who had just discovered their unique abilities. Boys often manifested their powers earlier than girls. Stan was nearing fifteen this summer, but unlike most boys at school, he had never boasted about his Gift. *Why was he keeping it a secret?* The potential answer was unsettling.

"Please, don't be upset," Elisa said, pulling Becca out of her reverie.

"Why would I be upset?" Becca asked in a weak voice, still reeling from the revelation about Stan.

"Because you look upset."

She exhaled deeply. "Even if he erases your memory of last night, it won't solve anything."

"Why not?"

"You might forget that your mom passed away last night. But you won't forget your entire life with her. You'll start asking questions, and people will eventually tell you the truth. In the end, it will hurt just the same."

"Everyone who can tell me the truth is here, in Triville. If Stan erases my painful memory just before I leave for the Middle Lake, I'll be okay."

"No, you won't," Becca insisted. "Picture waking up in an orphanage, not remembering anything. Won't you have questions?"

"I will," Elisa agreed. "But I'm still a child, and I won't be able to travel back to Triville alone for another four years. By then, I'll have grown up and be ready to face the truth."

"Believe me, loss never feels easier. It doesn't matter how old you are; it always breaks your heart into shards. If you agree to this memory erasing, in addition to the painful discovery, you'll live in the dark for all these years."

Elisa placed her hand on her chest. "This pain is too much, and I can't make it go away!"

"I understand. But you're not alone, Elisa." Becca reached out and touched her hand, infusing some of her Light energy into Elisa's palm. Mages were typically advised against sharing their Light energy without urgent need, as the reactions between different energies could be unpredictable. However, Becca felt compelled to share her energy to support Elisa. "Can you feel my Light?"

Elisa nodded. "It's warm."

Becca's head spun, and she withdrew her hand. "See? We can help each other heal. It's a gradual process, but it works. You just need to trust in it."

"I have no idea how it works."

"Then trust *me*. I'll do my best to support and guide you through these difficult times. I'll be by your side for as long as you need."

"Not always. They'll send me away from Triville, and I'll be alone."

"They won't. Even if your aunt doesn't come, I'll make sure you stay here until you're ready to move on."

"Really?"

"Of course," Becca promised. "You can stay with me for as long as you need."

Elisa set her plush bear aside and embraced Becca tightly. "Thank you, Becca."

Becca patted her gently on the back. "Always."

When Elisa finally fell asleep, Becca left the bedroom door slightly ajar. The pink glow of the time crystal on her nightstand offered a sense of comfort, and she hoped it would help chase away Elisa's nightmares. Quietly, she made her way downstairs to the living room.

The sight of a man's silhouette seated in a chair startled her. Becca yelped and instinctively reached out, attempting to recall a Paralyzing spell. Unfortunately, she found herself unable to conjure it. Perhaps sharing her Light with Elisa had left her weak.

The man rose from the chair, and a red, sparkling Light emanated from his palm, illuminating his features.

"Stan!" Becca's heart raced as she remembered he had a Hypnotic Gift. "What do you want?"

Stan appeared puzzled. "You told me to come by at ten in the evening. Don't you remember?"

She nodded, recalling their conversation from that morning when she had accompanied Elisa back from the church shelter. Little did she know that Elisa would uncover Stan's secret. Now, Becca was unsure of what to do next – should she confront him? Inquire if he was the one who assaulted Mina? It all felt surreal, and she doubted Stan would ever reveal the truth.

The truth. Becca's gaze shifted to the kitchen entrance. The potion she had used for the pie still sat on the top shelf of the cabinet, concealed from the rest of her family. If she were to add a few drops to a drink...

"Becca?" Stan's voice brought her back to the present. "Is everything alright?"

"Of course," she replied, her expression serious. "I just thought my scream might have woken the children."

She didn't lie. Elisa was peacefully asleep in her room, and her younger brother Kyle had long since drifted off in his own bedroom. Becca needed to check on them, ensuring their safety. It also gave her a moment to compose herself before confronting Stan about the unsettling truth she had uncovered.

Stan glanced up the darkened stairs. "I can go check on them."

No, she couldn't risk allowing Stan near the children. "There's no need. Could you please go put the kettle on instead? We can have our talk over a cup of tea."

"That sounds good," he replied with a smile.

As Stan headed to the kitchen, Becca ascended the stairs. The sight of her sleeping sibling brought a sense of relief. Both Elisa and Kyle were safe and undisturbed. She took a moment to gather her thoughts before facing the challenging conversation that lay ahead.

She could force Stan to confess using a potion of Sincerity. Then, after the truth would be revealed, he might attempt to erase her memory to get rid of the witness. Becca raised her hand and checked her palm. Apparently, she wasn't skilled enough in spell-crafting, so neutralizing him with a Paralyzing spell wasn't an option. *What shall I do, then?*

As Becca neared her parents' bedroom, she recalled her father's memory crystal. He often used it to record the voices of the perpetrators during interrogations, aiding in the creation of detailed reports. With the crystal, she could capture Stan's words, ensuring she had a record of his confession even if he managed to make her forget.

If it's Divine's will, Becca thought, *I'll find the crystal easily*. She opened the door to her parents' room and stepped inside. The memory crystal sat on the bookshelf, its creamy-white walls gleaming in the moonlight. Becca smiled. "Here we go."

38

Liquid Truth

The tea pleasantly warmed Becca's palm as she sipped it. Stan sat across from her, holding his cup and studying his drink. *Does he suspect that this drink contains more than just tea leaves?* she wondered. When Becca had returned to the kitchen, she had sent Stan to the washroom to wash his hands. Seizing the opportunity, she added some of her potion of Sincerity to his drink. It was about to start working.

She discreetly checked her dress pocket under the table to ensure that the memory crystal was activated. The crystal glowed pure white, indicating that she could begin her interrogation. "Stan, I wish things were different. But breaking up is the right decision. You're too focused on your studies, and I only distract you."

"This is what you wrote in the letter. And I'm still not convinced. Did you ever truly love me?"

She exhaled a sigh. If she had to admit it, she was prepared. "Alright, you caught me. I love someone else."

His jaw dropped as he stared at her.

"I understand this is difficult for you, but it's not easy for me either."

Stan's eyes narrowed. "Who is he?"

Becca hesitated. She couldn't risk revealing Mira's name, especially not with the recording device active. It was time to shift the focus and make Stan answer her questions. "Why do you ask? Do you think you can make me forget about this person?"

"Maybe," he blurted out, then quickly covered his mouth as if he couldn't believe he had revealed something so important so carelessly.

"Relax, I know about your Hypnotic power." Becca took a sip of her tea, watching him closely, before continuing. "Why didn't you tell me about it?"

"I didn't want anyone to know. If I confess, the doctor will send my records to the Guardian House. My Gift is potentially very harmful, so it needs to be monitored. If a crime occurs and the victim claims they were manipulated, I'll always be a suspect."

"We have check-ups every September, so they'll find out eventually," Becca pointed out.

"I was fortunate to discover my Gift in early November, and I began learning to control it on my own. I just wanted to delay being placed on the guardians' 'special list.'" He paused, then asked, "Wait, how did you find out about it?"

"Elisa told me."

"I see... I thought that girl could keep a secret."

Ignoring his dismissive comment, Becca pressed on with her questioning. "Did *you* rape Mina?" Her question rang out like thunder, its weight hanging in the air. She knew she had to ask, even if the truth tore her apart. She hoped it was merely a coincidence that Stan possessed the same power that could have been used against Mina. Her heart raced as she awaited his response.

Stan gritted his teeth, his eyes widening before he finally nodded.

Becca set her teacup down and coughed. "I'm sorry, you must have misheard me."

"No, I heard you correctly." Stan's face now contorted with anger, his neck pulsing as he tugged at the collar of his T-shirt, perhaps trying to calm himself down. "I don't know why I feel compelled to tell you this, but I'll be honest. What do you want to know? How exactly did it happen?"

Becca nodded in silence, urging him to continue.

"That night, after the circus show, I walked you home," Stan began, his eyes fixed on a point in front of him as he delved back into his memories. "Then I returned to my house. My parents were out for the night, so I was alone. I was still upset about what those girls did to you, so I went to the kitchen cabinet and grabbed a box of beer. Sometimes, I drink to calm my nerves. My father says it helps him."

"Okay," Becca responded softly, guiding the conversation to the events of that fateful night. "What about the twins?"

"Right, the twins. I was sitting on the porch when they walked by. I was surprised to see them because it was past midnight. They were both agitated, so I suggested we have a drink to help them relax. They agreed, and we chatted for a while. Eventually, we moved the gathering inside to avoid drawing attention from the neighbors. You know how they can be, always ready to complain to their parents. And mine."

"It sounds like you had a good time," Becca commented. "Why did you assault one of them?"

Stan clenched his fists. "Because Mina crossed a line, okay?"

Becca remained silent, refraining from further interruption. Whatever Stan revealed would be captured on the recording, and that was all that mattered.

"In the living room, we finished off the remaining beer bottles, and I went to the kitchen to fetch more. On my way back, I overheard them arguing. It turned out that one of them wanted to seek revenge because I had 'rudely interfered with their prank.' It was Mina, the more cynical of the two. She had convinced her sister to remove their tops. As I got it, they intended to embarrass me by making me strip naked. They planned to laugh at me and then flee.

"Naturally, I was enraged. However, I remained calm until the twins removed their tops and were left in their bras. I then entered the room and asked them to leave, explaining that I had no desire to harm or engage with them in any way. It upset Mira, and she left.

"I chased after her until she stopped at her house. I questioned Mira about why they caused trouble for everyone and why they behaved so poorly. Mira explained that her sister could be uncontrollable at times and might need to learn a lesson. It was then that I realized Mina, the other twin, was still at my place. I made a promise to teach her a lesson, and I couldn't risk Mira remembering any of it. That's when I erased her memory, just slightly, for a few hours, to ensure a smooth outcome.

"After Mira fell asleep on their lawn, I returned home to find Mina in my kitchen, dressed only in her underwear. She was sitting on the kitchen table, drinking my father's expensive whiskey. I... I lost my temper. I grabbed a towel and warned her that I would tie her hands and take advantage of her if she didn't leave. In response, she laughed and called me a pathetic, impotent fool."

Becca took a deep breath, shocked by the disturbing revelations he had shared. It wasn't easy to hear his confession, but she knew she had to see it through. "Then you raped her," she said.

"Because she requested it."

"Huh?"

"She asked me to tie her up and engage in rough sex. And I thought, why not? I knew that I wouldn't be her first lover, so I assumed she enjoyed that kind of intimacy," Stan explained, swallowing hard before continuing. "It was bizarre! Throughout the process, she complained that I wasn't hard enough!" His eyes welled up with tears as he kept confessing. "She cursed at me and called me pathetic. I couldn't even bring myself to finish."

Becca shuddered at his words. "If Mina gave you her consent, why did you erase her memory then?"

"Because after I began to dress, she accused me of being a terrible lover and threatened to expose me to everyone at school if I didn't agree to become her boyfriend," Stan explained, shaking his head. "I felt... powerless. However, I could control the situation using my Gift. It was better to erase that memory from her mind. Once I was certain her memory was effectively wiped, I carried her back to their lawn. I suppose I was too anxious and overused my power."

Becca swallowed, stunned by Stan's confession. It was far from what she had anticipated. She now understood his truth, and it painted a different picture than she had initially thought. Stan wasn't a rapist; he was a man who had been manipulated and taken advantage of. "I understand why you acted the way you did with Mina. You were backed into a corner. Stan, you didn't assault her, as you believe. You are the victim in this situation."

"Don't say that! You don't know what it's like for a man!" Stan took deep breaths in an attempt to calm himself. "It's so humiliating... I don't know why I told you all of this. Maybe Mina was right – I'm not a real man. I'm too weak, and I couldn't bear to keep this secret any longer."

"You aren't weak, Stan," Becca reassured him. "I gave you a potion of Sincerity, which is why you are being so open with me now."

"A potion?!"

Becca nodded. "Sorry about it. When I discovered what Gift you possess, I got worried. But now that I know the truth, I see that you are a good person who made a mistake. You didn't deserve what happened to you."

"That's why you chose another man," Stan remarked, his disappointment evident in his voice.

Becca lowered her gaze, feeling her cheeks flush. After everything that had been shared, keeping her secret felt unfair. "There is no other man, Stan. It seems that I'm just not interested in boys," she confessed.

"What does that mean?"

"I love a girl," Becca revealed. "And she'll never love me back."

"Whoa... wait... I think I know who she is."

"We all have our secrets. And no magic can erase them. We can only strive to understand and support each other."

"So you'll keep mine?" Stan asked.

"Of course," Becca assured him, reaching out to touch his hand. "In fact, I've realized that there isn't much difference between men and women. We try to conform to different standards – you're expected to appear strong, while I'm supposed to be obedient. Both of these roles can be equally damaging."

"And there's nothing we can do about it."

Becca let out a heavy sigh. "I would give my life to change this."

"Let's just be ourselves," Stan suggested. "We can continue to discover who we are, and we can support each other when needed. We can remain friends. Perhaps that's all we need to make a difference."

"Agreed."

After Stan departed, Becca retrieved a memory crystal from her dress pocket. She deactivated it, halting the recording of their conversation. The yellow sparkles of the message now shimmered within the crystal's milky walls.

She had no wish to share it with anyone. It held not only Stan's secret but also hers – about forbidden love. However, there was one person who needed to know the truth about what had happened to her and her sister.

Mira had been restless in recent months, and it would be selfish to keep her in the dark. Becca must show her the memory crystal, even if it meant facing judgment and being labeled a 'weirdo' for the remainder of her school life.

39

Reflections

The bedroom, filled with plush toys, was dimly lit by the dull sunrise. Lana sat in a comfortable chair, yawning.

"I'm sorry I asked you to come so early," Mina said. She sat in the opposing chair, holding a milky-white crystal in her trembling hands. The crystal shimmered, keeping a message that clearly concerned her.

"It's okay," Lana replied with a small smile. "When your sister woke me up, I thought something terrible had happened. Again."

"Well, it's partially true."

"What's the matter?" Lana inquired. "From what Mira briefly explained to me, I gathered that Stan confessed to erasing your memory. She asked me to help you, but I'm not sure what I can do."

Mina placed the crystal on the side table. "Well, you are the only trustworthy person I could think of."

This compliment was pleasant yet unexpected. "What makes you think so?"

"You already read my memories when I was asleep, yet you never betrayed me by disclosing everything to the church community. So, you most likely won't do it now. Unlike my therapist, whom I've been talking to for these past few months."

"You mean... She shared your personal information with those judgmental women?"

Mina grinned. "Exactly. See? You get me."

Lana shook her head in disbelief. "That's completely unethical. She is a doctor and is bound by the oath."

"Well, as it turns out, that oath doesn't seem to matter when there is a crime or anything harmful involving a teenager." Mina sighed. "It's a good thing I didn't tell her the worst part... When it all began."

Lana ran her hand along the plush chair handle, deep in thought. In reality, she had never fully delved into this girl's mind, and she doubted if it was even possible. The human mind was too intricate to comprehend entirely. Lana had only skimmed the surface to learn what had happened prior to the memory erasure incident. It seemed that Mina assumed Lana knew more than she actually did, which was why she trusted her. Lana couldn't betray this trust now. If Mina discovered she knew nothing, she might never fully open up, hindering her healing process.

"I can keep your secrets," Lana assured with a nod. "You don't need to worry. Which episode did you want to discuss?"

Mina lowered her murky gray eyes. It still struck Lana as odd how much she resembled her sister, except for the missing mole over the left eyebrow. Despite the physical similarities, Mina was a completely different person with her own traumas and secrets that she was struggling to cope with. "The first one."

"Are you sure you're ready to discuss this?" Lana asked, trying to navigate the conversation despite being in the dark about the specifics. "It sounds like there's a lot of pain associated with it."

"Well, maybe you can help end that pain."

"First, you need to talk about it. Whenever you're ready," Lana encouraged her.

"Okay." Mina nodded and began recounting, "It happened when I was ten. During a harvesting event in town, Mira and I went to see the farm zoo. There was a man who showed us the sheep and chickens. He then promised to show us the bunnies if one of us went inside his trailer. He explained that the bunnies were small and would be scared if too many strangers were in the room."

Lana swallowed, dreading where the story was leading. "You went inside first?"

She nodded. "I was so foolish and naive. I didn't suspect anything when he locked the door after we entered. It wasn't until he pushed me onto the bed and began touching me that I realized something was terribly wrong." She shivered and hugged herself, seeking comfort in the retelling of her painful experience. "I screamed... I screamed for help, but there was no one nearby except for Mira. He then covered my mouth with his hand and demanded that I stay quiet. He threatened that if I didn't comply, he would harm Mira. So, I stayed silent.

"When I returned home, I kept the incident to myself. That man had warned me that if I told anyone, he would come to our house and harm Mira. I was terrified. It took me some time to realize that it was an empty threat and that he had manipulated me. However, by the time I understood, it was too late – he already left town, and no one would pursue him. I attempted to confide in a priest once. He said that a woman must remain pure until marriage. I was told that it was all my fault."

Lana gazed at Mina, astonished by the burden this girl had carried for so long. It was no wonder she exhibited hostility at school, as Becca had mentioned. Despite enduring such trauma, Mina continued to put on a facade of normalcy, concealing the pain that consumed her. "Mina, I am truly sorry... You were just a child, yet you did everything in your power to protect your sister. You are incredibly brave."

Mina wiped away the tears streaming down her flushed cheeks. "I've never shared this episode with anyone... And I don't know how to move past it. I wish I could erase it, like that foolish night when I tried to manipulate Stan to make him mine. That's what I've discovered from that recording Becca gave us."

"You don't have to forget it. It was a situation you were not prepared to face at that time, but you are stronger now and can confront it," Lana reassured her.

"How?" Mina's voice quivered as she clutched the Memory crystal tightly. "How can I confront it, knowing what I'm capable of?"

"Sometimes, we can begin with offering a genuine apology."

"I've already apologized to the people at school whom I was rude to, just as my therapist advised. I also wrote letters to those I couldn't reach in person. While it provided some relief, it –"

"You've overlooked one person. The most important one."

"Perhaps I need to apologize to Stan. Now I understand why he's been avoiding me for all these months. But I doubt it will cancel what happened to me."

"I meant yourself. You need to forgive yourself."

"For what?"

"For everything. Mainly, for being inexperienced and naive. Throughout our conversation, you've blamed yourself for that. Can you forgive yourself?"

Mina hesitated, then shook her head. "No, I can't. It seems I'm just a monster who brings misery to others. I despise it, but I can't seem to change. I thought I had a chance, but that..." She gestured towards the crystal. "It proves that I don't deserve any chances. I suppose I'm not meant to live."

Lana rose from her chair and sat on the floor in front of Mina. "It's okay to be angry with yourself. I understand. When my mom left us, I couldn't bear to talk to the girls at school anymore. Every time they mentioned their mothers or complained, I just wanted to lash out at them!"

Mina's eyes widened. "Really?"

"Oh, they infuriated me," Lana said, her breathing quickening as she recalled that time. "I resented that they could carry on with their lives and even complain about it while I'd lost the most important person in my life. I wanted them to feel the pain I was experiencing."

"I can't believe you could conceal something like that."

"I wasn't very good at hiding it," Lana admitted. "After a school fight that I instigated, my father sent me to a therapist. You see, even though it manifested as an emotional issue, deep down, my body was tense from the betrayal and hurt I felt. I needed to learn how to express my anger in a healthy manner without causing harm to those around me."

Mina's eyes narrowed, a glimmer of hope flickering within them. "How?"

"Watch," Lana said as she stood up. She walked over to the nearest shelf and grabbed a plush teddy bear. With all her strength, she hurled the toy against the wall.

"Lying bastard!" Lana shouted as the toy bounced on the carpet. Feeling a sense of release, she turned to Mina. "Give it a try!"

Mina hesitated, slowly rising to her feet. "Throwing toys? That sounds ridiculous."

Lana handed her another toy, a fluffy pink bunny with adorable button eyes. "Imagine this is your assailant, the one who harmed you. Channel all your anger into your throw."

Hesitant, Mina clenched the toy in her hands, then with a sharp intake of breath, she hurled it against the wall, screaming, "I hate you!"

"Very good," Lana praised, handing her another toy. This time, it was a yellow plush dog. "Now try this one."

Mina grabbed the toy and flung it against the wall with a victorious yelp.

After half an hour, they lay on the carpet, surrounded by a pile of toys. Mina was breathing heavily, drained from the activity. "That was the silliest thing I've ever done."

Lana turned to her. "How do you feel now?"

"Surprisingly better," Mina said after a moment. "I don't feel the urge to yell at people anymore."

"Well, whenever you feel that anger rising, you can do this instead."

Mina chuckled. "Okay."

"It took me nearly a year to manage my anger. This is how I began my healing process," Lana shared as she rested her head on her elbow. "I know my situation is nothing compared to yours, but with time, you'll start to feel alive. Eventually, you'll find your way back to normal."

Mina sat up. "I don't know. Lately, I can't stop asking myself, 'Why'? Why did all of this happen to me? I was just a girl."

"You're right. You didn't deserve any of it. The truth is, life can be filled with darkness and pain, and tragedies can strike anyone, even the kindest people."

"Then what's the point of being a good person if it doesn't offer any protection?"

"Unfortunately, being good doesn't shield you from life's hardships. However, the essence of being a better person lies in how you *choose* to navigate and cope with your pain. Over time, we grow more resilient – the things that once caused us immense pain no longer hold power over us. Furthermore, once we have healed, we can extend a helping hand to others, guiding them towards light. This is how we prevent the darkness from prevailing."

Mina regarded her with interest. "I understand. You've healed, and now you are helping me."

"I suppose so," Lana replied, her heart swelling. "Today, you've also helped me in a way."

"Me?" Mina's eyes widened. "How?"

Lana placed her hand over her heart. "I was filled with anger towards Charles after our breakup. However, I've found a sense of relief now. I've decided to let go of my foolish notion of ruining his career. I won't stoop to his level and will allow him to carry on. In the end, his ambitious nature will likely lead him to make a misstep."

She smiled. "I believe it was for the best that you left him behind. He truly doesn't deserve someone like you."

Lana chuckled. "I can't argue with that."

40

Leaving Behind

The road leading out of Triville started at the top of the hill. Sometimes, Becca came here to enjoy the spectacular view of the town. Today, she had come to say goodbye to her best friend.

As she walked along the trail, Becca stopped by a puffy blossoming tree. Its petals were silently dropping and twirling in the air before landing on the lush grass. Despite the beauty of nature surrounding her, her thoughts were elsewhere.

After giving Mira the crystal containing Stan's confession, both she and her sister had been skipping classes for the entire week. Becca knew they needed time to process everything, and Lana had been doing her best to help Mina heal.

However, the waiting was making Becca anxious. She had no idea how Mira would react after hearing the recording. Perhaps they would no longer be friends. With Lana leaving soon, Becca feared she would be left alone. Well, not entirely alone – she could always chat with Stan after school. Though, Stan would likely stop talking to her as soon as he learned that she had given away the recording with his confession.

The only positive thing that had happened that week was regarding Elisa. Upon receiving Lana's letter, her aunt had come to Triville and provided a testimonial as a witness of domestic abuse. She was now in the process of officially adopting her niece. Furthermore, she had decided to stay in Triville, finding the town more suitable for them than the noisy capital where crimes were rampant.

"Hey, weirdo!" The sound of Mira's voice made Becca flinch.

She turned to see Mira, who looked stunning in her pretty white dress with a chamomile pattern. Her raven hair was adorned with tiny plaits, and she was as beautiful as ever, while Becca still felt like the school freak.

Mira approached her. "Sorry. I didn't mean to offend you. It was a bad joke."

"It's okay," Becca said, unsure of what to expect next. "I'm glad you're in a cheerful mood. How is your sister, by the way?"

"Much better. Your crystal helped a lot. Lana helped, too. Now I can really see the progress."

Becca nodded. "That's why you came – to say goodbye to Lana."

"Not only." Mira took Becca's hands, causing her heart to melt. "I wanted to talk to you for a while. I just didn't know how to say it."

"You just said it. That I'm a weirdo," Becca reminded her.

Mira's sad gray eyes locked with hers. "Then me, too. I don't fit."

"You fit just perfectly," Becca reassured her. "It's me who will never be welcomed in this community. Not after so many people learned my secret."

"Then I must tell you mine to be even, right?" Mira's lips, coated in an attractive shining balm, trembled before she confessed, "I love you. And not just as a friend."

Becca blinked, unable to believe it wasn't another prank.

"I never thought I would love someone so deeply," Mira continued, "but you're the kindest and bravest person I've ever met. Sometimes I acted jealous, but it was because I was upset. I just knew that you would never love me back."

"Why not?" Becca asked, taken aback by such an incorrect conclusion.

Mira exhaled a sigh. "Because on the recording, you said you were already into someone. I know I can't just replace this person who isn't capable of seeing your true beauty. But I can be by your side. I'll always support you, no matter what. Because that's what love is."

Becca breathed out, her heart overflowing with joy. She had never seen Mira like this – so open and strong at the same time. Her gray eyes sparkled, and they didn't lie. Nothing but love could transform her in such a beautiful way. Knowing that Mira truly loved her... it was priceless.

Not wasting any more words, Becca leaned in and kissed Mira's lips. They were tender and sweet because of the balm. This sensation sent sparkles all over her blood, making this moment magnificent.

They were sitting under the tree, holding hands and quietly talking, when Lana showed up. She walked to them along the trail, holding the reins of her horse with only two bags attached to the sides of the saddle.

As Lana noticed them holding hands, she smiled widely. "Aww... You two finally made it out!"

Becca and Mira exchanged glances in silence. Then it hit Becca – when she was testing a potion of Sincerity for the very first time, Lana had mentioned that she had read Mira earlier and learned about her love. Becca had always assumed it was just an innocent lie meant to support her.

"You knew?" Mira asked in disbelief. "Why didn't you tell us?"

Lana kept smiling. "I didn't want to ruin your moment. I bet it was amazing."

"It was," Becca agreed.

"See?" Lana gave Mira a mischievous look. "It feels so much better when you figure it out on your own, without any hints from others."

"Well... Probably," Mira said, then rushed to hug Lana.

Becca joined them, and they stood like that for a minute, silently saying their goodbyes.

"I'll miss you so much," Becca said when they split apart.

"Don't be. I'll write you letters," Lana promised, her brown eyes glossy from tears. "And you two will be just fine here. Please, take care of each other."

"We will," Mira assured her.

"I'm sorry it didn't work out with Charles," Becca added.

Lana shifted her eyes to the Triville scenery. The generous sun shone bright in the clear-blue skies, making the neat roofs shine. Among them, there was the roof with the sparkling metal dragon on it – a Guardian House. "I guess this wasn't supposed to work out."

"Why not?"

"Because Charles seemed perfect from the very beginning. And it all was fake." She turned back to them. "I think a real relationship is always a bit flawed. It's full of awkward moments and misunderstandings that we must work on. This is how we fall in love with our partners – through overcoming our flaws together."

Becca smiled in agreement. This was exactly what had happened between her and Mira.

"You shouldn't go so easily," Mira said. "Charles hurt you, and you must make him pay for everything."

Lana gave her a sad look. "I thought of it. But you know what? This story taught me that the only way to eliminate the darkness is not to hold it within."

Mira frowned. "What do you mean?"

"When someone hurt your sister, Mina, she started being hostile towards others, and it almost destroyed her life. When we suspected Burke, we acted too boldly, and we almost destroyed *his* life."

"True," Becca agreed. "But what about Elisa? Was it our fault, too?"

"If I'd followed my initial plan and talked to him about parenting rights, it might have ended differently. Instead, I chose to follow Charles' aggressive approach, and... you know how it ended."

The girls exchanged glances in understanding.

"You see," Lana continued, "If women truly want to make a positive change, we must act with care. We must choose the right ways of resolving things, no matter how difficult it may seem. Every action must be carefully planned, and every intention must be based on love and kindness. To do that, we must learn to let go of our anger and frustration. We must heal our hearts because the only way for light to triumph over darkness is to become the light."

"I'll remember that," Becca said, pressing her hand to her chest. "You have really grown, Lana Morris."

Lana chuckled. "I hope so. From now on, I'll focus on my studies and start building my career as an architect."

"You're really going to give up on solving mysteries?" Mira asked, doubt evident in her voice.

"Yes..." Lana exhaled a sigh. "I've outgrown it, too."

Her response didn't convince anyone. Mira continued to eye her. "In case you forgot, you are going to the capital, a criminals' nest!"

"So what?!"

"Okay, stop arguing." Becca waved her hands, trying to change the subject. "We don't know what will happen next. But I'm sure that if helping others is your destiny, then it will happen. Wherever you go and whatever you do."

"I think I'll agree with this," Lana said, relaxing. "Well, it's time to go now."

Becca watched Lana mount her horse. Then, Lana waved and rode forward along the forest trail, not looking back.

"How long do you think it will take until she enrolls in another investigation?" Mira asked as Lana disappeared among the trees.

Becca turned to her. "The studies will start in the fall, so I guess four months. Okay, six tops."

Mira laughed. "I think so, too."

To be continued...

Appreciations

THANK YOU, DEAR READER!

Thank you so much for reading the opening novel in my fantasy series *Two Worlds*!

Just before I started working on *Reading You*, I joined a volunteer program aimed at helping women who have experienced domestic violence. They sought to break free from toxic relationships and begin the healing process. Sadly, even in our modern era, in the 21st century, we still witness numerous cases of crimes against women – from the violation of basic human rights to silencing their voices.

Being among these women in a support group, I was struck by their resilience and courage. I also learned another truth – all the progress we have made towards equality did not happen spontaneously. Throughout history, starting from the first feminist movement, we have been inspiring each other and striving to make the world a better place.

If women had never stood up for themselves and if we had surrendered our hopes of pursuing our passions to blindly follow all the rules of patriarchy, we would be living in a much darker reality today. The idea of sharing this insight was invigorating, so I decided to do it in the most creative way possible – through a story.

Reading You is the very first story I attempted to write, and it took me almost six years to piece it together before it could see the light of day. In sharing this story, I also share the light that was sparked by the stories of many other women who found their way out of the darkness.

If you enjoyed reading this, please consider leaving a positive review on the platform where you purchased it or on Goodreads website. Your support is greatly appreciated, as it helps the story reach new readers!

Sincerely yours,
-Lubov Leonova

I always loved reading. I guess all the books I've ever read impacted me greatly - they let me expand my worldview and inspired me to pursue my dreams despite the obstacles.

Born in Russia, I immigrated to Canada in 2014, where I faced multiple challenges, including building my own life from scratch and figuring out what career path would let me use my full potential. My searches led me to feministic studies in college and volunteering in female support groups.

My experience slowly formed into ideas for my fantasy series *TwoWorlds*, where females shape the sphere of justice using their natural talents.

Today, I live on the East Coast of Canada with my husband, Alex, and my bunnies - Boris and Flora.

LET'S CONNECT!

Do you want to win Giveaways for my books and receive daily inspirational content? Yes? Then follow me on any of these platforms on your preference:

Instagram - author's official page
https://www.instagram.com/authorleonova/

Instagram - 2 Worlds Series
https://www.instagram.com/magical2worlds/

Facebook
https://www.facebook.com/magical2worlds

Twitter
https://twitter.com/LeonovaLubov

Also, I have a **Goodreads** account where you can always get the newest updates on my stories release:
https://www.goodreads.com/author/show/21216748.Lubov_Leonova

Curious what will happen next?

MERCY HOUSE

Beginning Series, book 2

Lana now lives in the capital and aspires to become an architect. However, her destiny has other plans for her. One day, Lana learns about a woman who died under suspicious circumstances at Mercy House, a facility for young women struggling to control their magic.

To unravel the mystery, Lana agrees to become a Mercy Sister. As she delves into her undercover work, Lana uncovers the shocking truth that her best friend Becca had also been held captive at the facility. Furthermore, everything she thought she knew about Mercy House was a deception.

Will Lana be able to save her best friend and survive the dangerous secrets lurking within Mercy House?

MERCY HOUSE

Chapter 2. Back to Passions

"And how exactly was this building robbed?" One of the students asked in curiosity after Lana had revealed the history of this landmark.

She waved her hands in explanation. "That's a good question. They have special crystal sensors, and the security guard is constantly watching the hall. They are all strong and educated mages who can freeze you with a single finger click. When the mysterious crime happened last year, the guardians couldn't resolve the case. You see – no one was hurt, and no one could describe the criminals. They only discovered the robbery at the end of the day when the cashiers were checking the gold inventory after closing."

"Then they must have been hypnotized," someone suggested.

"Not really." Lana walked along the porch, capturing all their attention. "Usually, when people fall under hypnotic charm, everyone experiences different kind of illusions. However, all the witnesses' reports match, which means they never were charmed."

"What about the energy traces?"

"They had been erased," Lana explained in a mysterious tone.

Oliver took a step up on a wide stair, taking the spotlight. "Yes, we like talking about the guardians and criminals, but let's not forget that we came here to discuss the architecture." He gave Lana a strict look before shifting his attention to the group of students. "This building was designed by one of the most famous architects – Hofstongen. He created this unforgettable old style that we call 'Gothic.'"

Lana stepped aside, covered her mouth with her palm, and let out a yawn. Sometimes it was hard to imagine that this subject could spark any interest in anyone. However, when Oliver talked about the architecture, his words piqued the students' attention. *And why is this subject so boring for me?*

Even after a year of studying, Lana still had a strong desire to fall asleep each time she had to listen to a lecture about the local architecture styles. She only managed to accomplish this project because she chose buildings based on their criminal history. *It was a good compromise; however, adult life isn't supposed to be all fun*, she reminded herself.

Before the gloomy thoughts about the boredom of adult life started creeping in, Lana looked around the street to distract herself. Her gaze stopped at the carriage at the corner. It had been parked there since they arrived, and the coachman seemed suspicious. He wore black clothes and a hat. His unfolded newspaper covered the lower part of his face as he periodically glanced at them.

Lana blinked. As a person who loved mysteries, Lana knew one thing – with time, criminals got smarter, and with the calm environment, business owners got less cautious. Who knew, maybe the bank decided to hire less security guards, hoping that the same crime won't happen again?

Oliver slightly poked her elbow. "Okay, we're done here. Let's go."

"Sure." Lana took a heavy sigh and glanced at her pinkish-red time crystal. *Almost noon.* She promised Captain Harrison not to be here longer than ten minutes, and her time was up. She had to leave all the foolish thoughts about the mysteries and return to her real life.

To find out what happened to Lana next, read *Mercy House: A Dark Castle Mystery.*
The story is available at multiple online bookstores!

Amazon Book Store:
http://author.to/lubovleonova

Check all my books on my official website:
https://www.magical2worlds.com/books

www.ingramcontent.com/pod-product-compliance
Lightning Source LLC
Chambersburg PA
CBHW030806210726
48290CB00002B/452